THE MARQUESS MARRIED A MURDERESS

The Brelsford Brothers, Book 1

Michelle McLean

ARE YOU SIGNED UP FOR DRAGONBLADE'S BLOG?

You'll get the latest news and information on exclusive giveaways, exclusive excerpts, coming releases, sales, free books, cover reveals and more.

Check out our complete list of authors, too!

No spam, no junk. That's a promise!

Sign Up Here

www.dragonbladepublishing.com

Dearest Reader;

Thank you for your support of a small press. At Dragonblade Publishing, we strive to bring you the highest quality Historical Romance from some of the best authors in the business. Without your support, there is no 'us', so we sincerely hope you adore these stories and find some new favorite authors along the way.

Happy Reading!

CEO, Dragonblade Publishing

Author's Note

This book was inspired by the 1993 cult classic movie, *So I Married an Axe Murderer*. While there is no on-page death of a spouse, the main character is a widow many times over and her widowhood and the deaths of her husbands are mentioned frequently. As this is a romantic comedy, this is done in what is meant to be an irreverent and humorous light. If you are sensitive to the subjects of death, death of a spouse, widowhood, dating after marriage, remarrying, murder, and related subjects, this is likely not the book for you. If you enjoyed the movie, then you should be fine.

<u>Trigger and Content Warnings</u>

- Death of a spouse (off page)
- Widowhood
- Remarriage
- Murder (discussion of a spouse's possible murder)

PROLOGUE

"COME ALONG, SELENA!" her cousin Anne called.

Selena hesitated, but Anne was having none of it and grabbed her hand, towing her to the alcove of the Tullys' salon where the fortune teller they'd hired for their dinner party sat at an ornate, velvet covered table.

"Everyone else has had their fortunes read already," Anne stated, pushing Selena into the chair. "Don't you wish to know if you'll marry?"

Selena softly snorted, forcing a nonchalance she was far from feeling. She did, in fact, wish to know if she'd marry. And who she'd marry. And if they'd be madly in love and live happily ever after like the princesses in the book of fanciful tales her grandfather had given her. But the last thing she wanted to do was ask the fortune teller, who even now looked at her with a raised brow and narrowed eyes.

What if the woman said no?

"Very well," she finally muttered with every ounce of confidence her twelve-year-old self could muster. "Tell me then."

The woman's eyes narrowed further, but she began shuffling the cards in her gnarled, papery hands, her piercing gaze never leaving Selena.

Selena gripped her skirts in her fists to hide the shaking of her hands as the fortune teller turned the cards over one by one.

Queen of Hearts…that one was good, she thought. Though…it was reversed. What did that mean?

Queen of Spades. The fortune teller frowned. That boded ill, did it not? Selena swallowed hard as more cards were turned. The Knight of Spades, reversed. Ace of Clubs, also reversed. She didn't know what they all meant, but she did know reversed usually meant the opposite of whatever the original meaning was. And that, along with the increasingly pinched look on the fortune teller's face, made the gnawing pit in her stomach intensify.

"Well?" Anne asked when the silence had stretched too long. "Will she wed?"

Instead of answering, the woman's hand darted out and snatched Selena's. She flipped Selena's hand over and flattened it out, running a dry finger over the lines of Selena's hand while she muttered under her breath.

Selena let the woman look for as long as she could stand the suspense, and then pulled her hand back, letting all the questions clouding her mind fill her eyes.

The woman tilted her head and gazed at her a moment longer and then gave her a sharp nod. "Aye, ye'll wed."

She sat back, her lips pressed into a thin line.

Anne and Selena waited. Surely there was more. She'd spun wonderful fortunes for all the other girls, full of details of the brilliant matches they'd make. Surely there was more for Selena than three short words.

"Is that all?" Anne asked.

The woman hesitated, her eyes darting between the girls, then around the room, as if she wished to ensure no one else would overhear.

"Ye'll wed. I see laughter. And happiness. But it'll require a leap of faith." Her eyes narrowed into tiny slits as she stared at Selena, and she suddenly sat forward, grabbing Selena's hand to yank her closer. "Trust your gut, girl. And choose wisely. Or you may find a few…bumps along the road."

Then she released her and started muttering under her breath again.

Selena stood there, thoroughly discombobulated. What…did that *mean*? Trust and wise choices? Leaps of faith? And what bumps along the road?

Selena wasn't sure what to make of it all. But as she walked away, the fortune teller's quiet mutterings turned into a chilling cackle, and she couldn't help but feel as if her 'fortune' had been more of a curse.

CHAPTER ONE

SELENA DAMPIERRE FIORENTINO Albescu MacLaren (nee Griffiths) watched the handsome men loitering about the ballroom, determined that none of them would be her next victim. Four—almost five—dead husbands were quite enough for one woman, thank you.

To say she was unlucky in love was an understatement of such a staggering magnitude the phrase was rendered nearly useless. Cursed, would be more apt. It might have taken her a while to learn that unfortunate truth, but she'd nearly come to terms with it. Nearly.

Unfortunately, there was a tiny shred of hope still lodged in her broken heart that she couldn't quite extricate. She sighed and took a deep sip of her lemonade. Try as she might, she couldn't let go of the dream of love. Marriage. Perhaps even a family. Despite her dismal attempts in the past.

"Stop it." Mrs. Jane Haddon, her sister-in-law (from her fourth marriage), came to stand beside her.

"Stop what?" Selena glanced at her, trying to ignore the slight twinge she always felt when looking at the woman who looked so much like her husband Charles.

"Thinking so hard," she said, her gentle Scottish brogue softening the underlying criticism of her words. "Ye're allowed to come out of seclusion, Selena. And even enjoy yourself occasionally."

Selena let out a slow breath. "I am here, am I not?"

Jane's delicate brow arched. "Due only to coercion and a few well-timed threats on my part."

Selena snorted softly. "Be that as it may, I am here, and I'm enjoying myself immensely."

"If this is you enjoying yourself, then I'm afraid I must inform you, you are dismal at it."

Jane could always be counted upon to point out the uncompromising truth. "Perhaps *immensely* is a bit of an overstatement..."

Jane let out a harumphing laugh, and though it had been relatively quiet, it still drew a fair number of glances.

Then again, Selena had been drawing glances since the moment she walked in the room. Her eyes darted about, not lingering on any one person too much. Though their eyes lingered on her.

She was a stranger in their midst, one who had arrived in a cloud of rumors. Of course they stared. A woman of barely five and twenty who had already been widowed? Multiple times? Their interest was not unexpected. Though that did not make it easier to shoulder. Few knew exactly how many times she'd been widowed, or the circumstances of her husbands' deaths, and she preferred to keep it that way. One freak accident was dreadful enough. But four? The tongues would never stop wagging.

Still. Just the fact of them was enough to set the gossips agog, even without the details. Even moving soon after each husband's demise hadn't stopped that.

Jane's sympathetic smile soothed her somewhat. "If their whispers bother you, we can leave at any time."

Selena let out a long sigh. "There will always be whispers, I fear. Leaving Edinburgh didn't stop them. Nor did leaving Bucharest, or Venice, or Paris. Or," she said with a grimace, "Geneva." The site of her most recent debacle.

Jane's loyal fury lit her face. "No one knows your real story. They wouldn't gossip so much if they knew."

They had had this argument before. And Selena still did not agree. "Knowing the truth wouldn't stop anyone from spreading any tidbit they might have picked up. No matter how untrue, or hurtful, it is. In fact, I think they prefer it to be so."

Jane couldn't argue with that, though Selena could tell she wanted to.

"I had hoped London would be different," Jane finally said. "My offer stands, if you would like to leave."

And she meant it too, though Selena knew her sister-in-law would prefer to stay. Truth be told, Selena wished to stay as well, despite all the stares and whispers. She had been under self-imposed exile for far too long. The loneliness was beginning to eat away at her. If she indulged in it much longer, there would be nothing left.

"Thank you. Perhaps I—"

A blond gentleman across the room, lankier than she preferred but handsome enough, caught her eye and gave her a slow smile that sent faint but definite interest swirling about in her head. She blew out a sharp breath through her nose and hid her suddenly flushed face behind her fan.

"Yes?" Jane asked, her amused tone letting Selena know her razor-sharp eyes had missed nothing.

"I—" Selena cleared her throat and looked away, refusing to look back at him. "I think I should like to stay, for a little while longer, at least."

"I'm glad to hear it," Jane said, a sly smile on her narrow lips.

Selena grimaced at her, which only made Jane laugh. They both knew she wasn't going to leave. She just couldn't help herself. She was in love with love. Or the idea of love, in any case. Or perhaps she was just dreadfully lonely and the sight of any kind face sparked interest.

But interest from afar would have to be good enough. She'd tried, and failed, too many times to put herself back on the marriage mart. Not that anyone would have her anyway. Not with the rumors of her past swirling about her. That would prove even worse if they discovered the truth.

Saying "I do" to her was as good as a man signing his death warrant.

Jane called such thoughts maudlin and dramatic. But Selena could not stop them from intruding. She might not have physically killed her men, but she *had* been cursed. That was evident enough. Every one of her husbands had perished before the ink was even dry in the marriage register. As far-fetched as it seemed, what other explanation was there?

She'd given fate enough chances. She was done. Finished with silly dreams. Hopes for a happy future with a loving husband. She'd find her own path to happiness. Alone.

Which was why she'd ventured to London. Hundreds of miles away from the string of misery she hoped to leave behind.

"So. See anything you like?" Jane said.

"Absolutely not." Selena tried to inject as much polite horror into her voice as possible. "I've had enough of all that, thank you. I've given up the quest for matrimony… while there are still men left alive in the northern hemisphere," she added under her breath.

Jane, with her ears like a fox, heard her anyway. "There's always the southern hemisphere."

"Jane!"

"Oh, don't go working yourself into a lather," Jane said, waving her off. "I merely jest."

"Um hum," Selena rumbled.

She adored Jane, but if her parents had hoped Jane would prove a sobering influence on her, they had been sorely misled. Perhaps willfully so. After marrying their daughter off multiple times only to have her return home to lick her wounds time and again, they hadn't protested too vehemently when Selena had voiced her desire to return to England to stay with Jane after her disastrous fifth attempt at wedded bliss.

They had agreed with alacrity. She couldn't truly blame them. After all, how many times must they give her away before she stayed gone?

"Make what excuses you like," Selena said, "but *I* am the common denominator in my past relationships. I think at some point we must acknowledge that I am obviously a danger, a threat. Like an unlucky coin that keeps turning up."

"Oh tosh. You are nothing of the sort. Though you *are* maudlin this evening."

"With cause."

Jane scoffed. "Very well, I will admit you've had a bit of bad luck—"

"A bit?" Selena said with a mirthless laugh.

Jane pursed her lips together and glanced at her side eyed. "All right. Perhaps a bit more than a bit."

Selena snorted delicately, a noise Jane steadfastly ignored. "Charles would want you to find some happiness," Jane said, leaning toward her to speak quietly.

Ah Charles. Her favorite of her husbands. The only one she might have truly loved, given time. Not that it had made one lick of difference in the end.

"I tried that. I gave it one more chance after Charles. And I was left with nothing but an empty church and a host of regrets."

Jane's petite face grew fierce. "The only regret you should have when it comes to Otto von Richter is that he didn't die like the rest of them."

"Jane!" Selena gaped at her, truly stunned.

Jane pursed her perfect, bow-shaped lips together and then huffed. "My apologies, Lena. But the man was a scoundrel. I will never understand why you agreed to marry him."

Selena sighed. "Neither will I, in truth. It seemed a good idea at the time."

Jane harumphed and took another sip of her lemonade.

It always seemed like a good idea. With the promise of that fortune teller ringing in her head, that she would marry and find happiness if she trusted her instincts and took a leap of faith, she'd jumped into relationships with all of them.

She just never seemed to realize, until it was too late, that her instincts were abysmal and she leapt way too far. Too quickly.

Then again, it was rather difficult for one's instincts to warn one of impending doom when each of their deaths seemed more a stroke of cruel fate than anything she could possibly control. All the more reason to avoid such possibilities in the future. At least Otto had left *before* the wedding, rather than risk leaving her a widow for the fifth time.

"It had," Selena insisted. "Otto was so dashing and…spontaneous and exuberant. He was a breath of fresh air after my melancholy over Charles's death."

Jane's exasperation softened at the mention of her brother, and she reached out to squeeze Selena's arm.

Losing Charles had deeply saddened Selena. The others…oh, she'd regretted their deaths, of course. They'd been good men. But little more than strangers when they wed. Each one had swept her off her feet and whisked her through whirlwind courtships that had gone from bridal veils to widow's weeds in distressingly short periods of time.

Their intervals together had been quite diverting. While they'd lasted. But the gold dust would likely have fallen off the pig soon enough, as her mother would say, had they not shuffled off this mortal coil so quickly. Though their families had all made good on her husbands' promises of security upon their deaths. Despite the brevity of the actual marriage. The reason she'd agreed to wed them all in the first place. Well, one of the reasons. But as a woman, it was an important one. So. There was that.

"I know how much you cared for Charles," Jane said. "And how lonely you've been since his death."

Selena blanched, chastising herself for being so obvious. She did try to hide her more morose moments. Especially from Jane, who mourned her brother dearly.

"And if you are going to stay to enjoy yourself this evening, well…" Jane shrugged a shoulder. "You are too young not to enjoy such bounty." Jane made eyes at a shy-looking young man who blushed and hurried to the refreshment table to drown his reddening cheeks in punch.

The women laughed, but Selena shook her head. "While you are not entirely incorrect, I think I've given fate enough chances to be kind to me. I'd rather not tempt it again."

Though speaking of temptation…

A tall, broad-shouldered man with thick, wavy brunette locks and a jawline that would be at home with Michelangelo's *David* sauntered into the room. He glanced about, one brow raised over a twinkling eye as if to say *"Behold, I have arrived!"* As if he thought the festivities could not begin without him.

Though, in his defense, if she must be charitable, he *did* command a justified, if unseemly, amount of attention. The eye of every unwed lady in the ballroom was upon him. And the eye of more than a few wed ladies as well. Of all ages, she noticed, her lips twitching when she spied the ancient Lady Collier making moon eyes over her fan at the gentleman.

"He would be a lovely treat," Jane whispered to her.

"Jane! Really," Selena whispered back.

Of course…he *would*. His hands alone, with those long, strong fingers encased in their pristine white gloves as he clapped a friend on the shoulder, were large enough to—

No. She nipped that thought in the bud, appetizing as it may be. All of that was beside the point.

Jane leaned toward Selena again. "No one is saying you have to marry again. However. A few discreet liberties with a handsome gentleman now and then wouldn't be so unusual."

"Jane!" Selena exclaimed again, trying to keep her voice down.

Jane simply shrugged. "You're a widow, dear sister. One with adequate means and little supervision. Take advantage."

Selena clapped her hand over her mouth to keep her scandalized laughter muted. Jane winked at her and turned to survey the room once again.

Her dear sister-in-law might have been purposely baiting her to pull her from the doldrums. But she did have a valid argument. Selena had money, courtesy of her husbands—a sizeable inheritance from Charles and small settlements from the families of her other husbands. Generous of them, considering most of her marriages had very obviously not lasted long enough to actually consummate them. Not enough to entice any reluctant bridegrooms, but enough to live comfortably for the rest of her life.

Her only chaperone was Jane who, as a married woman and her relative by marriage, might do for propriety's sake but was proving to be more of an instigator than a deterrent. And, more relevantly, the loneliness that was Selena's constant companion had grown nearly unbearable of late. It was the greatest reason she had agreed to visit Jane, in fact. She needed to move on from her parents' home. Build a life for herself. As she did not intend for that life to include a husband, she would like to find friends. Companions. Worthy occupations with which to pass her time.

And…

"Perhaps a moment or two of discreet companionship now and then wouldn't be the end of the world," she said quietly.

"That's my girl," Jane whispered back.

Selena shook her head, but with a fond smile. "As long as I take the proper precautions, of course."

"Of course," Jane nodded sagely.

"And never allow it to become more than that," Selena added.

Jane's dismayed groan made Selena smile. But she was resolute. "I'm sorry to disappoint you, but I will not yield on this. I will *never* marry again. My heart has been through enough."

"I hate to hear you say that, but…I can't say that I blame you," Jane said, patting her hand.

"Besides," Selena muttered, "I am running distressingly short of countries in which to become a widow. I cannot return to France, Italy, Wallachia, Bavaria…Scotland." She gave Jane a sad smile. "If I bury a husband in England, I'll have to relocate to the

Americas."

Jane clapped a hand over her mouth to muffle her amused snort, then shook her head. "Now that *would* be a real tragedy."

"Mrs. MacLaren, Mrs. Haddon," Lady Persing said in greeting as she approached.

Selena and Jane both startled, too lost in their own conversation to have noticed their friend. They smiled in welcome as the older woman sidled up to them with a mischievous smile.

"What has you looking so delightfully scandalized, I wonder?" Lady Persing asked.

Before Selena could answer, Jane piped up. "I have been trying to convince dear Selena that she mustn't become a recluse now that she has finally returned home. She seems distressingly determined to remain aloof. Despite the wealth of entertainment at her fingertips," she said, with a delicate nod at the mingling assembly.

"Oh, my dear," Lady Persing said, fanning herself gently. "I agree with Mrs. Haddon. If Lord Persing were to ever to depart this earthly plane…"

The three women looked toward Lord Persing, who had found himself a nice quiet corner, perched himself on a chair, and promptly fallen asleep, his head bobbing toward his rather rotund chest.

Jane and Selena joined in the laughter as Lady Persing giggled fondly.

Selena finally sucked in a deep breath and Jane glanced at her, eyebrows raised in question.

"Very well then," Selena said, with the air of one very much put upon. "Perhaps I shall attempt to be more open to any opportunities that come my way. I may even reconsider my status as the city's resident recluse."

Jane flashed her a delighted grin, which Selena couldn't help but echo.

She lifted her now empty lemonade glass and turned toward the refreshment table. "Just as soon as I—ah!"

She looked up into the stunned eyes of the handsome brown-haired gentleman she'd spied earlier, who was now standing before her, eyes wide, hands holding a half-empty glass of lemonade and an empty plate that had likely once held the cake that was now dribbling its way into her decolletage.

She glanced back at Jane, who for once in her life had been robbed of speech.

Selena grimaced as the sticky dessert slipped into her stays. "I've changed my mind."

CHAPTER TWO

EDWARD COLWYN LAURENCE Brelsford, Marquess of Lockhaven, stared in fascinated horror as the confection
previously on his plate slowly slid its way into the bodice of the
stunned woman before him.

"I am terribly sorry." He grabbed a passing footman and
deposited his now empty plate and half-filled glass on the man's
tray before sending him off for napkins. He whipped his handkerchief from his pocket and reached toward the woman but froze,
coming to his senses just before he began accosting the woman
further in an effort to clean the dessert from her—well, her…

He cleared his throat and looked with rising panic between
the three women.

The woman beside her—Mrs. Haddon, if he remembered
correctly—took the cloth from him with a distracted smile and
pressed it into the other woman's hand. She took it, but continued to stare at him with wide, piercingly sapphire-blue eyes that
were a stunning contrast to the nearly black ringlets that framed
her face.

"My sincere apologies," he said again, clasping his hands
behind his back to keep from reaching for her.

"That's… quite… all right," she stammered, turning her back
so she could attempt to repair the damages.

"It was so clumsy of me," he continued. "I'm afraid I didn't see you there."

That was a lie. He'd seen no one *but* her since he entered the room and clapped eyes on her. She was the entire reason he'd ventured to the refreshment table in the first place. So that he might get closer and hopefully garner an introduction. Anthony—Viscount Goodwin and his oldest friend in the world—was still in the corner struck dumb with shock.

So was Edward, to be honest. He hadn't gone out of his way to be introduced to a woman in…well, ever.

This one though…he had been moving toward her before he'd made the conscious thought to do so. Like a bee to a flower. A moth to a flame. A dog to a bone. He simply couldn't help himself and that fact alone made him more curious about this woman. And concerned. This was quite out of character for him. Perhaps he was coming down with something. He did feel rather ill. Though that might be more due to the terrible social gaffe he'd just committed than any impending illness.

A pity, that. A touch of the grippe or pleurisy, a bit of gout maybe, at least had some hope of being cured. Smearing one's pudding down a woman's chest—an activity he might relish under other circumstances—might be the social death of him.

He'd lost sight of her for a moment, however, when he'd turned his back in an effort to make their meeting seem spontaneous. And then misjudged her proximity when he'd turned back around. Horribly misjudged.

"I'm sorry, my lord, but are you ill?"

Edward glanced at Lady Persing, who was looking at him with stunned concern.

Right. Standing staring with one's mouth agape after committing such an atrocity likely did make him seem rather…off. To put it mildly. "Yes. Quite. That is no, rather—" He stopped and sucked in a sharp breath through his nose.

Contain yourself, man!

"I am dreadfully sorry. My apologies again…"

The poor woman turned back to him, her cheeks stained a

deep pink from scooping what she could from her bustline without totally disgracing herself in front of the entire ballroom. Though he'd at least had the presence of mind to position himself to block her from the view of most in the room. Still, she'd likely need to excuse herself before she could clean up completely.

He glanced back at Lady Persing, eyebrows slightly raised. The woman finally snapped out of her shock and cleared her throat.

"Yes, of course. Mrs. MacLaren, please allow me to introduce Lord Lockhaven," she said, her eyes darting between them with growing interest. Nothing got past the old gossip.

Edward kept his face as neutral as he could make it at the word *Missus*.

"It's a pleasure, Mrs. MacLaren," he said, bowing his head slightly before turning to the other woman at her side. "And Mrs. Haddon. I hope you are enjoying your evening."

"It has certainly taken an interesting turn, Lord Lockhaven." Her contemplative gaze raked over him. "Mrs. MacLaren has been a dear to keep me company the last few weeks. She is my sister by marriage," she said.

"Ah," he said politely, hoping he wasn't betraying his disappoint—

"She has decided to stay with us for a while now that my dear brother Charles is gone," Mrs. Haddon explained, giving him a conspiratorial smile.

Disappointment averted. Edward's eyebrows raised, and Mrs. Haddon softly smirked before turning to Lady Persing.

Well, well. It seemed Mrs. MacLaren was a widow.

And out of mourning, judging by the soft blue gown that cupped her curves and the generous sprinkling of diamonds and aquamarines at her throat, ears, and wrists. He should be ashamed of the hope that spiked through him. Flabbergasted was more apt, however. Utterly bewildered and confused. Hope for what? The most he ever hoped for when it came to a lovely lady was perhaps a lively dance, some innocent flirting, and then he was off to find some not-so-innocent activities in more experienced quarters.

Mrs. MacLaren, it seemed, was already proving quite the conundrum.

"I am sorry for your loss, Mrs. MacLaren. But delighted you have decided to grace us with your presence," he said, aiming his most charming smile at her.

What had gotten into him?

A quick glance at Anthony, who had moved closer and was now standing, mouth agape and eyes shining with something that looked like befuddled amusement, showed he wasn't the only one confused.

"Thank you, Lord Lockhaven. You are most kind." Mrs. MacLaren shot a desperate look at Mrs. Haddon, then glanced back at him with a strained smile. "If you will excuse me for a moment, I must...um..." Her eyes darted down to her gown, then back to him, then to Mrs. Haddon, before flitting back to his face.

"Of course, of course. My sincerest apologies again. Perhaps," he said, his words stopping her before she could turn away, "you'll permit me to make amends with a dance?"

Her mouth dropped open, and he feared imminent rejection, and rightly so after what he'd done to her gown, but Mrs. Haddon stepped in again.

"How lovely," she said with a smile.

He was growing quite fond of that woman.

"You would be delighted to accept, isn't that right, Selena?" she murmured to Mrs. MacLaren, though loud enough for him to hear.

When Mrs. MacLaren—*Selena*—continued to gape, Mrs. Haddon smiled at him.

"She would be delighted," Jane said firmly, ignoring the way Mrs. MacLaren's gaze jerked to her. "We won't be but a moment."

The women excused themselves and hurried toward the

dressing room that had been made available to the guests. Before they were fully out of sight, Anthony was at his side.

"That was an interesting strategy for getting a woman's attention, I must say," he drawled. "Accosting them with pastry…who would have ever thought?"

Edward scowled at him. "It was an accident."

"I should hope so," Anthony said with a snort. Then he looked around, eyebrows raised. "Is your continued presence in this corner an indication that you intend to wait for this woman to return?"

"Yes," Edward said warily. He already knew what his friend would say. And he wanted no part of it.

Anthony crossed his arms and shook his head, his expression almost awestruck. "I never thought I'd see the day."

Edward let out a sigh. "What day?"

"That the lover Lord of Lockhaven would be ensnared by a woman."

The eyeroll that remark elicited from Edward made Anthony chuckle.

"You are ridiculous," Edward said.

Anthony pursed his lips and nodded. "True. But *you* have been avoiding marriage since the day you came of age. This is a novel experience for me. I have never seen you actively pursue an eligible young lady. Or even dance with one more than once. Or voluntarily speak at length to one. You are far more wont to hide from them."

That rang a little too true for Edward's comfort. Though, *hiding* was too strong a word. He was still in full view of the rest of the ballroom. But he couldn't deny that his position in the corner with his back turned to most everyone but Anthony likely broadcast a certain message.

Still.

"First of all, I am not hiding." He ignored Anthony's snort. "Nor am I pursuing anyone. All I am pursuing is a dance. And secondly—"

"Thirdly."

He glared at the correction. "Mrs. MacLean is a widow."

Anthony's eyes widened further. "Oh, well now, that *does* present a few possibilities, I suppose. Or, at the very least, removes a few immediate expectations. As long as the lady isn't looking for another husband. In which case, you will be in much the same boat as with the virginal hopefuls over there," he said, subtly nodding his head over his shoulder.

Edward scoffed and turned back to watch the door through which Mrs. MacLaren had disappeared.

Though Anthony, yet again, wasn't wrong.

The sudden, intense, and wholly consuming desire to *know* this woman, the moment he'd clapped eyes on her, was both a familiar and totally foreign urge. He loved women. Everything about them. The way they moved, the way they spoke, the way they were somehow soft yet hard as steel. He loved conversing with them, dancing with them, dining with them. Making them come apart in his bed. As long as their liaison began and ended with the mutual agreement and understanding it would go no further than a blissful night or two.

And that conversation never happened at all if the woman in question was young, inexperienced, or would ever be in search of a husband. Because that man would never be he.

His interest in the raven-haired beauty who had drawn his eye was decidedly more intense than usual. And as he knew nothing at all about her—aside from her widowhood, which at least removed the inexperienced problem—this was more than a little concerning.

Yet still, he waited.

"Perhaps this interest means you are ready to—"

"You know me better than that, Goodwin," Edward said.

Anthony let out a sigh that could have come from his mother's lips. "Yes, I know. The word 'relationship' makes you nearly apoplectic."

"That is categorically—

"True."

"An exaggeration," Edward said with a chuckle. "I simply prefer my…interactions—" He ignored Anthony's snort at his refusal to even say the word relationship, "with ladies of a certain breeding to be brief in nature and heavily chaperoned. That way everyone is aware of expectations and there are no messy entanglements."

He would absolutely *never* dabble with a lady on the marriage mart whose reputation might suffer from his attentions. Attentions that might change that lady into a wife he had no wish for. He had too much regard for both their future and his own.

Anthony shook his head, disappointment weighing his features down. "Marriage might do you some good."

"Marriage," Edward said, the word sending a shiver up his spine, "is but a death knell to true passion. And sanity."

Anthony chuckled but Edward pressed on. "It is! I've seen it time and time again. From my father who will pine after my mother until the day he dies though she'll never feel more than a passing fondness for him…"

Anthony tilted his head to the side and pursed his lips with a grudging nod of agreement.

"To scores of friends and acquaintances," Edward continued. "Who, no matter how happy the union began, at some point all devolved into complacency at best. Outright hatred at worst."

Anthony scoffed, and Edward raised a finger before his friend could interject.

"And I have no intention of ever shackling myself so."

"Hmm," Anthony said, leaning closer. "Then how did one look at this mysterious woman suddenly spark such a marked change in your very nature, hmm?"

"That is a severe overstatement of the situation," Edward said, tugging on his cuffs to straighten his jacket as he waited to catch sight of the delectable Mrs. MacLaren again. "I merely desire a dance with her. As an apology for my little accident."

"That is all?" Anthony asked, one eyebrow quirking up.

"Yes." He paused. "Though, I will admit to a slight curiosity."

He scowled at Anthony's quick grin.

"Do not read too much into it. Judging from the looks that were aimed her way," Edward continued, ignoring his friend's smirk, "I'm not the only one who is curious about the lady. Mrs. Haddon said her coming here was returning home, but I've certainly never seen her before."

"Yes, well despite your obvious love of the fairer sex, even you do not know every woman in England."

Well, he couldn't argue with that. "Fair point. Hence, the mystery that may be leading me to be *somewhat* intrigued by the woman."

"Um hm," Anthony muttered. "Wait a moment. She isn't *the* widow, is she?"

Edward frowned. "*The* widow? How do you mean?"

Anthony's wide-eyed look of outraged shock would have been downright comical if Edward weren't so thoroughly confused as to his meaning. Well, it was comical anyway, but that didn't change Edward's confusion.

"*The* widow," Anthony repeated. "The one everyone has been talking about."

Edward squinted, still unsure as to what his friend referred.

"Oh, for the love of all that is holy, how you can be such a social hail-fellow and still be so sadly misinformed of the latest scandals, I will never know," Anthony said with more than a little mock disgust for Edward's failure.

Edward just chuckled and crossed his arms over his chest. "I have little defense. Of course, I *have* just returned from several weeks in the country and this is the first event I have attended since my return."

"Hmm, I suppose," Anthony grumbled.

"And," Edward added, "I have taken the utmost pains to avoid my mother and sisters who would be the most likely to supply me with such information."

"That is true enough," Anthony admitted. "Afraid they'll

have you married off before you can unpack your bags?"

Edward poured every ounce of his frustration into his grimace. Being the eldest unwed brother in a family with three elder sisters who had all already done their duty and suitably married made him the focus of far too many meddling mamas. His two youngest brothers had so far escaped the attention focused on him, and likely would until he, the heir, had married a suitable bride.

"You have no idea. They have been nothing short of militant."

Anthony laughed again.

"Well, enlighten me, my friend. What have I missed about this infamous widow?"

Anthony glanced about and stepped a little closer, lowering his voice. "According to several sources—"

"What sources?"

"Don't interrupt. According to these sources, there is a widow traveling about leaving dead husbands in her wake."

Edward squinted an eye. "So…the gossip is that this widow has dead husbands? Isn't that the very definition of the word?"

Anthony huffed, obviously perturbed that Edward wasn't taking this more seriously.

"It is the manner they became deceased that is at issue. And the number of husbands she has in that state."

Well then. That was enough to spark a little interest in Edward.

"I take it the lady has buried more than one husband then?" he asked.

Anthony nodded solemnly. "Upwards of twenty, I've heard."

Edward didn't bother to hide the mocking tone of his scoff.

"No! 'Tis true!" Anthony insisted. "And more than the quantity of poor unfortunates who have crossed her path is the fact that she has supposedly helped usher each of them into their graves."

Edward regarded his friend for a moment, not quite sure how to respond to such astonishing tidings. Though it *would* be his luck that the only woman who had spurred him to show genuine interest in more months than he could count could possibly be the actual death of him. Not just the metaphorical one should she ever trap him into matrimony.

"Well, well. You have me intrigued. Terrified," Edward said with a self-deprecating grin. "But intrigued."

Anthony's eyes flicked up, and he leaned forward, his smile flush with anticipation. "Well, gird your loins, my terrified friend. Your lady returns."

CHAPTER THREE

SELENA MARCHED BACK into the ballroom, her head held high. Her bosom might be red as a crushed cherry from the mostly futile attempt to remove every last tracing of icing sugar from her skin, but her dress, at least, was mostly intact. The dessert had kept its sticky fingers to the inside of her gown, so the outside was still presentable.

"I suppose I needn't wonder how many people saw that little spectacle," she muttered to Jane as they fully reentered the room. Every eye turned toward them, most widened in scandalized interest. More than a few fans hid the titters and murmured words of the amused throngs.

"Ignore them, my dear," Lady Persing said. "They are not worth your time. If you will excuse me, I must wake my dear husband before his snoring brings down the rafters," she said, giving Selena a supportive smile before moving off toward Lord Persing.

"Lady Persing is correct. Words can only hurt you if you let them," Jane murmured, glaring at the nearest pair of gossiping debutantes.

"That is depressingly untrue, my dear Jane, or I would still be in Paris."

Jane's brow furrowed at the mention of the setting of Selena's first disastrous marriage—and the reason for her abrupt departure from that city. But she couldn't respond further as Lord Lockhaven had caught sight of them.

Selena took a deep breath and tried to let it out as unobtrusively as possible. He was a handsome rogue, if the twinkle in those warm brown eyes meant anything. What on earth was she to do about him? She hadn't expected him to be still waiting for her to emerge. In fact, she'd purposely taken longer than necessary to ensure his departure. Most men's attentions waned quickly, and there were certainly more than a few women at this ball waiting for his notice.

"Perhaps we should have made our escape out the back entrance," she whispered to Jane behind her fan.

"Nonsense," Jane whispered back. "You came to enjoy yourself. So, go enjoy!"

Before she could get another word in edgewise, Lord Lockhaven came to a stop before them and bowed his head.

"I am glad to see that my clumsiness didn't cause too much damage," he said, his eyes lingering on her neckline.

A thrill skittered down her spine, and Selena clenched her fist around her fan handle. She wasn't quite sure what it was about him. He was handsome, yes. But she had been around handsome men before. Her husbands had been handsome, all. But none had wrought such a response in her. Was it the wicked gleam in his eyes when he looked at her? The crooked tilt of his lips when he smiled, as if he held a tantalizing secret he would share only with her? The confidence that bordered on arrogance in his demeanor that lent such a swagger to his step that her knees became weak?

Or was it the heat that filled his gaze when their eyes met? A heat that promised a pleasure she had only ever had a taste of before.

Her mouth suddenly parched, Selena swallowed with difficulty and snapped her fan open, hoping a bit of cool breeze would cool her thoughts. His mouth pulled into that slight grin again, and she sucked in a sharp breath she prayed he had not heard.

Perhaps Jane was right. A little *discreet* amusement might not be amiss. A few years ago, she would have used that fan to remind him where his eyes should be. She would *not* have stood there, letting him look his fill with hardly a peep. She certainly would not have taken a perhaps slightly deeper than necessary breath in order to ensure his view was…adequate.

A realization that had her flushing until her eyes watered and hoping no one else had noticed her brief foray into wantonness.

"Not at all, my lord. I have been assured the dress is salvageable." Her pride was an altogether different matter, but she was well accustomed to holding her head high despite her circumstances. Which were often dire. And ridiculous.

"Excellent news." He held out his hand as the band began the opening notes of a quadrille.

At least it wasn't a waltz. Had it been that, she might have lingered in the dressing room longer. Or taken advantage of the back door. A dance was one thing. But the waltz was so intimate. Scandalous. And dangerous. A waltz had been the main cause of her third marriage. Though even a quadrille was dangerous enough. It afforded far too many opportunities for conversation than some of the other dances.

She shut down that thought and slipped her hand into that of the waiting lord, scolding herself for her thoughts. It was a dance, not a marriage proposal. She might be a magnet for matrimony but surely even she could get through one dance without becoming betrothed. Again. Though, the way her hand tingled at his touch, even through the layers of their gloves, didn't bode well.

"How long have you been back on our shores?" he asked, his warm smile catching her off guard as they joined the other couple in their set to begin the dance. "I don't believe I have seen you this Season. Or prior to that, come to think of it."

"No, you wouldn't have. I spent my childhood in Wales. And have been abroad most of the years since. I've only recently arrived in London."

She smiled as she crossed the square made by the dancers,

hoping the expression covered the fact that her answer was only mostly truthful. She'd been back from the Continent for quite some time. But as she had no wish to discuss her time in Scotland as it would inevitably lead to discussion of her fourth husband, Charles, and possibly to the subject of her other husbands—or at the very least, thoughts of them, which would always be too painful—she saw no harm in a little interpretation of his question. One that would allow her to answer him—to do otherwise would be churlish and suspicious—yet remain sufficiently vague enough to protect her past.

"Months?" he asked as they came back together. "And I'm only now making your acquaintance?"

She cocked her head. "I was unaware you were in the habit of making the acquaintance of everyone in London, my lord. And upon their immediate arrival, no less."

He chuckled but the steps of the dance spun them away from each other for a few moments. When they faced each other again, he said, "Everyone, no. But I am acquainted with a fair many."

His flirtatious grin set her heart to fluttering.

"And I would have been foolhardy indeed not to make the acquaintance of such an intriguing woman as you," he murmured when the steps brought them close enough for him to lean down so she alone would hear him.

She flushed again, glad the steps of the dance took her away from him for a moment. Not that she wasn't enjoying his company. She was. Quite a bit more than expected. Or was wise. Aside from the blatant flattery he insisted on heaping upon her— and to be truthful, she didn't hate that as much as she should—he seemed a jolly sort. His ready smiles and shameless flirting amused her. And it had been a good long while since anyone had amused her so.

"You seem the type to find most women intriguing," she said, his playfulness making her bold.

"Some more than others," he answered, his smile drawing another one from her.

"Perhaps you *have* seen me and were too distracted by the others to notice."

"Oh no, I am certain had I seen you before, everyone else would have disappeared, as they have this evening."

She raised an eyebrow at that. "A woman could drown under such flattery, my lord. Are you always so…profuse?"

He chuckled. "Not always, no."

"Well, that is good to hear. I would fear for your health if you exerted yourself so copiously as a habit."

They spun away again, and Selena took the opportunity to gather herself. This interaction was bringing her far too much enjoyment. Danger lay behind those dancing eyes of his. Danger for her heart…and his life.

She was cursed in love. Fate had proven that to be true every time she'd taken that leap of faith into the promise of love. She'd do well to remember that.

"Tell me, truly," he said as they clasped hands and spun together. "I know you are widowed, if you'll forgive me mentioning it. But you are still young, and out of mourning." His eyes took in her attire with an interested twinkle. "Why haven't I seen you until this evening?"

His deep voice sent a delightful shiver through her.

"You are very forward, my lord. Shockingly so."

"It is a failing, I'm afraid." He flashed her mischievous grin. "One I rather like."

She bit her lip to keep from smiling. She rather liked it too.

"I tend to keep to myself," she murmured, trying to answer without answering. "I've seen little reason to venture out too often of late."

"Well," he said with another roguish smile, "I shall endeavor to give you a reason and entice you from hiding. There are far too many pleasures to be had to spend your days secluded."

Yes. There were. And it was those very pleasures of which she was afeared.

Even so, she found herself smiling more and more as the

dance progressed. And she wasn't the only one over whom Lord Lockhaven had cast his spell. He'd put their dance partners so at ease that the four of them twirled and weaved and clasped hands with much merriment, despite her being a stranger. One of which they hadn't been sure when she had initially joined them.

Not that anyone had been overtly impolite to her since her arrival. To her face. But no one had been overly friendly, either. And whispers and rumors followed behind her every time she passed. Yet, despite her misgivings, she couldn't regret agreeing to the dance. Or deciding to leave her self-imposed exile in Jane's house to venture out that evening. And it was all due to the dashing lord who clasped her hand like it was a precious thing and smiled into her eyes like she was the only one in the room.

A lady could far too easily get used to such treatment.

And this particular lady was already far too prone to fall for dashing gentlemen. She would be wise to guard her heart a little more carefully. As she had pledged to do not half an hour earlier. As she still intended to do…until Lockhaven flashed yet another brilliant smile in her direction that had her ready to throw all caution to the wind.

Perhaps she suffered from some malady of the heart and mind. There was certainly something in her that craved love and affection. It must be a defect in her. How else could one explain how her steadfast vows to remain aloof crumbled with such alarming ease in this man's presence.

He smiled again, his fingers tightening on hers ever so slight-ly, and she let out a shaky sigh.

Lord help her.

Because she certainly didn't seem capable of helping herself.

EDWARD WATCHED THE conflicting emotions play over Mrs. MacLaren's face and had to suck in a deep breath to tamp down his exuberance. The lady was obviously drawn to him. And equally obviously not happy about that fact. Or at least guarded. Confusingly so.

The reason for her hesitance nagged at him. As a widow, she was no blushing virgin who knew not of the ways of the world. Yet she seemed determined to keep him at arms' length. Even while her eyes begged him to draw her closer.

She was such an intriguing mix of contradictions. He wanted nothing more than to discover all her secrets. Oh, he didn't put any credence in the rumors floating around about her. There was nothing Society liked more than a good scandal that it could blow out of proportions. They heard of a woman who had buried a husband or two and suddenly she was a murderess hell-bent on matrimonial homicide.

The truth was rarely so titillating. It wouldn't even be out of the ordinary for her to have been married more than once. Likely, Mrs. MacLaren was like many other widows out there. Married off to an older man who unsurprisingly predeceased her only to be married off to another man who followed suit. He doubted there was more to the story than that. His own grandfather had been married no less than three times. Though granted, it was a little less usual for a woman. But hardly unheard of.

Regardless of the mystery surrounding her past, he wanted to make sure that he was part of her future.

That thought nearly made him stumble. Where had that come from?

Her *immediate* future. That was what he meant.

As the dance drew to a close and everyone bowed and nodded, he stepped closer to keep their words as private as possible.

"Thank you for the dance, Mrs. MacLaren. I quite enjoyed myself."

Her cheeks flushed becomingly but instead of glancing down shyly, as he expected her to do, she met his gaze, sending a thrill through him.

"As did I, my lord."

"I would like to continue our acquaintance," he said, heart pounding at his forwardness. "Would you permit me to call upon you tomorrow?"

Her full, perfect mouth dropped open in a slight *O*, and he could hear the sharp breath she sucked in.

"I…" She stopped, her eyes flashing to the waiting Mrs. Haddon before she cleared her throat. "I am deeply sorry, my lord, but I do not think that would be wise. Thank you for the request, but I…you must forgive me. But I'm afraid I must decline."

She dropped a quick curtsy and spun around, hurrying to her sister-in-law.

Anthony appeared at his side less than a second later.

"What just happened? I've never seen that expression from you before. Are you quite well?" he asked, peering at Edward like he'd developed the pox. Then his glance flickered to the retreating women and his eyes widened. "What on earth did you say to the poor woman to make her run from you so?"

As they watched, the women paused near the door while Mrs. MacLaren whispered vehemently to Mrs. Haddon who pursed her lips and finally sighed and nodded. Within moments, they had quit the room and were likely on their way out the door.

"I asked if I could call upon her," Edward said, still bewildered.

Anthony's eyebrows hit his hairline. "You did what? Wait. That is what sent her running?"

"Apparently," Edward said with a frown.

"Then I take it the lady declined your request."

"As much as it pains me to admit it, yes."

The blow to his ego was, admittedly, fierce. But all that aside, he had simply never heard of a woman declining such a request. Oh, he was sure it was done occasionally. But simple politeness dictated that a lady accept any such overtures. Nothing need come of them, of course. But to so bluntly rebuff a man…astounding.

"Interesting," Anthony murmured.

His friend's tone had Edward tearing his eyes from the door and back to Anthony, who was gazing at him with a tilted head and squinted eyes like he was trying to solve one of the world's great mysteries. "How so?"

Anthony quirked another eyebrow up at that. "First of all, I have never seen a woman run from you. Certainly not one in whom you have expressed interest."

"I am sure that isn't true," he said. Women had certainly rejected him before. Though admittedly, he couldn't think of such an instance at the moment. But even if he could, *running* was an extreme reaction.

"And secondly," Anthony continued, ignoring his comment, "I don't know that I've ever heard of a woman turning down such an offer from *any* man of similar standing."

"Thank you!" Edward said, his volume much louder than he'd intended. He glanced around, nodding and smiling at the people who had stopped their conversations at his outburst. "Thank you," he said again, much quieter. "I was of much the same mind. I am not so horrible, am I?"

Anthony snorted. "You are asking the wrong person."

Edward's scowl made Anthony chuckle.

"No, my lord," he said. "You have your faults but none so grievous as to spark such a reaction." Anthony tapped his finger against his chin. "In fact, 'tis usually *you* doing the running."

Edward started at that. "Whatever do you mean? I've never run from a woman in my life."

That elicited a full body chuckle from Anthony. "Oh, you most certainly do. Any time a woman gets even a fraction too close. The moment she or her parents start thinking your interest might be matrimonially minded, you are out the door with your coat tails fluttering behind you. And for the most ridiculous reasons, as well."

Edward scowled again. "You exaggerate."

"Do I? Very well, then. Lady Elizabeth. You danced with her

at three balls and called upon her twice. The columnists had you all but wed with eight children, yet at the fourth ball, the moment you saw her walk through the door, you went out the back."

Edward frowned, not liking where this line of conversation was going. "Her clothing was always covered in the hair of that dog of hers."

Anthony's brow rose again. "Dog hair?"

"Yes. I'm allergic. It makes me itch terribly."

"Your hounds will be surprised to hear that."

"They stay outside."

"You sleep with at least two of them."

Edward scowled again. It was impossible to argue with a friend who knew you so well. "The hounds are fine, it was that little ball of fur she called a canine that was the issue," Edward muttered.

Anthony rolled his eyes. "The only thing that makes you itch is the thought of marriage. The poor woman was mortified."

"I steered Lord Aberforth in her direction. It was quite the match, if I do say so myself. She is now much more happily married than she would have been to me."

"Hmm, most likely true. Perhaps you should hire out your services."

"Don't tempt me," Edward muttered.

"Very well. What about Lady Tabitha? She was lovely."

"Yes. But she also wouldn't stop quoting Shakespeare. I enjoy the man's plays but if I'd had to listen to one more sonnet…"

"Um hmm. Miss Catherine Bixby?"

"Too tall. I was constantly in danger of compromising the poor girl through no fault of my own because my face reached no higher than her bosom."

"The world will laud you for your suffering, I am sure," Anthony said dryly. "All right. Miss Tessmorton."

"Too religious."

"Miss Draper?"

"No sense of humor."

"No, the other Miss Draper."

"Ah, *too* humorous."

"Edward…"

"What? The woman never stopped giggling. I could barely utter a word without setting her off."

"Lady Constance?"

"She…had a chin hair."

"You can't be serious."

"Well, you didn't see it," Edward said. "It was two inches long and black as night, right in the middle of her chin."

"She could have plucked it."

"It would have grown back."

Anthony threw his hands up. "See. Ridiculous. You will find fault with any woman no matter how preposterous or absurd to justify permanent bachelorhood."

"I will not," Edward said, cringing at the petulant tone in his voice.

"So you say. But all evidence is to the contrary, my lord."

Edward blew out a breath, knowing Anthony wasn't entirely wrong.

It was true that he had never earnestly courted a woman. And perhaps the reasons he had failed to do so were slightly…finnicky.

But it was equally possible those women simply hadn't been right for him. Surely if he were truly drawn to a woman, he wouldn't focus on such trivialities. If he were to ever consider matrimony, and that was a big *if,* it would ideally be with a woman he could stand to be around for more than five minutes. He couldn't be faulted if he hadn't met such a woman yet.

His eyes were drawn back to the spot Mrs. MacLaren had last been. And he couldn't help but wonder if maybe he finally had.

It would be just his luck that the one woman he might want apparently did not want him in return. He wished to get to know her more. Allow her to get to know him. He would not pursue a woman who did not wish to be pursued. But he could have sworn there was interest in her eyes, a slight tremble in her hand, as they danced. He had not mistaken the enjoyment they had shared, he'd stake his life on it. Perhaps the lady was not so averse to him as that *no* had implied.

He could but hope that their paths crossed again. And with the rumors that followed her about like clinging shadows, that might not be as difficult as he might have feared. The rumors did give him a slight pause. Even if they were but partially true, the lady seemed to have an unfortunate habit of losing her partners. Therefore, pursuing her in any capacity, even one not matrimonially minded, was a risky endeavor. More so than usual, in any case.

But, foolhardy or not, for the first time in his life, it was a risk he might just be willing to take.

CHAPTER FOUR

T HE LIGHT BREEZE carried the scent of the waterlogged plants that were now stretching their leaves happily in the sun. Selena tilted her face to the light and followed suit. Breathing it in. Reveling in it. Despite the crowds she normally eschewed. After three long days of rain, the graveled paths threading throughout Kensington Gardens were clogged with people, seemingly as delighted as the foliage to be getting a bit of sun.

"I cannot tell if you are happy to be outdoors or not," Jane said, squinting her eyes quizzically. "You are smiling yet frowning at the same time. I cannot say I have ever seen that expression before."

Selena laughed. "I am glad of the sun and fresh air. All the people…a little less so."

"Hmm, I do understand that," Jane said.

"Not that I mind a crowd when the occasion calls for it, mind you," Selena said, her eyes glancing around the crowded paths. "The stares and whispers I could do without, however."

Jane giggled. "Yes, you *are* quite the attraction this afternoon. One would think that a stranger had never been seen in their midst before."

Selena nodded politely at a gentleman who was startled from his gawking and gave her a hasty nod. She had no doubt it was less her newness and more her so-called mystery that drew the glances. But that couldn't be helped. The truth of her past would only cause the tongues to wag faster.

"To be fair, I am being treated kindly enough, I suppose," she replied with a small sigh. "But all the stares do get tiresome."

Kind might be a little charitable, but it was true no one had been explicitly unkind.

"They'll grow used to you soon enough," Jane assured her, making her feel briefly mollified until she added, "though I doubt the stares will stop."

"And why is that?"

Jane stopped walking and glanced at Selena in surprise. "You, my dear, are a beautiful young woman shrouded in an air of mystery. Your face would garner enough interest. But throw in a mysterious past that has the gossips buzzing, and you have become the talk of the ton."

Selena pursed her lips against a moan. "I will never understand why anyone would find my past of such interest."

"It's because they do not know you," Jane said with a shrug. "What they do not know, they invent. And what little they have heard, they exaggerate."

"Lovely," Selena said with a groan.

Jane chuckled. "As if you wouldn't be right in the thick of it with them trying to figure out who this woman was, where she came from, and if it were true that she had ushered twenty men into their graves if your roles were reversed."

"*Twenty*? Is *that* what they are saying now?" Selena blew a puff of air through her nose. "Surely no one believes such nonsense."

Jane shrugged delicately. "You could put the rumors to rest."

Selena's jaw clenched so tightly it ached. She sometimes wondered if Jane could read her very thoughts. Or perhaps it wasn't so difficult to deduce her current line of thinking.

But on this matter, at least, her mind was made up.

She finally gave a jerky shake of her head. "I shouldn't have to bandy about my pain for their curiosity and entertainment." Her breath left her in a shaky rush. "Besides, the truth isn't nearly as salacious as their fictions. They'd likely ignore it no matter what I said in favor of the better story."

Though…it was salacious enough to have chased her from shore to shore. All the more reason to keep it to herself.

"Unfortunately, that is doubtless true." Jane just gave her a knowing look and looped her arm through Selena's as they resumed their walking. "You're new. Which is enough to raise anyone's curiosity. And you've kept yourself mostly away from everyone until the ball last week. Which I understand but certainly hasn't helped with the mystery they think surrounds you. Too few people have had the opportunity to meet you."

"I wouldn't have thought I was so interesting."

Jane chuckled again. "The attention will die down. Or some delightful new scandal will crop up to take your place. Something always does."

"Well, that is true enough," Selena said with a sardonic smile. "I shall endeavor to wait patiently until my turn has passed."

"Hmm, are you sure you want *all* the interest to disappear?" she asked.

The tone of her voice had Selena glancing at her inquisitively and then following her gaze across the path to—

Selena stopped walking with a quick intake of breath.

"As I thought," Jane murmured, ignoring Selena's gasp of outrage so she could send a welcoming smile toward Lord Lockhaven.

Selena's traitorous heart skipped a beat as he walked toward them, another gentleman in his wake.

"Mrs. Haddon, Mrs. MacLaren," he said with a courteous bow. "How very fortuitous. I was just mentioning to Lord Goodwin that I hoped you were out enjoying this beautiful day," he said, looking directly at her. Stunning her into silence. "A joy to see the sun after so many days of rain, is it not?"

Jane waited half a heartbeat, then answered for them in the affirmative when Selena showed no signs of doing so. Though

Selena didn't hear what she replied. Something suitably appropriate, she had no doubt. Her own attention was fully taken with staring at the man like a lovesick schoolgirl. She truly had no idea what sort of hold this man had on her. She was no inexperienced violet whose head was turned by every handsome gentleman who crossed her path. Many, admittedly. But not *all*. She had certainly grown more discerning after marrying—and burying— four husbands. And narrowly avoiding marrying a fifth. Though she hadn't appreciated his fickleness at the time. And she would have greatly appreciated if he had decided to run off *before* the morning of their wedding rather than waiting until she was already at the church.

Still. Better jilted than widowed yet again.

Whatever this strange attraction was between her and the devastatingly handsome Lord Lockhaven, she needed to regain some modicum of control. She could not, *would* not, allow there to be a sixth attempt. No matter how tempting.

Then again, it was rather bold of her to presume he might actually seek a match. She was of good family, certainly. But her father was a mere baronet; her mother the daughter of a country gentleman. They were wealthy, thanks to her father's investments and mother's small inheritance. But she was not of noble blood. And Lord Lockhaven was the heir to a duke. His family likely had higher designs for him than the likes of her.

"You mentioned you haven't yet been introduced to many people here, Mrs. MacLaren," Lord Lockhaven said, drawing her from her thoughts. "I hope you will permit me to help rectify that situation and allow me to present my good friend, Lord Goodwin. His sister, Lady Beatrice, is actually an acquaintance of Mrs. Haddon's, if I'm not mistaken."

"You are correct," Jane said, smiling benignly at both gentlemen. "She speaks very highly of you both."

Lord Goodwin chuckled. "Knowing my sister as I do, Mrs. Haddon, I am sure you are being kind to spare my feelings." Then he turned to Selena. "And it is a very great pleasure to make your acquaintance indeed, Mrs. MacLaren. Lord Lockhaven has spoken of little else since the Hayworths' ball."

Selena's mouth dropped open slightly, at both his admission and what it meant. Her eyes strayed back to Lord Lockhaven, who was glaring at his friend. The expression was so much the same as the one she'd aimed at Jane on frequent occasion, she had to bite her lip to keep from laughing.

Jane glanced around at everyone and then honed her attention on Lord Goodwin. "My lord, would you care to stroll for a moment? I would love to take in a bit more air, and I'm afraid Mr. Haddon will be occupied for quite some time," she said with a nod toward where her husband stood with several other gentlemen deep in conversation.

"I would be happy to accompany you," he said, amusement twinkling in his eyes as he flashed Lord Lockhaven a delighted grin before turning and leading her away. Leaving Selena and Lord Lockhaven to follow.

"That was subtle," Selena murmured.

Lord Lockhaven's chuckled heartily. "Yes, Goodwin isn't known for his finesse."

"Neither is Mrs. Haddon."

"It seems we are doomed to be the object of their machinations then."

"Apparently so."

His smile had her breath catching in her throat, and she turned to follow Jane and Lord Goodwin before she disgraced herself with an ill-timed fainting spell.

They walked in silence for a moment, long enough for her racing heart to calm a bit.

"I must confess, their less-than-subtle meddling aside, I am grateful for the opportunity to speak to you again," he said.

She raised her brows. "Are you?"

He nodded. "Indeed. It gives you the chance to experience all my considerable charms without the distraction of a dessert mucking about in your gown."

That startled a laugh out of her, and she clapped her hand over her mouth until she had it under control. "You seem to have an overly robust opinion of yourself, my lord."

"Do I?" he asked, flashing that grin that never failed to send her stomach spinning. "Or do I simply have a healthy familiarity with my effect on my audience."

She laughed again. "I suppose that is one explanation. Though, few people are so exuberant in their praise of their own appeal."

"This is true," he said with a sage nod. "Though I find most individuals' refusal to state their mind or insistence on pretense to be other than they are maddening. If one is a terrible bore or perhaps, on the other side of the coin, a charismatic, charming creature, for instance," he said, pressing his hand to his chest and bowing his head with a roguish wink, "it does no good to anyone to feign ignorance of the fact."

She chuckled quietly, more charmed and amused by their conversation than she'd like to let on. "Hmm, perhaps. Though I have found, more often than not, it is less a pretense and more a disheartening lack of awareness."

He glanced at her with elated surprise. "Another truth. I must say, Mrs. MacLaren," he said leaning in a bit closer, "I find myself delighted that we seem to be of much the same mind."

"Is it so rare an occurrence?" she asked, brows raised.

"Surprisingly, yes. I often find myself in the minority of popular opinion."

She watched him for a moment, brow slightly furrowed.

"What is it?" he asked.

She was silent a moment more, then lightly shrugged a shoulder and resumed walking. "I am trying to determine if you are being truthful or merely facetious."

He blinked at her, likely surprised at her bluntness.

"I assure you, I am many things, but I am always truthful. Painfully so, my mother often tells me."

Selena smiled, remembering her own mother's warnings

against her speaking her mind so blatantly time and time again. Another commonality between them, it seemed.

But while Selena had attempted to curb her tongue in her youth, she was now a widow several times over with no desire or wish for remarriage, one who had the means to live comfortably enough on her own terms. Frankly, while much about her circumstances distressed her, she found a great deal of it freeing. Speaking her mind as she pleased was the silver lining on a very large cloud, and she had every intention of exploiting it often.

"I am glad to hear it, my lord," she said. "Though I must say, I am surprised. As a wealthy, powerful man…"

He grinned and bowed his head toward her as if she'd just complimented him instead of stating a fact.

"…Surely most people fall over backwards to parrot your opinion."

He chuckled. "Well, I will admit to a certain amount of that, I suppose. In the interest of truth," he said, drawing a grateful nod from her. "I do pride myself, however, on spotting such disingenuity, and paying it no mind."

"A refreshing position, my lord."

And it was. She'd met precious few men who did not enjoy a little sycophantic validation at least on occasion.

They passed by a trio of women sitting on a bench and Lord Lockhaven smiled politely, giving them a nod when they tittered and aimed flirtatious grins his way. But those expressions became decidedly colder when Selena nodded politely as well. Lockhaven turned his attention back to their path, though his hand quickly darted toward the monstrous bonnet overflowing with flowers and ribbons that one of the women wore.

Selena glanced at him, eyes narrowed. What had he just done?

He waited a few moments until they had fully passed the women and then he glanced down at her with a mischievous smile. "For my lady," he said, presenting her a flower with a gallant flourish.

A flower that had previously been perched upon the head of one of the waspish misses.

Selena clapped a hand over her mouth to muffle her laughter, but accepted his offering with a smile of thanks.

The man was a rascal, through and through. Which only made her like him all the more.

Lord Lockhaven was proving increasingly dangerous by the minute. Not only did they seem to have a great deal in common, but she genuinely enjoyed his company. And that alarmed her so much more than if he'd just been a handsome face. A handsome face, she could ignore. Theoretically. A handsome face backed by a sharp mind and delightful presence? That was decidedly more difficult to disregard.

"Oh dear, Old Thackery is being a nuisance again," he said, drawing her from her thoughts.

"Old Thackery?"

"Hmm," he said, pointing to an area a few dozen feet away where a cantankerous old goose had begun flapping his wings and chasing a child about the lawn's edge. His nursemaid was shouting in French at the crusty old bird, waving her apron at it in an apparent attempt to get the thing to fly off. Instead, she only seemed to be angering it further.

Lord Lockhaven let out chest-rumbling laugh. "I shall return momentarily," he said, though Selena barely heard him through the blood thundering through her system.

Lockhaven approached the melee and began herding the goose away from the child enough that his nursemaid could gather him up. And then he laughingly ran as the goose turned its attentions on him. Onlookers laughed, pointing and cheering at the ridiculous sight of a grown man, running, knees exaggeratingly high, while a furious goose honked in displeasure at his heels. Lord Goodwin and Jane had stopped a few feet ahead of her, laughing along with the others.

Selena blinked, her gaze jerking toward the sound of hoofbeats. A rider approached, trotting faster than was prudent along the clogged lanes of Rotten Row. And Lord Lockhaven continued to run right toward the path, looking over his shoulder at the goose who pursued him, instead of ahead, at the danger that waited.

A danger that had already taken one man from her. Images from her wedding day to Louis flashed through her mind, stoking the dread building in her gut. Honking geese, stampeding horses, a runaway carriage…and her poor Louis, not seeing any of it until it was too late.

She stumbled forward several steps, hand outraised. "Attention! Le cheval!" she yelled, her panic reverting her speech to the French the nursemaid also shouted. "Le cheval! Le cheval!"

EDWARD LOOKED AT Mrs. MacLaren and then glanced over his shoulder at where she was gesturing.

There was, indeed, a horse and rider bearing down on him. Though not so quickly or closely as might warrant the frantic tone in her voice. Rather careless of him to not take more notice of his surroundings, granted. But she did seem quite a bit more distressed than he thought necessary. Hmm, perhaps she was more interested in him than she tried to let on. Her refusal to receive him during calling hours still stung. But she was obviously concerned for his safety. Overly so, truth be told. Surely that meant something.

He stepped out of the way, clapped his hands one final time at the goose to shoo it back toward the pond, and then looked up to flash a grin at Mrs. MacLaren. Only to find her whispering with Mrs. Haddon. She did glance up at him once, her face paling when their eyes met. And she attempted to return some semblance of a smile. Briefly. Before she turned back to her friend.

Anthony came to stand beside him, though his eyes were

trained on the women.

"Any idea what that's all about?" Edward asked, nodding toward them.

"I haven't the faintest idea. Perhaps your company has finally worn her down, and she's begging to make her escape."

Edward scoffed. "We were having a quite pleasant conversation, I'll have you know, before the goose decided to—"

He stopped, watching dumfounded as Mrs. MacLaren turned on her heels and hurried away, dragging Mrs. Haddon behind her.

"You were saying?" Anthony said, amusement coating his words.

Edward shook his head. "Whatever is the matter with the woman?"

"I told you," Anthony said with a chuckle. "She's likely had her fill of your presence and is taking advantage of the goose to escape."

Edward frowned, not believing that was truly what had just happened, though it certainly seemed that way.

"So odd," he muttered. "Things were going so well."

Anthony snorted. "If that is your definition of 'going well,' I'd hate to see your version of disastrous."

Edward glared at him, which only made Anthony laugh harder.

"Come along, Lockhaven. I'm hungry. Let's see if your cook has any more of those little cakes that I like."

"Always thinking with your stomach," Edward said, rolling his eyes to the heavens. He *could* use some cake, though. Perhaps it would soothe his bruised ego. He'd never had a woman literally run from him before. The sensation was both odd and wholly unappealing.

As before, he could only hope their paths would cross again and hope for a better outcome. Though it could hardly end worse.

CHAPTER FIVE

Selena kept to the perimeters of the room, sipping her lemonade as she listened to the talented string quartet masterfully executing a difficult Haydn piece. She let out a content sigh, letting the music soothe her frayed nerves. A few people had greeted her. With curiosity, of course, but kindly enough for all that. Enough to give her hope that perhaps she would be able to build a new life in London. An independent life, with her own household. If she could fill that life with enough worthy pursuits to occupy her time and friends to stave off the loneliness, she could live a satisfactory life indeed.

An image of laughing eyes and mischievous grin flashed through her mind, and she quashed it immediately. As best she could, at any rate. It was pointless to pretend to herself that she hadn't been looking for him every time she ventured out of doors. Even though she'd taken great pains to actively avoid him.

"He's not here," Jane said, coming to stand beside her with a knowing smile.

"I don't know what you're talking about," Selena muttered, burying her grimace in her glass.

"Hmm, of course not. It seemed as though you were looking for someone. Or perhaps hiding from them, back here in the corner of the room."

Selena let out a quiet groan. "I made such a ninny of myself the other day. Running from him as I did. I cannot face him again. It is better this way, regardless."

"Oh?" Jane raised a delicate brow. "And why is that?"

Selena pursed her lips and tilted her head as she regarded her sister-in-law. "You know why. I can't trust myself around him. I am…too drawn to him."

"And you do not wish to be?"

"You know I do not," Selena said with a vehement whisper, her eyes darting around to ensure no one was close enough to hear their conversation. "I will not risk it again. And after what occurred in the park, with the goose and horses…"

Jane's amusement faded and she reached out to grasp Selena's hand.

"It was too much like Louis," Selena said quietly. "I could see him being chased into the path of that carriage all over again and…I just can't do it again."

"I know, dearest. But…that was an accident. A terrible accident, yes, but surely not one that would ever happen again."

"Yet it almost did!" Selena exclaimed again, struggling to keep her voice to a whisper. She shook her head. "Perhaps if it had only been Louis, I would consider taking making that leap again. But…"

Jane squeezed her hand again, her eyes filling with sympathy.

Marius's and Francesco's deaths, also terrible accidents mere hours after their nuptials, were almost enough to make her give up on her dream of love and marriage. Until she'd met Charles. He had survived their wedding day only to die while consummating their marriage.

She shook her head. "It's painful to think of them. I don't *want* to think of it, and I don't want to give the gossips more ammunition than they already have."

"Is that why you will not speak of them?"

"Yes. But being around him—Lockhaven—it is remarkably difficult not to talk to him. He looks at me as though I were the most important person in the world. As if he cannot wait to hear what I will say next. And it makes me want to tell him everything. But I just…cannot." She took a deep breath and let it out slowly. "And yet, it is so difficult *not* to want to be with him. I cannot stop thinking of the aggravating man."

Jane chuckled. "Yes, they do tend to worm their way in, do they not?"

Selena gave her a wry smile. "Just so. Therefore, it is better if I avoid him altogether."

Jane sighed. "I do understand that dearest, but…" She pursed her lips, trying to find the words. "I hope you will forgive me being blunt…"

Selena nodded, and Jane continued. "I know that you were not in love with your husbands. Not even Charles, though I know how fond you were of him. And I did so hope that the two of you would eventually find that love for each other that I have with my own husband," she said with a fond smile, nodding at where Mr. Haddon stood jovially chatting with a group of gentlemen. "It is obviously no longer possible with dear Charles. But I do still wish that kind of happiness for you," she said, reaching for Selena's hand again. "I hate to see you give up on that."

Selena squeezed her dear friend's hand back. "I know you do. It is only that—"

She broke off abruptly, her heart skipping a beat before pounding furiously in her chest.

"What is it—oof!" Jane exclaimed as Selena yanked her behind the drapes.

Jane stared at her, eyes wide with surprise as Selena risked a quick peek through the crack in the drapes before pulling them shut again and backing up against the wall.

"Selena. Dearest," Jane said, gazing at her in the faint light provided from the bit of window the drapes covered. "What are we doing?"

"Shhh." Selena waved her hand. "Hiding," she whispered.

"Ah," Jane whispered back. "Because?"

Selena opened her mouth to answer, but footsteps stopped

just on the other side of the drapes, and she held her finger to her lips. Jane's eyebrow rose sharply, and her lips quirked into an amused grin, but she held her tongue.

"I could have sworn I just saw her," Lord Lockhaven said from the other side of the drapes.

"Perhaps you are seeing things, brother," another man said.

Lockhaven scoffed. "I may be a few years older than you, Hugo, but I am not senile yet. She was here."

"So you say. And yet, there was no way for her to escape without passing us, and she is nowhere to be found." There was a slight slapping thud, like the sound of a hand hitting a shoulder. "Do not fear, brother. There are a great many other ladies in attendance this evening. I am sure more than a few of them would be glad of your company. Though why, I will never understand."

Lockhaven snorted. "Of course you don't. Because no woman ever preferred yours."

Hugo chuckled. "I disagree. However, we are discussing who might prefer *your* company. And in that regard, perhaps it is best that you did not find whom you seek this evening."

"Why do you say that?"

There was a pause before his brother answered. "I cannot fault you for being drawn to a mysterious beauty, Edward. Many men are. But…all rumors aside, the woman is already a widow. And one who is—"

"Careful," Lockhaven warned.

"I was merely going to point out that our parents had a few other ladies in mind for their future daughter-in-law. Ladies who are perhaps a bit more suitable. So perhaps it is for the best that this particular lady does not seem to desire your affections."

Selena blanched, her chest constricting painfully. Oh, but she did return his affections. Unfortunately so. Her pulse pounded and her stomach clenched. Though she wasn't entirely sure if it was from dismay that Lockhaven's family apparently considered her to be an unsuitable match or from hearing that he held some affection for her.

Likely both.

She fisted her skirts in her hands and leaned her head back against the wall, forcing herself to breathe slowly and evenly so he wouldn't hear her through the wall of fabric that separated them.

Lockhaven was quiet for a moment, and when he spoke again his voice was low, gravely in its intensity. "With all due respect to our parents, I will keep my own counsel on who is or is not an appropriate match." He let out a breath. "Perhaps she stepped out for some air. I could use some myself."

Their footsteps moved off and Selena let out a breath, forcing her aching hands to release her skirts and relax.

"Selena…" Jane started, but Selena shook her head.

"As I was saying, it is for the best if I avoid his company. Even his family agrees."

Jane scowled. "Then his family is not as intelligent as I believed."

Selena gave her a fond smile before risking another peek from the drapes.

"Are we not going to discuss that the man obviously holds you in deep regard? Affection even?"

Selena bit her lip and then shook her head. "No. It is for the best, Jane. Truly. Come," she said, slipping out from between the drapes, ignoring the exasperated shaking of Jane's head.

Despite what she'd said, it would not be so simple to erase Lockhaven's words from her heart. Traitorous organ that it was. She would just have to do her best, for both their sakes. And since she had no confidence in her ability to do so, avoiding the tantalizing Lord Lockhaven was her only hope.

CHAPTER SIX

EDWARD WAS READY to revise his previous statement. Worse than Mrs. MacLaren running off at the sight of him was her avoiding him altogether.

He had seen her about town and at various societal functions no less than five times, and each time she had made sure to disappear before he could make his way to her. Quite impressively at times. At the FitzDowells' soiree, there had been only one exit to the room in which he'd spied her. An exit he'd had eyes on as he'd made his way into the room. Yet by the time he'd entered, she had disappeared. Unless she'd been hiding in the drape—

He stopped dead in his tracks, causing Anthony to nearly run into him.

She *must* have been hiding in the drapes; he was sure of it. There was no other explanation. And then she'd probably slipped out when he was on the far side of the room searching for her.

He shook his head with an amused smile, not sure if he should be insulted or impressed at the lengths she was apparently willing to go to avoid him. He should doubtless leave her be. And would if he hadn't caught her staring at him with the same captivated interest he felt when he caught sight of her. What did that mean? Was she just as wary of her growing interest in him as he was of his in her? It was enough to make a man's head spin.

It would be easier to ascertain the correct course of action if her feelings toward him were more apparent. The few times they *had* met, she seemed to enjoy his company. Before fleeing it, of course. Yet even that fascinated him instead of wounding him as it likely should.

His reactions to this woman were simply something he had never experienced before, and he wasn't quite sure what to do about it. There was something about her that refused to release him. He could not get her out of his mind. And he had tried. None of his usual amusements helped.

Instead, he found himself looking for her everywhere. Wanting to share everything with her. Whenever he saw something particularly beautiful or interesting, he found himself wishing she were there so he could discover her thoughts and feelings on it. Did she enjoy the vibrant sunsets? Or did she prefer watching the sun rise?

When Anthony had told a particularly raucous joke a few days past, Edward's first thought was to wonder if *she* would have found it amusing. Would she have laughed? Been scandalized? What were her thoughts about the vicar's sermon this Sunday past? Was her favorite color the shade of green she had worn that day or the deep blue she had worn at the FitzDowells'?

He wanted to know everything with a desire that was beginning to make him feel quite unhinged. Perhaps he should not be so eager to share her company again. It could prove detrimental to his health. Yet his morbid curiosity couldn't wait to see what else the woman would do.

"Remind me, why we are here?" Anthony huffed, his eyes glazing over as he viewed one of the masterpieces hanging before them.

"It's the Royal Academy's annual exhibition, Anthony. We always attend. It makes a nice change from the usual soirees, does it not? And with the Prince Regent unveiling the new statue he commissioned, everyone who is anyone is here this evening. And therefore, *we* must be in the thick of it," Edward explained, though truly no explanation should be required.

They had always flocked to the biggest crowds like kittens to cream. How else could they see and be seen? Really, it were as if Anthony didn't even know him sometimes.

Plus, in addition to Edward's usual social tendencies, there was a very good chance of happening upon the elusive Mrs. MacLaren again. It had been far too many days since that brief glimpse he'd had of her at the FitzDowells', and his mind had dwelled upon nothing else since the moment she'd turned tail and run from him. Fascinating woman.

Not that he'd admit any of that to Anthony.

"Besides," he continued with a laugh, "a little culture and sophistication wouldn't hurt you, you know."

Anthony was many things, but a connoisseur of art, he was not.

"I'm sufficiently sophisticated, I'll have you know," Anthony argued. "I just do not see the point in standing about staring at paintings all night when there is fun to be had out there." He pointed in the direction of the door, no doubt thinking of his favorite gentlemen's club that wasn't too far from the gallery.

He dropped his arm abruptly, a delighted grin breaking out over his face. "I retract my objection. I think this evening is about to become very entertaining indeed."

The absolute glee in Anthony's voice made Edward frown in concern. Nothing Anthony anticipated that much could be goo—

Oh.

Down the long hall, Edward caught sight of what had given Anthony such a change of mind.

Mrs. MacLaren. *Selena.* Standing in front of a painting, mesmerized, while the throngs of people parted around her like a river around a stone.

Oh yes. This evening had just grown tantalizingly more interesting. At least for him. He frowned at Anthony.

"I know why I am happy to see her, but I fail to see why you are so. As far as I am aware, you have no interest in the lady." He hoped, in any case. The both of them hadn't been interested in the same woman since they were twelve, and they had nearly come to blows over it. Until they'd realized the lady in question didn't know either of them existed and had no inclination to change that state of affairs.

Anthony smirked. "Only insomuch as pertains to you."

"Me?"

He nodded sharply, his amused gaze still bouncing back and forth between Mrs. MacLaren and Edward. "I have never, in all the years I've known you, seen a woman reject you so quickly. Not only once, but twice. Literally running from your presence. And she's done all in her power to avoid your company since then. Yet, you still crave the lady's attentions. And from the look on your face, you're about to return for a third helping, which will amuse me very much, indeed. In fact, I find this entire situation utterly riveting."

Edward glared at him through narrowed eyes and opened his mouth to respond and then thought better of it. For one, his friend wasn't wrong, as aggravating an admission as that was. For another, he had much more delightful plans for entertainment for the evening than arguing with Anthony. He'd leave his old friend to his own devices. And would try to ignore the fact that *he* was Anthony's entertainment.

He flashed Anthony one last scowl and then made his way through the crowd, nodding to people here and there but not pausing until he came to stand beside Mrs. MacLaren.

He didn't say a word, and she made no acknowledgment of his presence aside from a slight stiffening of her posture. At least she wasn't running away or hiding behind columns. Instead, she just continued to stare at the painting.

He turned to peruse it with her, glancing at the gold placard beneath it.

"Ah. *The Grand Canal in Venice,* as I thought. By Francesco Fiorentino. Talented chap, wasn't he?" He took in the scene, the boats floating in the canal overlooked by the grand Basilica of Santa Maria della Salute with its beautiful blue-domed roof. "It's lovely. Doesn't quite capture the vibrancy of the place," he said, his eyes shifting to her. "But it's quite a beautiful rendering."

She nodded, almost absentmindedly. "I miss it." Her words were so softly spoken that he might have missed them had he not been looking directly at her.

"You have been to Venice?" he asked, delighted to have discovered even this slight morsel of her life.

She raised startled eyes to him, staring at him for a moment before glancing back at the painting. "I...yes, I have been there."

There was more to that answer lingering in her eyes but before he could ask anything further, she abruptly straightened and moved to the next painting, pausing briefly before moving to the next. And the next. He had no choice but to follow or lose his place at her side. Though he couldn't help but notice the small bubble of space around her. People didn't hesitate to stare. Some deigned to nod or otherwise greet her. But most seemed to give her a wide and wary berth, all the while gazing at her with rampant curiosity.

His eyes narrowed at a particularly rude woman who stared at Mrs. MacLaren with open interest before whispering furiously into the ear of another woman whose mouth had dropped open with a scandalized gasp. That they would conduct themselves so toward a woman who had done nothing to harm them set a fire in his gut that he had to grit his teeth to quell.

How often, he wondered, must she suffer such behavior? Too often, he feared. Yet from everything he'd seen, she remained respectful and kind to everyone. She didn't need his protection, but it made him want to offer it all the same. He would protect her from any unpleasantness that came her way if she would let him.

The moment the women caught sight of him and noted his disapproval they bobbed a tiny curtsy and moved along.

The soft touch of a hand on his arm brought his attention back to Mrs. MacLaren.

"I appreciate the gallantry," she said, dropping her hand, "but it's not needed. I am well accustomed to the stares and whispers."

He frowned again. "So you have said. That does not excuse their behavior. In fact, your very graciousness about it makes their comportment all the worse. Honestly, it's as if they have never seen a young widow before."

She glanced at him curiously, eyes narrowed, forehead creased, and head tilted in a delightfully inquisitive fashion before she shook her head and smiled. A gentle smile that spread across her soft lips and sent his heart pounding like it was trying to punch its way through his chest.

But she said nothing, turning back to the still life of fruit and flowers they were viewing.

"You said you missed Venice," he said, hoping to spark a conversation and gather a few more details of her life. "Have you visited there often?"

"I…" She paused, glancing up at him. "I lived there for a time."

Her gaze shifted away from his and she moved to another painting, pausing before it with a smile.

"This one is one of my favorites," she said, looking at a sunny landscape with a church and rainbow in the distance with evident pleasure. "It always brings me joy."

He recognized the change of subject but short of pinning her place and torturing the information from her, he couldn't force her to answer his questions more fully. And he could be gentleman enough to move on. No matter how greatly his curiosity was killing him.

"It is quite lovely," he said, though he wasn't looking at the picture.

"I agre—"

"Why did you run from me at our last meeting?" he asked, unable to stop the question from erupting. Apparently his gentlemanly restraint only stretched so far. "And you have avoided me since."

She glanced up at him with wide, startled eyes. "I…" She

looked back at the painting. "I must apologize, my lord. I hope I did not offend you. I suppose I have been embarrassed. The incident with the horse…it reminded me of something. I'm afraid I let my emotions get the better of me and felt the need to excuse myself."

"With impressive speed," he said, trying to bring the smile back to her lips.

"Yes." She did smile, but it had little amusement in it.

That just wouldn't do.

He turned back to the painting and quietly perused it with her for a few seconds. Then he leaned a bit closer to her, giving their conversation an air of conspiracy.

"Have you ever been told that you shouldn't touch a painting with your bare hands?" he asked.

She blinked a few times at the sudden change of conversation, but she followed along good-naturedly. "I don't believe so."

"It seems the oils from one's skin can mix with the paint and smear it if one is not careful."

"Oh, my, that is—"

"Touch it." He jerked his head at the painting.

Her shocked gaze jolted to him. "What?" she asked, her voice little more than a whisper.

He leaned in a little closer. "Aren't you curious?" He gave her a conspiratorial half-grin that had her biting her bottom lip, her teeth sinking into the plump flesh so sweetly it made him bite back a groan.

"Perhaps. Do you always break the rules simply out of curiosity?" she asked.

"Frequently. I find it immensely freeing."

She raised a gloved hand to her mouth, her eyes shining with amusement. Much better than the melancholy that resided there only a few moments ago.

"Very well." He pulled his glove off and glanced about. "Is anyone watching us?"

Her eyes darted about, and she snorted softly. "Yes, quite a few people."

"Hmm." He angled his body so that the painting was blocked from the view of at least the people behind him. "Ready?"

"My lord," she said laughing, "you mustn't."

He reached a finger out to touch the painting and—

"Lord Lockhaven," a man's voice said.

Edward pivoted on his feet, clasping his hands behind his back so he could greet the Earl of Chesmorton whilst shoving his hand back in his glove. A more difficult task than he would have thought as he discovered when the earl left with a nod, and Edward turned back around and held up his hand.

"Well, that doesn't seem right," he said, looking down at where four fingers were tucked inside the glove, though none in their correct places, and his pinky was bare to the world.

Mrs. MacLaren's laughter rang out in earnest, a delightfully hearty belly laugh that he would pay a hefty sum to hear every day. His heart soared at the sound.

He might not know everything about her just yet. But he *had* made her laugh, which, surprisingly, filled him with more satisfaction than anything he had done in a very long time. And he *had* discovered some information, scant though it was.

She'd been married. At least once, possibly twice. He had a suspicion she had lost someone close to her in a horse or carriage accident. She spoke French. She'd lived in Venice, therefore likely also spoke Italian. She enjoyed art. And the color blue, judging by how often she wore it. A woman who was very well-traveled and well-cultured. Kind. Gracious. Elegant. Intelligent. Curious enough to break a few rules, though hesitant to do so. And heart-stoppingly beautiful.

It was more than he'd known about her a few weeks ago. It was enough.

For today.

"Allow me to call upon you tomorrow," he said.

Her smile dimmed slightly, and he inwardly cursed himself for his hasty request. He'd meant to wait until she'd grown more comfortable around him before he asked again. Skittish creature that she seemed to be. But being in her presence did something to his senses. He simply wasn't himself. Was it the air of mystery about her? Those piercing blue eyes framed by their dark lashes? Or simply the fact that he enjoyed conversing with her far more than anyone else he'd met in the last...well, ever. Hell, he enjoyed standing in total silence with her more than he enjoyed conversing with anyone else.

He didn't know what it was about her. But he was desperate to find out. Something that would be far easier away from the prying eyes of the ton. The semi-privacy of a salon was hardly ideal either, but a far sight better than this crowded hall.

"I...um..." Her eyes darted around, looking at everything and everyone but him. "I..."

She backed up a step, right into a pedestal that held a bust of some statesman or other.

"Oh!" she exclaimed as the thing tottered on its perch.

He leapt forward, arms outstretched just in time to catch it before it fell completely.

There was quite a bit of commotion as the crowd bustled in closer, trying to get a look at what was going on. Thankfully, several other gentlemen stepped forward to help him replace the surprisingly heavy chunk of marble. In just a few minutes, they had everything set to rights.

But when he turned, it was to find Mrs. MacLaren had vanished.

CHAPTER SEVEN

W ELL, MRS. MACLAREN hadn't completely disappeared.

There was a path through the crowd through which she had apparently pushed, and he just caught sight of her skirts and raven curls as she reached the exit.

Edward leaned to the side slightly, enough to keep her in view as she hurried through the door and out into the night. Anthony came to stand beside him, leaning in a similar fashion to take in the view of the now empty doorway.

"She keeps doing that," Edward said, utterly baffled, his eyes still trained on the door through which she had just disappeared.

Anthony shrugged, needing no explanation as to what he referred. Of course he didn't. The entire room had seen her bolt.

"Perhaps she doesn't fancy you."

"No, that can't be it," Edward scoffed.

Although…could it?

No, surely not.

"You aren't nearly as charming as you think you are," Anthony said with a chuckle.

"I used to be," he muttered.

He'd never questioned his charismatic personality in the past. His ready wit and brilliant smile had gotten him out of more than one scrape. Even one involving the royal guard and a vastly unfortunate misunderstanding with the queen.

But now, damn the woman, she had him questioning every-thing about himself. And damn himself for enjoying every moment of it.

"You know, I never thought I would say these words to you," Anthony said, "but perhaps this is not the best time to change your usual inclinations when it comes to courting."

Edward squinted at his friend, thoroughly confused at the sudden twist in argument. "You despise my usual inclinations. I do not court as a general rule."

"Exactly. And while I know how you enjoy a good rule-breaking, perhaps just this once you should follow it."

Edward couldn't do much more than blink at his friend for a full three seconds before gathering his thoughts enough to respond. "I beg your pardon. Are you ill? You must be ill. You cannot have possibly just suggested that I cease pursuing a woman when you have spent no less than the last decade of our friendship castigating me for doing that exact thing for any number of what you call ridiculous reasons."

Anthony grimaced. "I am aware."

"Then explain," Edward said, squinting at him suspiciously.

"I am not ill. I am concerned."

"About what, exactly?"

Anthony shrugged again. "I'm not one to put too much stock in rumors, mind you. However, *if* the rumors about your Mrs. MacLaren are true, then she has helped quite a few hus-bands...gain their eternal reward, shall we say. Perhaps she flees due to a guilty conscience. Whether it is a compulsion she cannot help, some otherworldly curse, or even good old-fashioned rage or greed, you could be very well in danger if you persist in pursuing her."

Edward shook his head. "You cannot truly believe what they are saying."

"I am not saying if I believe it or not, just that the situation bears a touch of caution. And if you have finally decided to court a woman in truth, there are others who would prove less hazardous for your health than your Mrs. MacLaren."

Edward coughed out a breath. "I confess, you have me truly stunned. An allergy to a woman's cat is too fantastical for you, but a murderous widow you find a credible excuse."

Anthony just shrugged again with a self-deprecating grin. "I am simply urging caution."

"When you usually urge rashness."

"I wouldn't say that."

"That is exactly what you say. And you have always been wrong. As you are in this case."

"I hope so, my friend."

"Wrong about what?" a feminine voice said behind him. "And why is he calling Mrs. MacLaren *your* Mrs. MacLaren? Who is Mrs. MacLaren?"

Edward closed his eyes in a fleeting grimace and then turned, his most charming smile in place, to greet the woman who had stopped beside them.

"Mother," he said, trying to make his tone sound much more welcoming than he felt. Until he glanced over her shoulder and saw the entire entourage milling about behind her. "Did you leave anyone at home?" he asked, taking in his father, two of his three sisters, and both younger brothers as they wandered about the hall, mostly ignoring the masterpieces on display in favor of socializing.

His mother, unfortunately, ignored nothing. She tilted her head, waiting for him to respond.

"This wouldn't be…" she glanced about before leaning in closer to mock whisper, "*the* Mrs. MacLaren, is it?"

Edward cocked an eyebrow. "I have no idea to what you are referring, Mother, but as I am only acquainted with one Mrs. MacLaren, I shall hazard a guess that the answer is yes."

"Oh dear," she murmured, then let out a sigh. "Leave it to you to strike up a romance with the one woman in the city from whom I would rather you keep your distance."

His other eyebrow rose to join the first. "I am quite sure there is more than one woman who fits that description," he said with a laugh. His mother just pursed her lips with a harumph. "And who said anything about a romance?"

His mother snapped him on the arm with her fan. "You always were an impertinent young pup. Don't you go playing the fool with me now. You've been romancing any poor woman with a pulse for more than a decade," she grumbled. "Though precious little has come of it. Your father and I would like to leave this existence knowing that our family name, title, and estate are intact, and we'd like to see some grandchildren before we are too old to enjoy them."

Edward stifled the urge to rub at his now aching brow. "Mother, you and Father won't be going anywhere anytime soon. You exaggerate worse than Lord Goodwin."

She snorted delicately but didn't look mollified.

"And you already have a whole parcel of grandchildren thanks to Louise, Mary, and Elizabeth."

His mother let out a long-suffering sigh. "Yes dear, but we need heirs. Which, unfortunately, only you can provide."

"That's not true. They come after me," he said, nodding toward his brothers. "Hugo and Arthur are just as capable as providing heirs as I. They would no doubt be thrilled to be put to the task."

His mother just stared at him and then called over her shoulder to where her husband stood a few feet away.

"You deal with him, my lord. I do not have the energy to expend any longer."

His father, George Brelsford, Duke of Haltham, chuckled as he came closer. "My dear, if you have not been able to sway him to your liking yet, I certainly will not be able to." He stopped at her side and looked Edward over before nodding slightly. With approval, Edward hoped.

"What is the trouble now?" he asked.

"Mother would like more grandchildren, apparently," Edward said, dryly.

"Yes," she said, "and I would prefer their mother not be a known murderess."

Edward's gaze snapped to her. "Mother! I am shocked you put so much store into idle gossip. Mrs. MacLaren is many things, but a murderess is not one of them."

The words were out of his mouth before he had a chance to think about them, and he froze, the implication of what he'd just said reverberating in his mind. He could only hope his mother hadn't noticed that he did not immediately protest the possibility that Selena could be the mother of his children.

Could she be? Had that possibility truly crossed his mind? The thought wasn't causing the usual wave of nausea he typically felt when faced with the possibility of marriage and parenthood. What did that mean? Did he…did he truly mean to court her in earnest?

He thought he actually might.

But he would have to revisit that revelation later. One mother-induced crisis at a time.

"It is not idle gossip, Edward. I have it on good authority from no less than three people who either saw her themselves or know someone who did, in at least two separate countries with at least two different men. Neither of whom were this Mr. MacLaren who also supposedly left her a widow."

Edward stared at his mother, stunned into silence. For a very brief moment.

"I…" He sighed and gave into the urge to pinch his nose between his fingers before trying again. His father just watched with amused sympathy, tinged with a look of contemplation Edward didn't like.

"Mother, I cannot speak as to what your friend's cousin's wife's aunt may or may not have seen whilst traipsing about the Continent. But I do know for certain that Mr. MacLaren *did* indeed exist and did indeed leave Mrs. MacLaren a widow. As she is accompanied everywhere by her sister-in-law, Mrs. Haddon. Mr. MacLaren's *sister*. I see no reason why Mrs. Haddon would be part of some strange conspiracy to make Society believe her brother had been married to this woman if he had not indeed wed her."

His mother frowned. "I suppose. But that does not explain the rest."

"The rest is nothing more than idle gossip."

"Even if that is true, you will be the next Duke of Haltham. Your wife should be above reproach and of impeccable bloodlines."

Edward shook his head. "She's a woman, Mother, not a horse."

His mother snorted softly. "When it comes to matrimony, my son, the conversations are more alike than not. What about Lady Charlotte, the Earl of Craston's daughter? I've heard she's quite an accomplished embroiderer."

Edward blinked. "Fascinating." He shook his head with a tired smile. "I shouldn't keep you any longer, Mother. You will miss the unveiling of the new statue the Prince Regent had commissioned."

"Oh, goodness, is it time already? Thank you, Edward." She half turned to go before glancing back at him. "But this conversation isn't over."

He leaned in to kiss her cheek. "Of that, I am painfully aware."

The sigh he let out as she walked away on the arm of his father, the rest of his siblings trailing after them like ducklings, dragged from the bottom of his soul. He loved his family, dearly. And his parents, unlike some highborn couples, loved their children fiercely and were unashamed to show it.

But there were times when he wished his mother loved him just a little bit less. Or at least was less interested in his life.

"Come along, Lockhaven," Anthony said, clapping him on the shoulder. "I think you could use a drink."

Truer words had never been spoken. Though he kept his mouth shut while Goodwin dragged him out into the night and toward the nearest club. His friend certainly didn't need to be told he might be right. Anthony would enjoy that far too much, and Edward would never hear the end of it.

Still. Despite what he'd said to Anthony, Edward *was* attuned enough to his own failings that he could admit there was a small percentage of the population who would not find his particular brand of charm…well, charming. And had it been anyone else, he might consider the possibility that an extreme dislike spurred Mrs. MacLaren's flights from him.

But she—*Selena*—was surely not one of them.

Not with the way her eyes flashed when they spoke, the way her cheeks heated when he was ever so subtly inappropriate, the way her breath hitched in her throat whenever they chanced to touch.

No. She was just as taken with him as he with her, he'd stake his fortune on it.

Either that or Anthony was correct, and she was fleeing from his presence for his own good. And he just couldn't live in a world where Anthony was correct.

His determination to court this woman was something he didn't want to examine too closely. It went against his very nature. Not only to try and court a woman, but to court one who, judging by her tendency to hastily quit any room containing him, did not wish to be courted.

But those moments before she fled, he was quickly beginning to live for them. So, for better or for worse, he would follow his gut. It had served him well in the past.

He could only hope he wasn't dooming his future by following it now.

CHAPTER EIGHT

SELENA SHIFTED IN her seat, one she'd chosen on a sofa as far from everyone else as she could get. Difficult to do as there were scarcely more than a dozen people in attendance at Lady Tresscott's musical soiree. Jane had hoped that a smaller gathering would allow for better opportunities for Selena to make some friends. A noble endeavor from a dear friend who wished to see her happy. But one that seemed doomed to failure.

Everyone still treated her with a sort of sympathetic wariness that filled her with endless frustration, but amusement as well. No one wanted to be outrightly cruel to a widow. But their uncertainty as to her role in her husbands' demises tempered their friendliness. A brave few had thrown caution to the wind, however, and made some friendly overtures, so perhaps her cause wasn't completely lost after all.

"You seem to be enjoying the evening," Jane said, settling beside her during a brief intermission between performances.

Selena gave her sister-in-law a grateful smile. She could always count on Jane. "I am, I think."

Jane's sweet titter of a laugh had Selena's smile widening. "You do not know your mind on the matter, hmm?"

"Of course I do. It is merely that I am of two minds on the subject. I do so love music. It has been a treat to hear such talent tonight," she said with utmost sincerity.

Their hostess had arranged an evening of musical guests for them, ranging from a quartet group to an incredible opera singer newly arrived from Paris. Selena had reveled in every moment. Before all her tragedies, she had actually spent a great deal of time taking in all the operas, plays, and musical performances that she could. Moments she had sorely missed. She *had* been hiding herself away too much of late.

"Though," she continued, "I do feel a bit like the oddity on display."

"Yes, there does seem to be a fair bit of that going about." Jane glanced around, returning any stares that lingered too long until they moved on with a shamed blush to their cheeks. She finally sighed and patted Selena's hand. "I am glad you are enjoying your evening otherwise though. How are your parents doing? I saw there was a letter from them in the post this morning."

"They are well. Mother worries, as usual. But says that my father has recovered nicely from his cold, and they would like to come for a visit soon. I didn't want to presume but—"

"Of course, they are most welcome to stay with us," Jane answered before Selena had a chance to ask. Her sister-in-law was a saint, truly.

"You are too kind, Jane. Thank you, I shall write tomorrow and let them know. Or…perhaps in a day or two."

Jane's laughter pealed out. "Surely, they aren't that bad."

"Not entirely," Selena said with a small smile. "But my mother does have a tendency to hover. And she worries that I have no wish to wed again. Despite my relative security, she will not rest until she sees me safely married to a suitable gentleman. She simply will not accept that I have no wish to marry again. Or need to, if I am careful."

"Is it not a mother's place to worry about her daughter?"

"Naturally. And I do love that she cares. I would just prefer if she cared a *little* less."

Jane laughed and this time Selena joined in.

Truthfully, she was gratified that her mother cared for her future so much. But it did grow frustrating when she refused to accept Selena's choice to remain firmly in her widowhood. Dooming a fifth husband to die seemed cruel and unnecessary. And based on past experience, her marriages wouldn't end any other way. Why tempt fate?

"Oh!" Jane's delighted gasp drew Selena's curious gaze. "Perhaps the newest guest to arrive will improve your evening," she said with a mischievous smirk.

What?

Selena's heart raced before she even turned to look. Who else would Jane be so teasingly smug about?

She glanced up and met the gaze of Lord Lockhaven. Who still seemed delighted to see her, despite the fact she'd run from him on no less than three occasions.

Of course, she kept running precisely because *she* was equally delighted to see *him*. Frighteningly delighted, in fact. She had tried to deny it to herself over and over, but there was just no help for it. He made her laugh. He brightened her day every time she saw him. Their conversations were entertaining and stimulating. And that smile of his, the slight brushes of his hand when he thought he could get away with it, those heated looks of his, stimulated parts of her she hadn't been aware *could* be stimulated.

And she couldn't help but crave more.

"Oh, I believe I see Lady Hayworth. I really should go and give her my condolences on the death of that cranky old parrot of hers. I won't be but a minute," she said, already rising and hurrying away.

"Jane, wait, I—"

"Mrs. MacLaren."

Lord Lockhaven's deep voice seemed to reverberate right through her chest, and she took a deep breath to steel herself before glancing up to meet his gaze.

"Lord Lockhaven," she said, her voice quieter than she'd like, but steady, at least.

"I was unaware you'd be attending this evening. How very fortuitous, meeting you yet again." His half-crooked smile sent a fine tremble through her. One he noticed, if his widening grin meant anything. He leaned in slightly closer, just on the wrong side of appropriate. "It's beginning to feel like fate."

Her heart pounded and she closed her eyes, looking down. "Or a curse," she muttered.

For what else could it be when any future between them spelled catastrophe for him. The pattern had been repeated too many times already. And each time it had only proven that the fortune teller from her youth had indeed taunted her with promises of happiness and then cursed her that it would never be so.

"Lord Lockhaven, would you mind keeping Mrs. MacLaren company for me?" Jane said. "I do so hate to leave her on her own, but I must..." Her eyes darted around while Selena's narrowed. "Go...over there, for a moment," she finally stammered with a huge grin.

Selena silently plotted revenge while Jane made her escape. Though it was somewhat Selena's fault. She hadn't shared with Jane the outcome of her last meeting with Lord Lockhaven. She hadn't mentioned she'd seen him at the museum at all. The embarrassment was too much to be born. Frankly, she was astonished that Jane hadn't heard about it yet. Though perhaps she had and had simply decided not to broach the subject.

Selena discarded that notion before it fully took root. Jane would have asked. And Selena should have told her the moment she'd arrived home. But she truly didn't know what had happened. One moment she'd been trying to formulate a response to his request to call and the next she was tripping over a pedestal and fleeing out the door once again, skirts in hand and pride in tatters.

"The music is lovely," Lord Lockhaven said to her, his quiet voice only loud enough for her to hear.

"Yes, it is," she said, swallowing hard, glancing about to see if anyone noticed their furtive conversation in the back of the room whilst one of the guests played a charming Beethoven piece.

"Forgive me for being forward," he said, sending her heart pounding with anticipation. "But I do not wish to continue to foist my presence upon you if you truly not desire it. Do you find my company abhorrent?"

Her gaze snapped to him. "No. Not at all!" she whispered.

His full lips stretched into a slow smile that filled her with a delicious warmth. A warmth that quickly evaporated with his next words.

"Then why do you run from me? I must know."

Her breath caught in her throat, and she looked away, anywhere but at him. She couldn't answer him. Not here. Not ever. How could she tell him it was because of how he made her feel? That she ran because she truly wanted to stay. She ran because if she didn't, then she would only grow more attached, crave him more.

It didn't help matters that each instance had been preceded by a moment that had reminded her about her painful past. A past he could never know about. He'd never look at her the same way. He'd certainly never speak to her again. No man wants to be the sixth man in a woman's life. Or discover that the others had all met untimely ends.

Then again, why should she ever need to tell him? It wasn't as if she would ever agree to wed him or anyone else. Not that he was asking. The man only wished to call on her. Perhaps she was over thinking all this. After all, Selena had been in London long enough now to know that Lord Lockhaven had a certain reputation. He was popular with women, was a great flirt, and likely a great lover as well. Though to his credit, he didn't attempt to truly court any eligible young ladies. He never gave the women false hope. But women seemed to give themselves enough of that without his help.

But she couldn't just sit there and not say anything. He was already looking at her like—

"Mrs. MacLaren? I'm sorry, I didn't mean to pry. But if it is something that I am—"

"No, no," she said, waving her fan along with her shaking head. "It's not you. I just…"

"Mrs. MacLaren," a woman said, drawing Selena's startled gaze. "We'd be honored to have you play for us. Please," she said, gesturing to the pianoforte.

Selena glanced about, finally seeing Jane who was smiling at her with gritted teeth and trying to subtly nod her head in the direction of the instrument at the front of the room while everyone politely clapped for her.

Oh, dear heavens.

Selena very belatedly realized her waving her fan about must have been construed as an offer to play for the assembled group. She couldn't back out now.

Lord Lockhaven stood and bowed, holding his hand out to her in a silent offer to escort her to the front.

She swallowed hard at the lump of nerves clawing at her throat and slid her hand into his. He squeezed her fingers ever so gently as he helped her to her feet, and their gazes met. And held. His smile was benign enough, but the sudden flash of heat in his eyes was not. She could only hope her audience assumed the flush in her cheeks was due to nerves and did not deduce the real reason.

That the heat that flooded through her was because of a simple touch from the enigmatic man at her side. A touch that made her tremble, and her core tighten with need.

He deposited her on the stool before the pianoforte and went back to sit on their sofa. A lucky thing. She didn't think she'd be able to command her hands to play a single note had he been within her line of sight.

She took a deep breath and slowly released it, placing her hands on the keys. And then she played.

She didn't consciously choose the song. It was simply one

that often played in her head. A song Marius, her third husband, had often played for her during their whirlwind courtship. A song he played for her at their wedding. Before his unfortunate accident.

Though really, if you get drunk enough at your wedding feast to try and wrestle an ornery horse...well, one could hardly be surprised if the horse wins.

Still, the song had been a source of comfort for her since then and she often played it. But typically, only when she was alone. Not with an audience. Certainly not with a person who drove her to such distraction in the audience. But it was what flowed from her when her fingers brushed the keys. And she let it come.

The melody was beautiful, slightly haunting perhaps, though a bit playful, as was Marius himself. She played with her eyes on her hands, though she didn't need to see them to strike the correct notes. Music had been a comfort to her, her whole life. And as she played, she took a deep breath and let it be so now. She let the music flow through her and sweep out all the tension, the uncertainty, the lingering sadness, the indecision. And when the last note was struck, she glanced up...and met the gaze of Lord Lockhaven.

This time she didn't think, didn't worry, didn't contemplate future consequences. He amused her, made her laugh, interested her, entertained her, made her feel alive again. Made her feel...many things. And she was tired of pretending otherwise. So instead of dropping her gaze and sinking back into her demure, respectable widowhood, she kept her eyes locked on his. And smiled, slow and sweet.

His answering smile sent fire rippling through her veins.

Politely exuberant applause broke the spell and Selena stood, her hand resting on the pianoforte to steady herself. She smiled at her audience and dropped into a small curtsy.

"That was so beautiful," Lady Tresscott said. "I don't believe I've ever heard it before. Have you?" she asked another woman at her side who shook her head.

"I believe I have, though it was several years ago," Lord Tresscott said, then turned to his wife. "When I was in Bucharest a few years back. There was a composer there. I believe he played it during a small concert I attended. What was his name…" He thoughtfully tapped his chin.

The blood drained from Selena's face so quickly it made her head spin. She opened her mouth, but it took two tries before she could speak. "Marius," she said, her voice faint. "Marius Albescu."

"Yes!" Lord Tresscott said with a huge grin. "That was it. Well done. Quite a talented fellow. I'm glad to hear his music being played."

Selena smiled faintly, her eyes darting around the assemblage for Jane. Instead, they met those of Lord Lockhaven again, and she sucked in a sharp breath.

He was at her side in a moment.

"Mrs. MacLaren are you well?" he said, his eyes roving over her with concern. "Allow me to escort you back to your seat."

"Thank you, my lord. But I think I should like to get a bit of air."

"Of course," he said, all gentlemanly graciousness though his eyes watched her with a burning fire. "I believe I saw Mrs. Haddon heading toward the refreshment table," he said. "I would be happy to take you to her."

"Thank you, that would be most kind, my lord."

He bowed his head to her and then nodded to Lord and Lady Tresscott before turning to escort her from the room toward the small salon where a table of refreshments had been set up.

But the moment they were out of the room, he glanced about, then wrapped his hand around her upper arm and gently pulled her into an alcove.

"My lord?" she gasped.

His eyes searched hers before he reached out and brushed a curl from her face. His hand lingered for a moment, and she gritted her teeth trying to resist the urge to lean her cheek against his palm.

"My apologies," he said, his voice deeper, gruffer as he tried to keep his voice down. "I merely wished to ensure you were well. You looked as if you could use a moment."

He let his hand drop, and she mourned its loss.

This was madness. If anyone saw them, pressed so close together in the shadowed alcove, what reputation she had left would be in tatters. Yet, she couldn't bring herself to push him away. To insist he let her pass. Return to the others.

It was simultaneously impossible to draw a breath. And yet, for the first time in months, she felt as if she could truly breathe.

"Thank you, my lord," she said. "I…it has been a while since I have played."

"You did so beautifully."

"Thank you. I shall have to ensure I purchase a pianoforte when I set up my household," she said with a smile she hoped was steady.

"Well, if you have trouble procuring one, let me know. I can always steal that one for you," he said, with a nod toward the salon.

That surprised a laugh out of her. "Do you often procure items that do not belong to you?"

He gave her that mischievous grin that never failed to set her heart pounding. "It has been known to happen on occasion. But only for a good cause," he said, leaning in with a conspiratorial whisper.

His gaze roamed over her face, his smile fading slightly as his eyes creased in concern. "Are you sure you are quite all right?"

Selena nodded. "Yes. I suppose I did get a bit overheated."

He tilted his head slightly, regarding her. "Is that all it was? It seemed as though something had distressed you."

"Oh," she said, her cheeks growing warm. "No. I was not distressed, exactly. Contemplative, perhaps."

"Did you know the composer Lord Trescott mentioned? This Albescu?"

She blinked, her chest growing tight. "Why do you ask?"

"Curiosity," he said, lightly shrugging one shoulder. His eyes roved over her face, lingering on her lips before returning to her gaze. "You played the song so beautifully. It seemed personal."

She sucked in a shaky breath. "Forgive me, my lord, but I find this all…"

"Impertinent? Rudely over-familiar?" he asked with a roguish smile that drew an answering one from her own lips.

"Perhaps."

"Again, my apologies. Truly, my only wish was to ascertain your wellbeing. Not distress you further."

She nodded, her thoughts a jumble as she tried to decide what to tell him. What would ease his concern without divulging secrets she had no wish to share. Finally, she gave him a soft smile.

"I lived in Bucharest for a time. It is a period of my life that I prefer not to dwell upon."

"Very well." His eyes searched hers again. "I will escort you back to the others, if you wish."

Her heart thundered so loudly he surely must hear it. "Perhaps not just yet."

That slow, crooked smile of his sent her heart skittering again. He picked up her hand and brushed his thumb across her knuckles. "Permit me to call upon you," he said, leaning down to press a kiss to her hand.

Selena sucked in a breath, her hand tingling where his lips had lingered. "My lord." Her voice was hardly more than a tremulous whisper.

This. This feeling. She hadn't felt anything like this. Ever. Not in any of her four marriages. Not with the man who was almost her fifth husband before he abandoned her. Not even with dear Charles. And Lockhaven had barely touched her.

But oh, she wanted him to touch her again.

Yet she daren't. Mustn't.

He straightened. Looked into her eyes. And before she could second guess herself or change her mind, she raised on her toes and crushed her lips to his.

For a few brief, glorious seconds, their lips pressed together, moved over each other, sending a tingling heat cascading through her that she had never experienced before.

She broke away with a gasp, looked into his startled face…and then turned and ran out the door.

CHAPTER NINE

EDWARD HANDED HIS coat and gloves to the waiting footman and then joined a grinning Anthony who stood leaning against the grand staircase banister waiting for him.

"My lord," Anthony said with a slightly mocking bow. Edward scowled at him, making Anthony chuckle. "I do not believe you've ever accepted one of my mother's invitations for her little gatherings before," he said. "I wonder what has changed."

"Do you really?" Edward asked, dryly.

Anthony's grin widened. "Come along," he said, instead of answering. "She's out on the back lawns."

"She?" Edward knew that Anthony knew why he was really there. Especially as Anthony had sent a message over just that morning to casually inform him of the rest of the guest list for his mother's afternoon tea party.

But apparently it was far too entertaining for them both to pretend otherwise.

"My mother, of course," Anthony said, continuing to feign ignorance. "And her other guests. I'm sure they'll be quite thrilled you have deigned to join them."

"Um hm," Edward muttered, trying to tamp down his impatience to see Selena again.

He couldn't think of her by any name other than her given Christian name since she'd given him the surprise of his life and kissed him when they last met. He'd played that moment over and over in his mind during the last three days. She had fully captivated him even before that moment. From her quick wit, her humor, her intelligence and talent—hell, the woman could speak at least three languages that he could deduce and played the pianoforte like a virtuoso. He would have been impressed and intrigued with even half as much to go by.

But the moment her lips had touched his…she'd ignited a fire within him he hadn't even realized existed. He *had* to have more.

It had been all he could do to keep himself from storming the doors of her house and continuing where they'd left off. Before she'd run from him yet again.

He really needed to get her to stop doing that.

He followed Anthony through halls of Goodwin House and to the back lawns where multiple shaded tables had been set up amidst refreshment tables and various lawn games. One group was bowling. A fair temptation as he excelled at the game. However, another group was preparing to play battledore and shuttlecock. A favorite of his.

He kept them both in mind. But his eyes didn't stop searching until he found her.

She looked up at the same moment and froze, their gazes locked.

"Hmm, the lady is looking rather fleet of foot this afternoon," Anthony said, leaning over to whisper in his ear. "Shall I have the servants block the exits?"

Edward gave him the scowl that comment deserved—though he couldn't deny it was tempting—and then turned to join Selena on the lawns, barely acknowledging anyone he passed. And not caring a whit about the stir his behavior would surely cause.

"Mrs. MacLaren," he said, coming to a stop before her.

She dropped a shallow curtsy. "My lord."

Her voice was strong and steady, though there was a faint blush to her cheeks, and she wouldn't quite meet his eyes again.

"I trust you are well?" he asked.

She gave him a soft smile. "Quite well, thank you."

He nodded at the battledore in her hand and grinned. "Fancy the game, do you?"

Some of the tension eased from her shoulders and she smiled back. "I do, yes."

"Well then," he answered, grabbing his own battledore from a servant who was handing out the rackets. "Prepare yourself. I am quite good."

She cocked an eyebrow. "Is that so?"

Anthony and Mrs. Haddon joined them, along with several other guests whom Edward quickly greeted.

Anthony nodded. "For once, Lord Lockhaven isn't exaggerating. The man has an uncanny knack for whacking these things about," he said, tapping the feathered and corked shuttlecock on the face of his racket so it bounced repeatedly in the air.

"As, apparently, do you, my lord," Selena said with a quiet laugh.

The whole group quickly discussed whether they wanted to play together or split into smaller groups. Edward, of course, voted for smaller groups, with he, Selena, Mrs. Haddon, and Anthony comprising theirs. Playing with a large group was quite entertaining. The more people who played, the more difficult it was to keep the shuttlecock aloft as it was hit back and forth between the players.

But it would also make conversing with Selena more difficult. And as that was his real aim, smaller groups were a necessity. Thankfully, the others agreed, and their foursome split from the other group.

"I propose a challenge," Edward said, an idea seizing him.

Anthony eyed him with suspicion. "What sort of challenge?"

"Instead of us all playing together, we pit the talents of Mrs. MacLaren and I against you and Mrs. Haddon. Whoever keeps the shuttlecock up the longest, wins."

"That doesn't seem fair," Mrs. Haddon said, coming to stand beside Anthony. "To you and Selena, I mean. I'm quite good."

Anthony laughed. "Well, then. I suppose that means your challenge is accepted, my lord. Prepare to be defeated." He tipped his head gallantly to Mrs. MacLaren and then tossed the shuttlecock to Edward, snagging another one from the servant who was holding the rest of the supplies.

Edward turned to Selena and held up their shuttlecock. "My apologies for not asking your thoughts on the matter first," he said. "But the opportunity to put Goodwin in his place was too tempting to ignore."

She chuckled. "Not at all, my lord. I am always up for winning a challenge."

Just when he thought he couldn't be drawn to her further.

He held up the shuttlecock and glanced over his shoulder to be sure that Anthony and Mrs. Haddon were ready. "Is everyone ready?"

At everyone's eager nods, he grinned. "Very well. Begin!"

He tossed the shuttlecock in the air and lightly tapped it, sending it to Selena while Anthony and Mrs. Haddon did the same.

"One," she said, tapping it back, sending it flying in a perfect gentle arc to him.

He hit it back. "Two. You *are* good at this."

"Three. Yes, as I said. Four," she said as he hit it back to her. "Pay attention."

"Five. I am."

"Six."

"But," he said, letting her keep count while he talked, "I would hate to waste such a perfect opportunity."

"Nine. Opportunity for what?" she asked, her words ending on a small grunt as she hopped over a couple inches and stretched out her battledore to keep the shuttlecock aloft.

"Sorry," he said, hitting it a little more gently on the return volley.

"Twelve over here!" Anthony called out.

"Fourteen here," Edward said with a competitive grin,

though he kept his eyes on his partner. "Our record is eighty-seven."

Selena's eyes widened. "Quite impressive."

He shrugged, then lunged with a gasp, the tip of his battledore just catching the corked bottom of the shuttlecock in time to keep it aloft. "The wind caught that."

Anthony laughed again. "The only wind out here right now is coming from you with your jabbering."

Edward rolled his eyes, but Selena cocked an eyebrow. "He has a point you know. Twenty-one." She lobbed it in his direction, and he tapped it back with expert precision.

"Are you calling me a chatterbox, Mrs. MacLaren?" he asked with mock outrage, delighted to hear her laughter ringing out again.

"I am merely pointing out that your aim is much better when you are concentrating more on *hitting* the shuttlecock and less on nattering on about it."

"Ah, yes, I do have a tendency to let my mouth run away with me. Thirty-five." He tapped it back and watched, admiring her form as she sent it sailing back to him. "My tutors were always complaining to my parents, but they knew a lost cause when they saw one."

"Oh? Thirty-nine. And are you a lost cause, my lord."

His breath quickened, though it had little to do with the physical exertion of the game. "I believe I might be, Mrs. MacLaren."

She froze for half a second, springing into action just in time to keep the shuttlecock aloft.

"And…why is that my lord?"

He moved a little closer, as close as he could while still allowing enough room to swing his racket.

"After what occurred when we last met, must you really ask?" he said quietly. "Forty-eight."

She visibly swallowed, her cheeks growing delightfully pink, and they volleyed the shuttlecock between them twice more before she answered. "Fifty-one. I…must apologize for that, my lord. It was unforgivably forward and—"

"Extraordinary. Nothing short of staggering. Quite possibly the best thirty-five seconds of my life to date."

"Did you say thirty-five?" Anthony asked. "We're up to sixty!"

"No," Edward said. "Stop eavesdropping. Sixty-two."

"My lord," Selena said, dropping her voice so low he could barely hear her. She whacked the shuttlecock toward him, her aim slightly less steady than it had been. "I appreciate you trying to be kind—"

"Sixty-three," he grunted. "I'm being nothing of the sort," he said, even his stellar skills being tasked by trying to focus on the shuttlecock while finally engaging in the conversation he'd wanted to have with her for the last several days. "I have wanted to do the same thing since the moment we met."

"What?" she asked, just as she swung. His response had obviously shaken her. Because instead of her battledore connecting with the shuttlecock…it connected with Edward's face.

He dropped to the ground, one hand to his now throbbing cheek. "Sixty-four," he said, holding the shuttlecock aloft with his other hand. "We may need to pause for a moment."

"Oh!" Selena dropped down beside him, gently prying his hand from his face so she could look at the damage. "My lord, my sincerest apologies. I didn't realize I was standing so close and—"

He chuckled though the movement hurt his throbbing cheek. "Well, now you *have* to permit me to call upon you."

She scowled down at him and dropped his hand. "Is that all you can think of? I've just struck you in the face."

Anthony peered down at him. "Hmm, I think she has improved your looks, Lockhaven. The patchwork pattern is a nice touch. Well done," he said to Selena.

"Ignore him," Edward muttered.

"Oh, do not fear, Mrs. MacLaren. It certainly isn't the first time a lady has struck him. Nor will it be the last, I wager,"

Anthony said with another chuckle.

Mrs. Haddon, the only one with her head on her shoulders it seemed, appeared beside him with a towel that must have been soaked in the cool creek water. "Here, put this on your cheek. It should help with any swelling."

"My thanks, Mrs. Haddon," he said, sitting up and resting his arm on his upraised knee as he pressed the towel to his tender flesh.

"I know this isn't the moment," Anthony said, holding up his shuttlecock. "But I do believe Mrs. Haddon and I won our challenge with sixty-eight."

"I call a rematch," Edward said, grunting as he got to his feet. Selena reached out to help him, so he took his time about it, reveling in the feel of her hands on his arm as he stood.

Mrs. Haddon bit her lip to keep her smile from spreading too far and bless the woman, she drew Anthony away to celebrate their victory, leaving him alone with Selena.

"Did you mean what you said?" she asked.

"About the rematch? Absolutely. I simply cannot live in a world in which I have been bested by Anthony. He'll never let me hear the end of i—"

"No," she said, some of the tension draining from her as she laughed. As he'd intended.

"I meant when you said—"

"I know what I said." He removed the towel from his face and gazed down at her, nearly trembling with the urge to pull her into his arms. "And yes, I meant it. You have captivated me from the moment I entered that ballroom. And it only grows stronger the more time we spend together. I would have been more direct about my interest, but I didn't wish to appear too vehement and frighten you off."

Her cheeks flushed again at that, likely in remembrance of all the times she'd literally run from him. But she wasn't running now.

"I would have spoken sooner than later," he said, his smile

making his face smart. "But you were more courageous than I."

"More forward, you mean," she said with a grimace that drew another smile from him.

"More blunt, perhaps. But welcomely so. And had you not broached the subject, so delightfully, I might add…"

Her cheeks flamed crimson at that, and he chuckled again. "I would have done so. My patience is great, but where you are concerned, I find myself sorely tested."

She sucked in a breath, and he could almost hear her heart racing. As was his.

"What do you say, Mrs. MacLaren? You won't allow me to leave here with my pride completely in tatters, will you? Having to deal with Goodwin's gloating is punishment enough for whatever sins I've committed that have kept me from your door thus far. I must see you again."

He didn't even request to call upon her. At this point, they both knew their interest went deeper than that.

"Very well," she said. "Come tomorrow."

CHAPTER TEN

THE NEXT AFTERNOON, Selena's mind was still spinning at Lord Lockhaven's—Edward's—parting words. Everything she had ever been taught said that she should have been shocked. Offended. Horrified at his forwardness, and his insult to her delicate sensibilities.

Her past experiences had taught her she should run, far and fast, for her sake and his own. She fell in love too easily. Well, infatuated, at the very least. In love with the possibility of what the men in her life presented. And every man she had married had died. Every last one. Her curse was unrelenting. And there was precious little left of her heart with which to gamble.

But apparently she hadn't yet learned her lesson—and her sensibilities weren't all that delicate—because she wanted nothing more than to embrace this man with both arms and explore whatever this connection was between them. So she'd said yes. Invited him to come.

And now she sat in Jane's parlor, her palms sweating so much she could scarce hold her teacup.

She wanted to see him, yes. But before anything went any further, she needed to make sure he understood that this was merely…

She let out a long sigh. She didn't know what this was. Or what she wanted it to be. A discreet liaison perhaps? A prospect which filled her with both trepidation and excitement. To take her pleasure as men often did would be intriguing. Frankly, it was a prospect that didn't seem possible. Certainly not practical. While she had no doubt it would be enjoyable, it could have long-reaching and possibly catastrophic consequences. All it would take was one marriage proposal—which she couldn't seem to resist—and husband number five was as good as dead. Her curse had never yet failed.

And yet she couldn't help but long for just such an association. If it were even possible.

She did, at least, know what couldn't be between them. It couldn't be real. Couldn't lead to marriage or even courtship. Not that he'd offered that. But if she were anyone else, his intense interest, his insistence on calling, not to mention that kiss in the corridor (even if it had been her fault)—any one of those things was a near guarantee of a proposal. Yet that was the last thing she wanted. And if his reputation was anything to go on, he would be of much the same mind.

Then again, according to everything she'd heard from Jane, who had been gossiping with Lord Goodwin, Lord Lockhaven was behaving in a manner heretofore unseen by his friends and family. They were as stymied as she.

Perhaps they had all gone mad. Perhaps they—

The door opened, and she shot to her feet.

Jane reached out with a steady hand and quiet chuckle and took her teacup from her, setting it down on the small table beside the sofa.

And then he entered, his eyes going immediately to hers as the footman announced him.

He bowed. She curtsied, wincing slightly at the sight of the bruise blossoming across his cheek. Jane mumbled something that neither of them paid any attention to. Mr. Haddon, who Selena had completely forgotten was still in the room, said something by way of greeting that Lord Lockhaven nodded absently at.

And still they stared at each other.

Finally, he spoke, breaking the spell. "Mrs. MacLaren, I hope you will not find me too forward, but I had hoped you would perhaps show me the library? My mother tells me Mr. and Mrs. Haddon keep quite an extensive collection," he said, with a smile at Jane, "and I do so love a good library."

"That is very kind of her. We would be honored if you would like a tour. I'm sure Mrs. MacLaren would be very happy to show you about," Jane answered for her. Not that Selena would have answered any differently. "Selena, dear, please show his lordship my collection of Cavalier poets. It is a particular favorite of mine. They are so beautifully bound, and the content of course is superb."

And she shooed them out the door before either could get another word in edgewise. Though that was just as Selena wished it. Her nerves were so raw her body nearly vibrated with tension. But something about his presence calmed her as well. The sheer contradiction of it all made her head spin.

Lord Lockhaven, bless him, didn't speak right away. He followed her down the hall and glanced around appreciatively as they entered the library. They wandered through the large room in total silence. Long enough that some of the tension in her shoulders began to ease. Her nerves began to calm. The library wasn't so large as some she had seen. Certainly not as large as Lord Lockhaven's she'd wager. Which meant he'd probably asked for a tour just so they could be alone. Away from any eyes that might have been watching.

Finally, she took a long, deep breath and released it slowly.

Only then did he smile at her in that way he had that sent the butterflies in her stomach rioting. Though he kept his hands firmly clasped behind his back as they walked, she could still feel the warmth of him as if he were enveloping her.

"Mrs. Haddon's favorite collection is this way," she said, leading him up a corkscrew staircase to the upper gallery.

They reached the shelf holding the Cavalier poets—a shelf

located toward the back corner near a recessed alcove with a reading bench. Selena shook her head. Mrs. Haddon took meddling to an extreme that was frankly impressive.

Lord Lockhaven nodded appreciatively as he glanced over the books. But they apparently weren't what was on his mind.

"I am glad you agreed to see me today," he said.

Selena bit her lip, her pulse racing though she was still somewhat bemused that he was there in front of her. "I feel I should apologize again for my behavior at—"

"No." He stopped and turned fully to her, his eyes boring into hers. "No apologies are necessary."

"Does…" She took advantage of their lack of audience and raised her hand to lightly touch his cheek. She wanted to soothe the pain she'd caused. And, frankly, she just wanted to touch him. "Does it hurt?"

He smiled, the movement causing his face to push into her palm. But instead of moving away, she could have sworn he leaned into her touch slightly. "Not as much as it looks like it should, I assure you."

Guilt filled her nevertheless, and her brow creased in a frown.

His thumb brushed across her forehead, smoothing the frown away. "I swear to you, I feel no discomfort."

She cocked an eyebrow, not bothering to hide her skepticism, and he chuckled.

"Very well, perhaps a slight discomfort. More damage was done to my ego, I assure you. Lord Goodwin has been insufferable."

She couldn't help but laugh at his forlorn expression, even as a light shiver ran up her spine at his sweet touch. She wanted to curl against him like a cat, rubbing her face into his chest while he stroked her hair.

That mental image startled her so much she stepped back, putting a few inches between them. But before she could move too far, he reached out and gently seized her hand.

She froze, her entire being focused on his hand encapsulating hers.

"Don't go," he said, his voice suddenly low, its quietness lending an intensity to the words that took her breath away.

Before she could foment another thought, he pulled her into the alcove, captured her face between his hands, and kissed her.

If their first brief kiss had shaken her, this one was a veritable earthquake, rocking her very foundations. Everything she'd previously thought, desired, dreamed, feared—It all came crashing down. She'd thought she knew what to expect. But that brief kiss before had barely been a taste, a hint, of what lay in store.

His lips moved over hers, sending her heart thundering. She leaned into him, seeking more, her mind a cacophony of emotion and confusion and sheer *need* that overrode everything else. Her entire world narrowed down to that moment. His touch. *Him.*

The rest of the world be damned.

She had been alone so long. And she was tired. Tired of the sadness. The loneliness. The longing for something she might never get. Well, here it was. A moment of joy. Of passion. For just this moment, at least, she was going to revel in it. Even if she couldn't let it ever go past this moment.

They finally broke apart, gasping for air. He kept her cheek cupped in his hand and rested his forehead against hers, his thumb brushing against her skin ever so gently. Their breath mingled as she leaned into him.

"Selena," he whispered, sending her heart soaring. "Marry me."

Her breath stopped altogether.

She pulled back, her eyes searching his. He hadn't just… He didn't just… "What?" she asked, the sound more a gasp than a word.

He looked startled himself for a moment, eyes wide and mouth open. As if he couldn't quite believe what he'd just said. But then he blinked and looked at her with renewed intensity, taking her face in both hands. "Marry me. We could be so good together. You enjoy my company, do you not?"

She frowned. "Yes, but—"

"You do not abhor my touch," he said, leaning in to press another kiss to her lips.

"No," she murmured, grasping his wrists as his hands still cradled her face, her entire body crying out for him to continue his exploration.

He broke away with a groan, then grinned. "You find me amusing, handsome, reasonably intelligent." His crooked half-smile sent her heart spinning and would normally have pulled an answering smile from her lips.

But she was still too stunned to do ought but whisper again, "Yes."

"Then marry me." He kissed her again. "Say yes," he whispered against her lips.

For one brief, glorious moment, she let herself sink into him. Luxuriate in his touch. Consider the madness he was suggesting, all the possibilities it entailed.

Good…very, very good.

And bad.

She pulled back.

"No."

His eyes widened, then narrowed in confusion. "But—"

She exited the alcove and hurried to the staircase. With a quick glance over her shoulder, she said, "I'm sorry, my lord. But I…I cannot."

"Selena." He held out a hand, beseeching her to return.

But she took step back, her heart that had been soaring only moments before now cracking.

"I'm sorry," she said again before whirling around and descending the winding stairs so hastily she had to close her eyes against the brief dizziness that resulted once she reached the bottom.

He stood there, staring down at her, confusion rife on his face.

She gave him one last glance and then ran from the library.

Damn it all to hell in a handbasket!

She gathered her skirts and hurried back to the salon, part of her hoping he'd follow her. But a larger part praying he wouldn't. If he asked again, she wasn't confident she'd be able to say no again. And she needed to. She couldn't let him become yet another casualty to her curse.

Everything had been going so well. And then he had to go and ruin it with a proposal!

Argh! She didn't want to let herself think of it.

How had she managed to find the one rake in London who would turn all noble and propose after one kiss?

Well, two, she supposed, or three. Not that she wanted to put too fine a point on it.

What she wanted was… She stopped, her hand resting on the salon's doorknob, and let out a deep sigh.

What she wanted was to say yes.

But that would doom them both.

She turned the knob and went inside. Jane was already on her feet, her eyes alight with curiosity.

"Well, what happened?" Her piercing gaze took in Selena's likely disheveled and distraught appearance, and she frowned, crossing her arms. "Oh, dear, you didn't run from him again did you?"

"He asked me to marry him!" Selena said, by way of explanation.

Jane, however, didn't seem to understand. She clasped her hands together with a delighted gasp, her face lighting in a smile.

"Who asked you to marry him?" another voice said.

Selena spun with a gasp, bringing her face to face with her mother.

"They arrived just after you left to show Lord Loc—where is he?" Jane asked, leaning slightly to look over Jane's shoulder at the open salon door.

The faint sound of the front door closing carried into them, and Selena winced. "I believe he has just departed."

"What? Why?" Jane frowned.

Selena rubbed a hand over her forehead and looked past Jane to the small table set near the salon's bay windows. "Hello, Father," she said, giving him a faint smile.

Her father nodded at her in greeting from his seat and raised his teacup to his lips, more intent on refreshing himself after their journey in from the country than haranguing her about what she'd unfortunately just let slip in their presence.

Her mother, on the other hand, had no such compunction.

"Yes, yes, hello dear," her mother said, giving her a kiss on the cheek. "Now, what is this about a marriage proposal?"

Her mother took Selena's hands and dragged her to sit beside her on the sofa. Jane sat opposite them, looking both amused and sympathetic. And full of curiosity.

Selena sighed, cursing herself for not being more aware of her surroundings before blurting out such news.

"It's nothing. A misunderstanding," she said.

Her mother frowned. "I don't see how it could be a misunderstanding. The man either proposed or he did not. Of whom are we speaking again?" she asked, turning to Jane.

"Edward, the Marquess of Lockhaven, Lady Griffiths," Jane answered.

"Lockhaven?" her father piped up, reaching across the table to pick up another slice of cake. "Is he one of the Brelsford boys, then? The Duke of Haltham's son?"

"Yes, Sir Rawley," Jane said. "The eldest."

"Well, now, that *is* good news," he said. "Well done, Selena. Quite a step up from the rest of the lot. Present company excluded, of course," he mumbled, apparently belatedly realizing that Jane might take offense on behalf of her dearly departed brother.

"Yes, indeed," her mother said, clapping her hands together. "My daughter, first a marchioness and then a duchess! We shall have the banns read at once. No lingering engagement. We don't want to tempt fate for a repeat of what happened last time with that—" She waved her hand in the air as if she were trying to shake off something unpleasant.

And while Selena didn't necessarily disagree with her mother's assessment of her brief and ill-fated engagement to Otto von Richter, she was missing the point.

"No! No banns, Mother. There will be no wedding. I turned him down."

Everyone in the room stopped and stared at her. Her parents in utter shock. Mr. Haddon, who was so quiet most of the time that Selena forgot he was in the room with alarming frequency, merely looked confused. Jane was the only one who didn't seem surprised. Sad, but not surprised.

"You did what?" her mother finally asked, a hand pressed to her bosom. "Why? Why would you do such a thing? He is a *marquess*, Selena!"

She dragged in a deep breath through her nose and waved her hand in the air, not waiting for Selena's reply. "Never you mind. I'm sure you can take it back. We'll all go to call on him, explain that there's been a misunderstanding. That you will of course marry him. I'm sure he'll understand. And then—"

"No, Mother," Selena said. "I cannot go through it all again."

Her mother stopped, her shoulders drooping slightly as she gazed at Selena with sympathy.

"Oh, my dear," she said, reaching over to squeeze her hand. "I know you haven't had the best of luck, but—"

"Haven't had the best of luck?" Selena scoffed. "I have been widowed four times, Mother. *Four*! Every last one of them on our wedding day. Or… soon after." Her cheeks flushed hotly at the memory of Charles's death on their wedding night. Her gaze flashed quickly to Jane and then away again.

"And the fifth," she continued, then shook her head. "Was a mistake. A mistake that Otto thankfully did not make worse by actually marrying me. He saved us both when he abandoned me on our wedding day. And I won't be tempting fate a sixth time. I am not normally one to believe in things like curses or even ill luck, but when it comes to me…to this…" She took another deep breath before continuing, letting it out slowly to calm herself before she became truly vexed. "It may have taken me a distressingly long time to learn this lesson but learn it I did. I was not meant for marriage. And I won't condemn another man to that fate."

Especially this man.

She blanched at the thought but forced herself to continue. "Nor will I subject myself to further pain or humiliation. It's better to just leave well enough alone."

Her mother's lips pinched, and she turned to her husband. "Rawley, talk some sense into your daughter."

Selena met her father's gaze, nerves gripping her stomach. But she held her shoulders back and kept her gaze steady. And after a moment, he smiled, his kind eyes crinkling gently, before looking back to her mother.

"Let it go, Catherine. She has security enough and is happy with her life, yes?" he asked, glancing back at her.

Selena only hesitated a second before nodding. If her father caught her hesitation, he didn't remark upon it.

Her mother scowled but stood, brushing her hands across her skirts. It seemed that for the moment at least, she would leave the matter alone. Selena let out a small sigh of relief as Jane also stood to summon the footman.

"Please escort Sir Rawley and Lady Griffiths to their room," she requested.

The boy nodded and waited as Selena's parents kissed her cheek and swept from the room.

The moment the door closed, Selena slumped back against the sofa and put her hand over her eyes.

She had scarce drawn two breaths when the cushions beside her dipped under Jane's weight, and she cracked an eye open to look up at her friend.

"Now," Jane said with undisguised delight. "Tell me every-thing."

CHAPTER ELEVEN

EDWARD PAUSED OUTSIDE the door of the salon at Brelsford House, his family's London residence, and took a deep breath, still bemused by what had just occurred. He probably should have returned to his own townhouse that he kept not far away. But his mother expected him to stop in when he was in the neighborhood. Besides, from the sound of things, his sisters were all visiting and his brothers were likely inside as well. Hopefully, the chaos that often ensued when they were all together would mask his entrance, and they wouldn't pay him any mind.

That hope was dashed the moment he walked inside the room, and they all stopped mid-conversation to stare at him. And then they converged.

Though it was difficult to make out exactly what everyone was saying, as they all spoke at once, the gist of the questions flying at him seemed to pertain to his visit with a certain woman. As he had just come from her house, they could only know about it if Anthony—

Edward glanced over to where his friend sat with his brothers stuffing his face with Mrs. Cook's famous tea cakes.

"Traitor," he grumbled to him.

Anthony just grinned and shrugged. "My apologies, my lord, but the rarity of what occurred today was so great I simply had to share the astounding news."

Edward sighed and dropped on one of the sofas. If Anthony thought the mere fact of him calling upon Selena was astounding, he'd need to be revived if he knew what had occurred whilst there. "You have no idea," Edward mumbled.

Anthony perked up at that. As did his mother.

"Why do you say that?" Anthony prodded.

"I proposed," Edward said, not really meaning to share that information but unable to keep it inside with his brain still swirly frantically.

The entire room went silent as they all stared at him again.

"You what, dear?" his mother asked. "Did you say you proposed?"

There was a half a second pause before sheer pandemonium erupted, and everyone in the room fired questions at him at once.

Edward finally stood and held up his hands. "Very well, you heathens! Quiet down!"

His mother blinked at him, thoroughly surprised but willing enough, it seemed, to hold her tongue a moment if it meant getting the information she craved. His sisters grumbled but likewise held their tongues. His brothers quietly laughed and elbowed each other, their delight at this turn of events evident. Anthony seemed torn between outrage at being chastised, concern (likely at the thought his friend might now be betrothed to a murderess), and utter euphoria at sheer improbability of what he was about to hear.

Lord, preserve him. Edward dragged a breath in through his nose and rubbed a hand across his now aching forehead.

"I called upon Mrs. MacLaren today," he said, ignoring his mother's quick frown. "And, over the course of our conversation, I, apparently, proposed."

Questions immediately erupted again.

"Why didn't you tell us you were going to propose?" from his father.

"When is the wedding?" from his brother Hugh.

"Was she very happy?" from one of his sisters.

"How did you ask? Did she weep?" from another sister. Likely Mary. She was the most romantic minded of the bunch.

Finally, his father cleared his throat. "I am assuming the Mrs. means the woman is a widow, and not that you are trying to steal another man's wife."

"Of course, Father."

"I'm not sure I've had the pleasure of meeting this girl. Nor her husband, that I recall. MacLaren? MacLaren? Scottish was he?"

"I believe so, yes," Edward said, belatedly realizing he wasn't all that sure who Selena's deceased husband was.

"Why do I know that name?" the duke asked his wife. Who still sat motionless staring at her son.

"*That* Mrs. MacLaren?" from his mother.

He squinted at her for that remark and held up his hand again. "I cannot hold a reasonable conversation with all of you shouting at me so. To answer the queries I heard…" Well, the ones he would deign to answer at the very least. A few of them, he wouldn't dignify with a response.

"I did not tell anyone I was going to propose for the simple reason that I had no intention of doing so. It is as much a surprise to me as to all of you. To the lady as well, apparently. Yes, Mother," he said, turning to her with a disapproving glance, "*that* Mrs. MacLaren. I do wish you wouldn't judge her so harshly based on vicious rumors. Or for the circumstances of her birth, for which she had no choice. She would make a fine duchess for all that her father is merely a baronet. For the rest of you, we could have avoided all this nonsense had Lord Goodwin kept his knowledge of my visit to himself."

Arthur snorted and elbowed Anthony. "Not likely," he muttered.

"There is truly nothing to tell," Edward said, throwing them a glowering look. "There will be no wedding." He swallowed past the embarrassed disappointment rising in his throat. "The lady refused me."

That shut them up.

Eight pairs of eyes stared at him in utter astonishment.

"She did what?" his mother finally asked.

He sighed and sat back down. "You heard me correctly. She does not seem inclined, at the moment at least, to agree to a match."

"Oh dear," she said, coming to sit beside on him on the sofa to pat his hand awkwardly. "Well, perhaps it is a blessing in disguise. I *have* heard some troubling things."

"Now, don't start on that again, Mother," Edward said, exasperated beyond endurance.

"Edward, I am your mother, and I love you. I want nothing more than for you to be happy."

"I'm rather sure our last discussion on this topic centered around your only wish being for me to settle down and start producing heirs. With a suitably noble wife. My happiness was not mentioned that I recall."

"Oh hush. You always were an impertinent boy. As I was saying, I only wish for your happiness. And, to that end, we might even consider a match with a woman who is not quite of your status if that is what your heart is set upon. However," she said, before he could seize that offer. "If even half the tales about this woman have some truth to them…well, I not only have doubts about your future happiness but fear for your safety as well."

Edward just shook his head and glanced at his father. Surprisingly, instead of siding with Edward in lambasting his mother's odd fixation on these rumors, his father simply frowned and folded his paper.

"I will admit that what we have heard is concerning, Edward," his father said. "I put no stock in rumors under normal circumstances. However, you are my son and my heir, and I would not lightly treat any woman you intended to marry. Any such woman needs to be above reproof and certainly scandal if she is to be your marchioness and someday the next Duchess of Haltham."

Edward frowned. "I understand that, Father, but the rumors about Mrs. MacLaren are simply that. Unsubstantiated rumors."

"Perhaps not so unsubstantiated," his mother said, nodding at his sister who handed her a sheaf of paper.

"What is that?" Edward asked, already dreading the answer.

"A scandal sheet that Lady Brighton brought back with her from the Continent."

"Oh?" Edward cocked an eyebrow. "Please tell me your source of prejudice against Mrs. MacLaren is not some rag from a foreign country."

"Edward," his mother said, sharply enough he looked at her with surprise. "It is true, under normal circumstances I would not come to you with such middling proof. But the coincidences are too great not to share with you if you are going to insist upon continuing your association with this woman."

"What coincidences, Mother?" he asked, unable to help himself.

"There is a woman purportedly traveling around Europe leaving a trail of dead husbands in her wake. They are calling her the Lady Death."

"Mother, really," Edward scoffed, but she held up a hand.

"I know it seems farfetched. But this woman supposedly finds wealthy men, marries them, and then kills them on their wedding day before running off with her inheritance."

"If she murders them on their wedding day, that doesn't give her much time to collect an inheritance, let alone run off with it," he pointed out dryly. "The paperwork alone would take a fortnight."

His mother ignored that. "She's been described as a striking woman with raven-black hair and piercing blue eyes," she said, reading from the scandal sheet in her hand.

And as much as it pained him, that made him pause. Still… "If the person reporting this is informed enough of the circumstances surrounding this woman to describe her, then why do they not merely mention her by name? Why the secrecy?"

"Oh, Edward, really," his sister Louise said. "They never mention the names. Just as the caricature artists never name those whom they draw. It's one thing to speculate. All in good fun. It's another entirely to outright accuse someone. That could start trouble, especially if they were wrong."

"Judging by the rumors running amok in this town, and the suspicion she is already under because of it, it looks like the speculation has already caused a great deal of trouble for Mrs. MacLaren, whether she's been named or not," Edward said, his eyes narrowing.

"It goes on to say," his mother continued, "that this woman has married men in at least three countries, and disappears almost as soon as they are buried, leaving their grieving families wondering just how much she had to do with their suspicious deaths."

"Very well," Edward said cautiously, "I will admit the description, at least, sounds like her. But other than the fact that she is a widow who has traveled more than the average woman, it could be anyone. Or no one. It is nothing but conjecture. We don't even know if the deaths occurred in the countries in which she lived."

"Well, one was in France. Has she lived there?"

"I do not know." For sure. But judging by her effortless slip into French that day with the horse, he could surmise.

His mother's eyes narrowed. She could read him too well. "You know something."

He let out an exasperated sigh. "I know she speaks French. But that is hardly damning. If that were the only criteria, then you would be on the suspect list as well."

His mother pursed her lips. "Perhaps. But I haven't been to Italy."

He opened his mouth to make another smart comment, but paused at the memory of Selena, staring at the painting of the Venice landscape. But, again, that was nothing but coincidence. Surely.

"Another murder reportedly took place in Bucharest. I'll admit that one may be a trifle more difficult to prove. I'm not sure I am acquainted with anyone who has been there recently."

Edward froze. That might be a bit more than a coincidence.

The haunting music that Selena played that night still filtered through his head in his quieter moments. That haunting but playful piece. The one that had made her seem sad. Contemplative. A piece by a composer from Bucharest.

It proved nothing. Even if she had been there, even if she *had* married these men, it meant nothing. Men died. It was a fact of life.

Was it odd that, if it were true, she was the widow of at least three, possibly more, men who had died suddenly on their wedding days.

Yes. He could admit that much.

Did it give him pause?

Truthfully, yes. Though he hated to admit it, even to himself.

He glanced at Anthony who was watching him with a speculative look in his eyes. As if he knew everything that was running through Edward's mind at that moment. And he probably did as he'd put half of the suspicions there with his earlier concerns.

"All I am saying, my son," his mother said, "is that you may not know this woman you wish to wed as well as you think you do."

"She rejected me, Mother."

The look his mother gave him was far more perceptive than he would like. "I know you, my son. You will not leave it at that, not if you truly care for this woman. And if you are intent on bringing her into our household, making her not just a part of this family but the future matriarch, perhaps we should look into her background before any more proposals are bandied about."

Edward was silent a moment, his mind still spinning. He could admit it did seem suspicious. But he wasn't sure he cared. *If* the mysterious Lady Death were even one and the same with Selena, there had to be a logical explanation. One that didn't involve her being a murderess. And it wasn't something he could exactly ask her outright, though he was tempted to do just that.

If the rumors were nothing more than that, then he could irrevocably damage their already delicate relationship. And if the rumors were true, did he really want to alert a possible murderess that he knew her secret?

Perhaps he should let his mother have her way. Even if he were to ask Selena, his mother would likely not accept her word on the matter. After all, if she *were* guilty, she would hardly admit it to the mother of her next intended victim.

This entire affair was nothing but nonsense. He was almost sure of it. It was that ever-so-slight possibility that it was *not* nonsense that had him slowly nodding.

"Very well. What exactly are you suggesting?" he asked, though he wasn't sure he wanted to know.

"I have a man," she started.

"Mother..." He dragged out the word, his tone coated with warning.

"He is very discreet," she assured him. "I am simply proposing that we let him dig around a bit. See what turns up. I know this is distasteful to you—"

"In the extreme," he said, fists clenched at his sides.

"And we understand that," she said, her face full of sympathy.

"However..." His father's voice brooked no argument. "This matter is too important to leave it up to your whims. The fact that we are considering this union at all is a measure of our affection for you. Or our desperation to see you wed," he added with snort. "This woman is untitled, unknown, and under a great deal of suspicion. If you want her, you will agree to our terms. We should, by all rights, be insisting upon a nice, titled, young virgin."

"Father!" Edward exclaimed, though it wasn't really so shocking.

His father just raised a brow and continued on. "However, as we've been trying for years to get you to settle down with *anyone*, a less-than-youthful widow will have to do."

"She's not yet thirty. She hardly has one foot in the grave," Edward retorted.

His father was already waving off his comment. "Yes, yes. As I said, she'll do well enough. However, we do draw the line at murderers."

Edward threw his hands up. "Oh, hell and damnation! She's not a murderess!"

"Edward!" His mother clutched her bosom, her cheeks bright red. "Your language!"

He scrubbed a hand over his face and took a deep breath. "My apologies, Mother. But this is ridiculous."

"Ridiculous or not, if you want to marry this woman, it is happening," his father said.

"Very well, Mother. Conduct your investigation, if you must. *Discreetly*," he cautioned. "I do not want the lady's reputation harmed more than it already has been."

"Of course, dear. It will be handled with the height of discretion."

Edward nodded again, avoiding Anthony's gaze. He didn't want to see the disapproval he knew he'd see there.

"If you'll excuse me," he muttered, rising to leave, though he knew it would be futile.

Anthony, of course, was right on his heels.

"Are you sure about this course of action?" Anthony asked the moment they were out of the room and away from any prying ears. "I can't imagine Mrs. MacLaren would be best pleased discovering you are having her investigated. Assuming, of course, you wish to remain in the lady's good graces."

Edward scowled. "My mother is having her investigated, not I."

"You agreed to it."

Edward snorted. "If you believe that my mother would have listened to me for one moment had I *not* agreed, you do not know her very well. Her investigation has likely been underway since the ball where we first danced."

Anthony chuckled. "You are doubtless right. Still—"

"I know," Edward said with a sigh. "But I am hopeful it will allay my parents' fears. And agreeing gives me at least the illusion of control of the situation."

"Perhaps," Anthony said with an amused grin.

"I must keep my mother happy, as well," Edward pointed out. "Then, when I next propose—"

"*When* you next propose?"

Where had that come from? "*If*, if I propose again," he amended.

Anthony pursed his lips and nodded slowly, watching Edward in that contemplative way of his that Edward didn't like. At least when it was aimed his way.

"Just be careful, Lockhaven. I know I've been pushing you toward that church for years now. But I rather hoped it would be for a wedding. Not a funeral."

"You are worse than my mother," Edward scoffed. "Far too susceptible to titillating gossip."

"Well, I can't deny that." Anthony's usual jovial smile was only slightly dimmer than usual.

Edward shook his head and took his leave, inwardly cursing himself for letting slip his plans to propose again. In fact, he hadn't realized he *had* plans to propose again until he'd said it. Then again, he hadn't meant to propose the first time, so perhaps making no plans at all was the best plan. He didn't seem capable of following them in any case.

Allowing his mother to investigate Selena did not sit well with him. But if and when he did propose again—assuming he was able to convince the lady to marry him—he wanted to be able to bring her to his family to be welcomed with open arms instead of ridiculous suspicion. They would not take her word for it on a matter such as life and death.

He could but hope that when he told Selena, as he must certainly do eventually, she would understand.

Or at least forgive.

CHAPTER TWELVE

SELENA SAT ATOP her horse, trying desperately not to fidget. Judging by the way the poor animal grew more and more restless beneath her, her efforts thus far had been in vain.

She smiled and nodded graciously at the other women who were starting to mount their horses in preparation for their ride. Lady Trescott and her niece, Lady Philippa, trotted by, feathers dancing jauntily in their hats as they passed. Mrs. Westley and her sister, Lady Rockford, waited for the grooms to help them mount. Their smart riding habits with their braided trim gleaming in the sun made Selena glad she had splurged a bit when purchasing a new habit for the trip. At least she looked the part of an accomplished member of the ton, even if she did not feel so.

The Misses Cherryfield—Fanny and Lucy, two spinster sisters who, by all accounts, were more than happy with their unwedded lot—greeted Selena warmly, and her stomach unclenched a little at their friendly smiles. Perhaps Jane's mission to make her friends wouldn't be as much a failure as she had feared.

Yet, despite the friendly faces that surrounded her, there *was* one face she missed. Though she hated herself for it.

He should have been out of sight, out of mind. But—she blew out an exasperated breath. He was never out of her mind.

Lord Lockhaven.

Edward.

Jane had, of course, invited him to the estate as well. Selena loved her dearly, but her misguided matchmaking attempts were enough to drive a woman to drink. Though, if the matchmaking attempts stopped, she might never see him again. That *should* be her preferred conclusion to all this madness. And yet...

She sighed. *And yet.*

Though she needn't have wasted her energies, because after all her angst and worry, Lockhaven had sent his apologies. He wouldn't be coming.

The crushing disappointment that had filled Selena had only proven to her that she was right in trying to keep her distance. She was already far too attached to the man. And that wouldn't end well for either of them. Something she assumed Edward must have decided as well as he had declined to join in their festivities.

It had now been far too many days since she had laid eyes upon him. Not that she was keeping count. She was too busy enjoying herself, mingling, making friends, enjoying the fine country air, to spend even a moment thinking about that man. In fact, she could barely conjure the image of his face in her mind. Nary a chiseled jawline or arched brow or thick, wavy hair to be found in the recesses of her mind. Nor warm, brown, laughing eyes either. Not a one! Her mind was a fortress, baring him entrance.

"I only have a moment, but had to issue you a quick warning," Jane said, bringing her horse to a sudden halt beside her.

Selena startled, her cheeks flaming, though Jane could hardly know the path her thoughts had taken. "Warning?" she asked with a frown.

"Yes. Brace yourself, my dear. *He* has arrived."

"He?" Selena's stomach bottomed out. She already knew. But she could not help but ask. "Who he?"

"*He.* Lockhaven."

Oh yes. She had been correct. Who he, indeed. 'Twas *the* he.

"He had a change of plans," Jane continued. "Arrived early

this morning, all devastating smiles and apologies. I did try to find you earlier."

"Devastating smiles?" Selena echoed numbly. As if she had no knowledge of the exact smiles of which Jane spoke.

She knew all right. They paired nicely with the smoldering looks that tested her knees' abilities to keep her upright.

"Yes," Jane answered, eyeing Selena with a mix of curiosity, concern, and growing amusement. "He had a change of plans—"

"Change of plans—"

"Yes, as I said, and he is now happy to attend our little gathering."

"Happy to attend?" Selena said, her voice a little stronger as her shock began to wear off.

"Yes. As I said," Jane said again.

Selena let out a sound that might have been a sigh or a growl. Even she could not tell. Her eyes narrowed as she scanned the courtyard.

"Aggravating man," she muttered.

"Quite right," Jane agreed. "He won't be joining the women for our ride—"

"He won't?" Selena blurted before she could stop herself. "I mean, of course not. Thank the saints."

If Jane heard, she ignored the comment. Aside from a noticeable twitch of her lips.

"He'll be with the men and their more *manly* pursuits," Jane said with a subtle roll of her eyes. Jane could outshoot the lot of them, though she did try not to upstage her guests. Hence, the leisurely ride about the grounds whilst the men amused themselves with the weaponry.

"That is all well and good, but that means he is still lurking about somewhere," Selena said, her eyes straining to see around every corner and bush whilst the gnawing pit of nerves in her gut grew more tenacious. An infuriatingly confusing predicament as, at this point, she genuinely could not tell if it was anxiety or anticipation.

She blew out a frustrated breath. Well. At least she now knew where he was—to some degree—and what he was doing. Perhaps her mind could cease its endless imaginings of various scenarios with Lord Lockhaven at the center. Being in his presence befuddled her, assuredly. But it was decidedly better than not knowing where the blasted man was. Waiting for him to pop up at every turn. No wonder she was a bundle of nerves!

Her mare shifted again, tossing her head against the tight grip Selena had on the reins. She forced herself to relax.

Deep breath in. Deep breath out.

"Are you well?" Jane asked, looking Selena over with a knowing eye.

Selena pursed her lips and didn't bother answering. She didn't need to. Jane, and anyone else with any sort of observational skills, could instantly see upon looking at her that Selena was, indeed, experiencing an attack of the nerves. But there was no help for it. She was finally making some headway with the other ladies—thanks in large part to Jane's efforts, culminating at this house party at the Haddons' country estate. And it was about to be ruined if she couldn't keep her emotions under control.

While Lord and Lady Trescott had always been friendly, the other ladies had been a little less so. But they, over the course of the last few days, had warmed to her considerably. A development Selena dearly wished to cultivate.

She had been dressed, ready to go, and looking forward to the company of the ladies, until *he* had decided to show his face.

Now, secreting herself away in the library seemed a more appealing use of her time.

"Are you truly so distressed by his presence?" Jane asked, a slight frown furrowing her brow. "I know I tease, but if you wish it, I will have Mr. Haddon send him on his way."

"No, no. I will be quite all right. I merely wasn't expecting to see him. Not here. Or at all. After…"

"Rejecting his proposal?" Jane asked, eyebrow raised.

"Yes," Selena answered through gritted teeth. Then she

sighed again. "I only pray I can make it through the next couple days with my dignity somewhat intact."

Jane laughed quietly. "You will be fine, I'm sure of it," she said soothingly. "He will hardly make a scene in public."

"My apprehension does not lie entirely with him," Selena muttered.

Jane's eyes widened. "Did *you* plan on making a scene?"

"Of course not." Selena frowned slightly at Jane. "Well," she said with a delicate snort, "I have no plans to. But when have my plans ever manifested in my favor?"

"What plans would those be?" Edward asked, his deep, grumbling voice materializing out of nowhere at her side.

Selena squeaked, accidentally yanking on the reins in her startled panic. Her horse reared, front legs pawing at the air as Selena held on for dear life.

"Whoa!" Edward jumped toward them, arms upraised as he attempted to calm the horse and grab the bridle.

Stepping into the path of a flailing hoof in the process.

Selena couldn't see exactly what happened. But one moment, Edward was at her side, trying to control the horse. And the next, he dropped to the ground like a sack of flour.

There was a flurry of shouting, and several grooms ran forward. They managed to calm the horse and backed her away from where Edward lay disturbingly still. But Selena had eyes for no one but the still figure on the ground.

"My lord!" Selena gasped in horror. She dismounted as quickly as she was able—ignoring the flash of ankle (and leg) she had likely given the poor grooms who managed to catch her as she launched herself from the saddle—and sank to her knees beside him, her hands moving over his face and upper torso searching for injuries.

"Saints preserve us," Jane said, hurrying to them. "I'll get more help."

Selena hardly noticed when Jane left, shouting orders to the footmen. And she disregarded the flurry of dismay coming from the other guests as they converged. Her entire being focused on the man before her.

"My lord?" she whispered, her hand cupping his cheek.

This was on her shoulders. If she hadn't been so ridiculously nervous to see him again, she wouldn't have been so startled. Would have had better control over her horse. The man had never been anything but kind to her. Forward, certainly. Determined, yes. Unnervingly so, on occasion. But kind, always. And while their last encounter had ended awkwardly, judging by his past behavior, he wouldn't have held it against her.

Conversing with him for a few minutes wouldn't have killed her. But her anxiety at the prospect could have killed him.

It seemed even without a marriage contract involved she was nothing but a menace when it came to men. Was her curse worsening? Was she now killing men before the marriage vows? How novel. She should join a secluded convent somewhere just to keep them all from harm's way.

She kept one hand on his cheek and one on his chest, just to assure herself that he still breathed. What had she ever done in her life to deserve such ill-fated luck?

She sat back on her heels and covered her mouth with her gloved hand, biting her lip against the laugh that threatened to bubble to the surface. Hysteria, surely. Though she did have a distressing habit of nervous laughter at the most inappropriate of times. She'd giggled through three of her four weddings. And one of their funerals. Though truly, amusement was the furthest thing from her mind on these occasions.

She would rather exile herself to the most remote corner of the world than see harm come to another man. Come to *him*. No matter how uncomfortable seeing him made her, it was certainly better than what had occurred.

And now, because she wished to spare herself a little embarrassment, Edward lay before her, his eyes still closed. Though he didn't have any wounds that she could see.

Jane arrived with several footmen in tow. She glanced down

at Lord Lockhaven, then glanced again, biting her lip as she directed the men to move him inside. Selena followed right on their heels, not stopping even when they reached his room. Nor when everyone left except for Jane. She simply waited, her heart in her throat, as Jane finished settling him in his bed.

"I'll...um...I'll have Mrs. Cowpry bring some cool cloths for his head," Jane muttered as she hurried from the room. Leaving them alone.

Selena raised her head briefly, staring in surprise at the door Jane had all but closed, leaving only a few inches open in a nod to propriety. She really should leave. Being alone with him, even in this state, flouted the rules of propriety. But she couldn't make herself go.

She leaned over Edward's still form, lightly placing her hand on his chest so she could feel the steady rise and fall.

And finally, she let out a long breath, her head hanging.

"This is my fault," she whispered.

"Yes," Edward whispered back, his eyes still closed. "Yes, it is."

Selena jumped back, slapping her hand over her mouth to mute her startled squeal. She looked more closely at Edward. At his chest that, upon closer inspection, rose and fell too quickly for someone unconscious. And his twitching lips utterly betrayed his true state.

"Ohh," she growled. She folded her arms, glaring down at him while he chuckled. "You, my lord, are a cad. A cold-hearted, weasel-livered, toad-eating, scapegrace!"

"Very likely." He didn't open his eyes, but he did speak. "That doesn't mean I am not grievously wounded, madam," he said, a slight smile belying his words.

"Um hmm."

He let out a sigh and opened both eyes, though he remained supine. "Did you call me weasel-livered?"

"Yes." It might not make sense, but it was the worst insult she could think of on such short notice.

"Ah, madam, you wound me. But surely you cannot blame me for such a small subterfuge."

"Oh, can I not?" She could, and she would. He'd scared a good nine years from her life.

"Had you known that my pride was more wounded than my body you would not have felt it necessary to be here so sweetly at my side, betraying your true emotions whilst—"

She gasped, outraged. "I am betraying nothing."

"But you are." He sat up, propping himself against the pillows with a wince that cooled her anger somewhat. The man obviously *was* injured, if far less so than he had let on. She let out a huff and reached over to help settle him.

"In truth," he persisted, capturing her hand so she couldn't move away again, "the very fact that you insist you are betraying nothing betrays the fact that you do in fact have feelings to betray."

"I…" She frowned, her head pounding from trying to follow his logic. Perhaps he was grievously injured after all. A head injury, undoubtedly. She pulled her hand from his grasp but stayed at his bedside. "That is too many 'facts' for me to follow," she said, rubbing at her temples.

He nodded as if he'd made his point. "Just so."

"No. You misunderstand—"

"Do I?"

"Yes!" She threw her hands up.

"Aha! Then you agree."

"No," she all but growled. "All the saints in heaven, you are the most aggravating man alive."

He nodded again. "I have been told so, yes."

"You needn't look so pleased about it."

He seemed to make at least some effort to stifle his smile, but to no avail. "My apologies, madam. It seems I cannot help myself."

She let out a delicate snort. "That is undeniably evident," she said with a shake of her head, biting her lip to keep from smiling.

She refused to encourage him. "I cannot believe you were lying there pretending to be injured—"

"I'm not entirely pretending," he said with a grimace, rubbing at his shoulder.

She frowned again, a knot of worry worming its way back through her.

"In my defense," he continued, his tone quickly dissipating her concern, "it seemed to be the only way to get your attention."

"That's not true."

"Is it not?"

"You always have my attention," she muttered, letting the truth slip out.

He froze for a moment and the air between them grew heavy. She had been a fool to admit such a thing.

Another heartbeat passed before he finally spoke. "You could have fooled me," he said, his flippant tone at odds with the sudden intensity of his gaze.

Her eyes narrowed. "Why do you say that?"

He coughed out a laugh, betraying a world of frustrated amusement. "You literally run from me every time we spend more than three minutes in close proximity."

"I do not," she said with an incensed gasp. Even though he wasn't completely wrong.

"I do hate to keep arguing, my dear, but you certainly do. You very literally turn tail and flee with nary a care for whatever innocent bystanders—or statuary—may be in your way."

Her mouth dropped open, the urge to contradict him burning through her. But, well, again, he wasn't mistaken.

She plopped on the bed with a huff. "Yes, well, you…"

He arched an eyebrow, his lips pulling into a half-grin that sent her stomach careening. "I what?"

She blew out another breath, exhausted from trying to deny what was becoming increasingly obvious to everyone. "You make me nervous."

His other eyebrow raised, joining the first in a look of delighted surprise. When he spoke, his voice had dropped an octave, and he leaned forward, his nearness sucking all the oxygen from her lungs. "And why is that?"

She struggled to suck in a breath. "I do not know."

"Oh, I think you do," he said, his eyes roving over her face, lingering on her lips.

Her heart thundered as she dragged in a stuttering breath. "Do I?"

"Oh, yes." He leaned in closer, until his lips were scarcely an inch from hers. And then he grinned. "You fancy me."

He sat back with a self-satisfied grin that had her sputtering. "I…I do not…" The argument sounded weak even to her own ears.

"I think you do." His smile grew even more smug. And damn it all, it somehow made him even more attractive. What was wrong with her?

"That is not what we are discussing," she insisted, trying in vain to salvage some modicum of composure.

"I think it is."

"It is not. We were discussing whether or not I run from you—"

"We've already established that you do."

"Well, if I do, it is only because—"

"You fancy me."

"No!"

"Yes."

She threw her hands up again. "Perhaps I was merely trying to escape from your *infuriating* presence."

"Well, that *is* a possibility. I do seem to have that effect on people, though you are the first to actually take flight to avoid me. Though even if my, shall we say somewhat *unique,* personality is partially at fault when it comes to your penchant for flight, I still contend that at least part of what chases you from my side is your growing desire to spend even more time in my presence because the prospect of that terrifies you for some reason to such a degree that you cannot help but—".

Selena lunged forward and kissed him, her mouth crushing to his in a sudden, intense, and wholly ill-advised fit of madness.

CHAPTER THIRTEEN

MADNESS, IT MIGHT have been. But it was passionate, exquisite, utterly delicious madness. She hadn't meant to do it. She'd wanted only to stop the never-ending stream of truth that seemed to pour from his lips.

Yet there they were. Kissing. Alone in his guest chamber. In his bed…

Selena jerked back, slapping her hand to her mouth. "My lord. I'm so sorry—"

He shook his head, trying to close the distance between them again. "Don't be."

"But I just…I kissed you."

"I'm aware. I quite enjoyed it."

"I didn't mean to. You were just talking so much and I simply…wished you to stop."

He chuckled. "So, you kissed me?"

She nodded numbly, and he laughed again. "Interesting strategy, but I must admit, it *was* quite effective."

"So it seems," she mumbled.

"Perhaps you'd better do it again, just to keep me quiet."

She shook her head, still horrified that she had done it the first time. Well, horrified was rather a strong word. Mortified, certainly. Though she couldn't quite bring herself to truly regret it. She'd been dreaming of just such a moment since the second he had sauntered into that ballroom so many weeks ago. And now, every cell in her body screamed at her to do as he asked and kiss him again. "I…I cannot."

"Are you certain?" he asked, capturing her hands and pulling her toward him as he leaned closer. "Because I do have a terrible habit of letting my mouth run away with me." He kissed each of her hands. Then turned them over and kissed her wrists, sending a riot of gooseflesh up her arms, and a bolt of heat straight to her core.

"In fact," he said, "I feel another bout coming on now, and who knows what sort of nonsense I might start spoutin—"

Selena didn't stop to think, she just lunged again. She was tired of thinking. She wanted him. They both knew it. Denying it was becoming exhausting. Soul crushing.

Their lips crashed together again, and he pulled her to him with a moan.

Sweet heaven, she could spend the rest of her life in that moment, wrapped in his arms, his lips moving over hers. How could something so simple be so shattering. Life-changing. Every brush of his lips against hers, every touch of his hands as they moved up her back and up to her face, every moment of their breath mingling as they explored each other branded her as his. And being his? She wanted nothing more.

But that was a fate that would only doom them both.

"Wait," she said, breaking away again. "We can't."

"Why ever not?" he murmured, kissing the corner of her mouth.

Her eyes fluttered closed again as she gave in to the utter elation of his touch. His arms wrapped about her, and she nearly sobbed when his tongue licked at the seam of her lips. She could do naught but open to him, sink into his kiss, and let herself drown in the exquisite bliss.

"My lord," she gasped, finally wrenching her lips from his and drawing back as she tried to drag enough breath into her lungs. Though that didn't stop him. He merely found other areas to taste, touch.

"What is it, love?" he asked, his hooded eyes, dark with passion, gazing down at her.

Her mind brought up one hazy argument after another why she should stop this, even as she arched her neck to give him better access.

She sucked in a breath with a near sob. How could such a simple touch feel so incredibly good. "I could be ruined."

"Hmm," he said, his mouth moving from her lips to the sensitive skin beneath her ear. "Only if I don't marry you."

She jerked back as if someone had tossed ice cold water on her. "You…you can't marry me."

Marrying him condemned him. Not marrying him—if they were caught together—would condemn her. A fate she preferred over his, certainly. But neither fate was particularly appealing.

Aside from the fact that they would be together. Nothing appealed to her more. But if the curse were to strike again, she knew with every fiber of her being, this time she would not recover.

"Oh? And why not?" He arched that brow of his again. "Have I not made my intentions obvious enough? I *have* asked you to marry me several times."

Selena frowned. "You've only asked me once."

"Truly?" Edward said with a frown of his own. Then he shrugged. "Once is usually all it takes in these matters, though I could have sworn it had been at least twice. In any case, I can remedy that. Marry me."

"My lord—"

"Edward."

She sucked in a breath through her nose, her head beginning to pound again. "*My lord.*"

He sighed and cupped her cheek in his hand, resting his forehead against hers. The sweetness of the gesture was enough to halt any further protests from her lips.

"If we are to be wed, I would like to hear you call me Edward. You've done it once or twice before. By accident, surely," he said with a wry smile. He moved his head to whisper in her ear. "I would like to hear it again. On purpose, this time. *Selena*."

She closed her eyes, a delightful shiver running up her spine despite her misgivings. "Edward."

He smiled and captured her lips again and for half a heartbeat she allowed herself to sink into him. Do nothing but *feel*. Pretend she could allow this to continue. Allow herself to do what she really wanted and accept him.

But her brain intruded yet again, and she once again jerked back. Damn the man and the spell he kept casting over her. "No. You can't mean—we cannot—"

He gave her an amused, but exasperated, look. "What? Wed? Of course we can. You just have to say yes. I'll even ask again."

He pressed his lips to hers in a kiss so sweet she nearly sobbed. "Marry me, Selena."

"I...I..."

He did it again. "You only have to say yes, and we can fully explore whatever this is between us without any danger hanging over our heads."

If only he knew how untrue that was. Even without the curse, what man wanted to be a woman's fifth husband? Otto had proven that when he'd left her at the altar. How could she begin to explain her tortured past? Saying yes to Edward meant not only putting his life in jeopardy but informing him of all the men who had come before him. She couldn't marry him without him knowing. And if he knew, he wouldn't want to marry her.

Which was perhaps the best reason of all to tell him everything. No matter how painful losing him would be.

His gaze turned worried the longer the silence stretched. "If you truly do not wish to marry, I will be with you in whatever way you wish," he said, his words somehow breaking and healing her heart all at once. "As long as we are together."

"But..."

"But," he echoed. "*My* wish is for you to be my wife." He

drew her into his arms again, and she could do naught but wrap her own around him. "Marry. Me." He kissed her between each word.

"Edward," she whispered, rising on her toes to meet his seeking lips with her own.

She had never felt such ecstasy. And they had barely touched. A few kisses, a brush of his lips on her neck, and she was ready to throw all caution to the wind, risk whatever curse she was under, flout society and the Church and anyone else who stood in their path, and give in to the enticing madness that was near drowning her.

She pulled away, whether to gasp for air or to give him the answer he sought, she wasn't quite sure. But—

"I do hope Lord Lockhaven is feeling better," Jane's exaggeratedly loud voice floated to them from the hallway, along with the sound of her stomping footsteps heading toward the room.

Selena gasped and jumped up, hurrying to the other side of the room as Jane reached the door and slowly entered, ensuring her body covered the opening while she quickly glanced around the room. Her eyes widened when she spied Selena, and a smile tugged at her lips. She tucked a nonexistent stray curl behind her ear, and Selena sucked in a breath, quickly patting her hair to make sure everything was in place.

Edward, damn him, just leaned against the headboard, completely relaxed and composed, as if they hadn't just been compromised. If it had been anyone other than Jane—

Selena met Edward's gaze, and had to bite her lip to stifle her outraged gasp when he grinned and winked, just as the door opened fully to admit Jane and the doctor.

EDWARD WATCHED SELENA while the doctor checked him over, not sure if he should laugh at her poor attempts to appear nonchalant and aloof, or chase everyone from the room so he could aggravate her into kissing him again.

Of course, he would far prefer to kiss her without aggravating her first—as amusing as that was. But she didn't seem ready to admit that she wanted him just as badly as he did her. Their sparring gave her the opening she so obviously needed to let her passions escape. Passions he wanted to stoke again. And would. As soon as the doctor finished with his interminably long exam.

The doctor finally stepped back with a satisfied nod. "You seem in relatively good condition, my lord, all considering. A few bruises, naturally. You'll be sore for a few days. I recommend resting for at least two days. Nothing too strenuous—"

Edward's gaze shot to Selena's, the rest of the doctor's instructions fading into the background as they stared at each other. Judging by the flush in her cheeks, he wasn't the only one thinking of certain strenuous activities that he had no intention of avoiding.

He managed to smile and nod at the doctor, mumbling some semblance of thanks as the man packed up his bag and left. A maid with a tray of food arrived shortly after…with enough for two. He glanced at Mrs. Haddon and had to quickly look away when he caught her mischievous grin lest he devolve into laughter. Still matchmaking it seemed.

Selena, who hadn't moved from her corner since the doctor had arrived, took a few steps toward the door. "I'll leave you to your—"

"Wait—"

"Nonsense," Mrs. Haddon said at the same time as his protest. "There is plenty of food for two. You hardly touched your food at breakfast, and I'm sure Lord Lockhaven would welcome the company as the rest of the guests will be out for a several more hours still."

Selena's eyes narrowed as she glanced back and forth between them, but they both donned their most innocent smiles. Finally, she huffed out a sigh.

"Very well," she said, moving to perch on the edge of the chair next to the table where the maid had set the tray.

"Excellent." Mrs. Haddon bustled back out the door. "I'll see to it you aren't disturbed. So you can rest," she said over her shoulder, smiling as she closed the door behind her.

Selena frowned and stood. She made it to the door before Edward managed to jump out of bed, suppressing the grunt of pain that threatened to erupt at such an ill-advised move. He pressed a palm against the door, preventing her from opening it.

"What are you doing?" she asked, tilting her head up to look up at where he loomed over her.

"I should think that is obvious," he said with a smirk. "Keeping you from opening the door."

Her lips pinched together as she tried not to smile, which only made him grin more. "I can see that, my lord, but it is hardly proper for us to be alone in this room together with the door closed."

"I know." He leaned down until his lips were a breath away from hers. "It's delightfully wicked. Though there is an easy solution to that. You need but accept it and we can be alone to our hearts' content."

She groaned. "I am not going to marry you." She tried to push away from him, but he caught her wrist and pulled her close.

"You've said that. But I know you wish to say yes."

"I…no…how do you…"

He pulled her against his chest and wrapped his arms around her. "Because you are trembling in my arms right now."

"Perhaps I am angry," she said, leveling a glare at him that only made him chuckle.

"I have no doubt of that," he said, sending another tremor through her as his breath whispered against her ear. "Though I do doubt that is the reason you tremble."

"Perhaps I'm afraid," she said, her breathy voice doing things to him that no other sound in the world had ever done.

"Perhaps," he said, leaning down to brush a feather-light kiss across her lips. "But not of me."

She hadn't tried to pull away again. If anything, she had moved a bit closer, her body soft and warm in his arms. This time when he leaned down to kiss her, she rose up to meet him, one arm slowly winding around the back of his neck as she melted into him.

He reveled in the feel of her for several moments. That's all he allowed himself to acknowledge. Not the arguments from his family or even the ones in his own mind on why wanting this woman was madness. He knew them all. He simply didn't care.

With Selena in his arms, her sweet scent enveloping him, her soft body pressed against his, he didn't give a cloud of flying flatulence in the wind about anything except ensuring this woman was *his* until the day he died. They could figure out the rest as they went along.

"Marry me," he said again, foolishly certain *this* time she'd agree.

She let out a small sigh. "No."

He let her go and spun away with a frustrated groan, only to spin right back around.

"You…*infuriating* woman. Why won't you just marry me?"

She planted her hands on her hips and leaned in. "It's not that simple!"

He leaned in until they were almost nose to nose. "Yes, it is! I know you have feelings for me."

She reared back, her jaw dropping open. "I…well…what does *that* have to do with anything?"

Edward froze, his entire body tuned into the words that had just escaped her lips. Because for the first time, she hadn't denied it. Exactly. "What did you just say?"

It was almost comical how wide her eyes grew when she realized what she'd said. "That's not what I meant."

He gave her a slight half grin that had her eyes narrowing. "Yes, it was."

"No, it wasn't."

"You admitted it."

She gasped. "I did nothing of the sort."

"Oh, the admission was there." He waggled his finger at her, unable to keep his grin from breaking out. "You have feelings for me."

The most adorable growl of frustration erupted from her. She covered her face with her hands and then threw them up. "Even if I do, they are irrelevant."

The words were vehement enough he feared she might actually believe them. A thought that filled him with an aching sadness. "Not to me."

She shook her head, covering her mouth with one hand, and all amusement faded from him when he caught the gleam of tears in her eyes.

"My darling," he said, gently taking her face in his hands and tilting it up so she would meet his gaze. "Talk to me."

Her smile echoed his, though it was full of a sadness he didn't understand. It made his heart ache for her all the same.

"You are right," she said finally, lifting a hand to briefly cup his cheek. "I do care for you. A great deal more than I would like."

His heart leapt at her words. And crashed just as quickly. "If you care for me, if you are feeling what I am feeling, then why—"

She shoved out of his arms with a sob. "Because I do not want to kill you!"

✦

CHAPTER FOURTEEN

EDWARD STOOD, TOO stunned and confused to respond for a moment. That didn't make any sense. Granted, he had always been of the opinion that marriage was a death sentence. But more in the abstract sense. It would kill his freedom. His passions. His relationship surely with whatever woman managed to wed him. At least at some point. He had no illusions that he would be easy to live with, let alone love for an entire lifetime, and frankly he pitied the woman who dared to try. Hence, why he had avoided the institution for so long.

Until *she* had come along. She was the only person who had ever made the risk seem worth trying.

But something told him that wasn't what Selena had meant.

He frowned, watching her pace the rug in front of him. "I think I may require a few more details."

She shook her head with a short, almost hysterical laugh. "I am quite sure you do. After all, a madwoman just told you she couldn't marry you because she didn't want to kill you. You must think…" She laughed again. "I can't even imagine what you must think. But you deserve the truth. I know that. It's only…it is painful to talk about my past."

Edward frowned again. "I have no wish to—"

"I've been widowed," she blurted out.

He nodded slowly. "I am already aware of that fact."

"More than once," she said, her voice hardly more than a whisper.

His heart sank. He'd heard as much, of course. The gossips did love to bandy about half-truths and salacious tales. Though he'd hoped for her sake it had been nothing more than rumors. No wonder she was so skittish about marriage. His poor, beautiful darling.

"Selena," he said, pulling her into his arms. She let him, though she placed her hands on his chest to keep some distance between them. "My heart aches for your losses. But that does not explain—"

"My last husband, Charles…he died on our wedding night. Right after…"

Her cheeks flamed red, and Edward steeled himself against showing any reaction. "Ah," he said. Though his emotions ran through the whole gamut. Horror, amusement, even—may God have mercy on his twisted soul—a touch of envy. Of her husband. If one had to die after all, it wasn't a bad way to go.

But the woman left behind, however…

"I have been afraid," she said, tripping over her words. "What if…what if it were to happen again?"

He reached out and tucked a curl behind her ear, caressing her cheek as he did so. "Selena, love, I can promise you—"

"No, you can't!" She grabbed his shirt in her fists with her sudden vehemence. "You can't promise me anything. You can't know the future. I am cursed."

He frowned down at her. "Selena—"

She shook her head, cutting off his words before he could refute her claim. "Charles was young and healthy, we should have had many years together, yet he still—"

Her voice broke on a sob, and he swallowed past the lump the sound brought to his own throat. He would raze the nation to the ground to keep her from ever again feeling that bone-weary sadness that coated every word she uttered. Even defying the Fates themselves. Yet, she was not wrong.

"I know there are no guarantees in life, love. But I also do not believe in curses. There must have been problems of which you were not aware." He stroked her cheek and moved his hands down to rub her upper arms, trying to soothe her. "Perhaps ailments of which not even he knew," Edward said.

"Yes, but—" She took a deep, shaking breath. "He wasn't the first husband I buried."

He frowned down at her and then understanding finally struck him, and he took her chin in his fingers, lifting her face to his.

"Is that why you are afraid? Why you think I'll die? Because it's happened before?"

"The men I marry die, Edward. It's happened more than once."

"That doesn't mean it will happen again, dearest."

She let out a sobbing sigh that tore at his heart, and he pulled her back into his arms. She laid her forehead against his chest, her hands still gripping his shirt.

"How can I take that chance? I do not think I could bear to lose you," she whispered.

Well, if his heart had not belonged to her before, it did now.

"Selena," he cupped her face so he could press tender kisses to her lips. "I know you have known heartache in your past. And whilst it is true I cannot promise you nothing bad will ever happen to me, I *can* assure you it is highly unlikely."

She tilted her head, eyeing him with a healthy dose of skepticism. And a glimmer of hope. "In my logical moments, I *know* that. But my heart…"

"Is more difficult to convince?" he asked with a knowing smile.

She let out a soft snort. "Yes."

"Let me prove it to you," he whispered.

"What?" She blinked at him, startled.

His hand came up to cup her face, his thumb stroking along her jawline until her mouth opened with a whimper. He captured her lips, exploring her mouth until she clung to him. God help him, but this woman was going to bring him to his knees.

"Stay," he whispered, kissing her again.

He leaned his forehead against hers, his eyes burning into hers, and waited. Giving her the chance to walk away. It would kill something in him if she did. But this needed to be her choice.

Her breathing grew ragged, and a tremor ran through her. But she didn't leave.

He reached down, letting his hand skim down her waist and hip, watching her, ready to stop the moment she asked him to.

But she didn't.

He met her gaze and for half a heartbeat she did nothing. Then she reached down, covered his hand with her own, and helped him drag her dress up her thigh.

The first brush of his hand on her bare skin had Selena clinging to him. He turned them so her back was to the door, and he pressed her back, letting the full hardness of his body settle against her. She arched into him with a moan. He covered her mouth with his own, swallowing down her cries as he kissed her, his fingers finding her already wet and ready for him. He groaned into her mouth.

She pulled away, turning so he could help her with her buttons. It took far longer than he would have liked, but he eventually loosened her gown enough to slip it from her shoulders. Then her stays.

Before he could do more, she moved away, divesting herself of the rest of her clothing until she climbed on the bed and lay bare for him.

"You steal my breath," he said. "You are so beautiful."

Hauntingly so. The image of her in his bed, her dark hair cascading over his pillow, would haunt his memories for the rest of his days. Whether this was the first of many times, or the last. It did not matter. This moment was forever etched in his soul.

She didn't move while he undressed, letting him look his fill as she watched him, her eyes devouring every inch he uncovered.

His heart thundered in his chest, his body warring against the desire to touch her. He wanted to memorize every line of her first. Just in case. He had a feeling if she ran after this, she would keep running. He would just have to do what he could to convince her to stay.

But until then, he would worship every inch of her. For as long as he could.

She raised a hand, beckoning to him. "Will you not join me, my lord?"

"Always," he said, smiling at her in that way he knew she loved.

He lay beside her, drawing her into his arms with a groan. The moment his arms slid around her, she turned to him, sliding one leg over his hip so her soft heat pressed against him. He ran a hand up her leg, squeezing her thigh to draw her closer. He had meant to take this slow. To savor every second in case. But she was just as impatient as he and apparently wasn't going to allow that to happen.

From the moment he'd met her, this woman had wrecked every plan he'd made. Delightfully. Diabolically.

He'd never meant to marry. Certainly never meant to fall in love. Yet there he was, near begging her to be his wife. Because planned or no, he very much feared she owned his heart. If she left, as she always seemed poised to do, she would take it with her. And he'd give it to her. Gladly. He wouldn't need it after she left in any case.

She arched against him again and he chuckled against her skin. God, but this woman was a gift. His lips touched the sensitive spot near her ear, pressing a tender kiss there before his tongue traced a gentle trail down the slope of her neck. The heat of her scorched him. Enveloped him, and he reveled in the burn. She shivered beneath him, tilting her head to give him better access, and he retraced his path. His fingers trailing along the lines of her body, his lips roaming over every inch of her, until she grew more and more frantic under his touch.

"Edward," she moaned, her leg tightening around him.

"Easy, love," he murmured. He didn't want to rush this. She might not be a virgin, but he knew it had been a while since she had lain with a man. He didn't want her to feel anything but pleasure at his touch.

He slid a finger inside and her hips bucked against him. Edward groaned, adding another finger to join the first as his lips moved back up her body, his mouth moving over her breasts, sucking each nipple into his mouth until she threaded her fingers through his hair, pulling his lips back up to fuse with hers.

Selena writhed beneath him. "Edward," she said, breaking their kiss with a gasp, "please."

"I know, love," Edward said, moving to cover her. He withdrew his fingers and Selena whimpered, almost sobbing at the loss.

He nudged her legs farther apart and she spread them eagerly to accommodate him. The hard, warm length of him pushed at her entrance and she wrapped her legs about his waist, lifting her hips to bring him closer. He tried to go slow, easing himself in slowly, an inch at a time, but Selena wasn't having that.

She arched, wrapping both legs around his waist to draw him in deep. He chuckled, the sound full of male satisfaction, as he finally slid his full length inside her. His laugh cut off as they both sucked in a ragged breath.

"Selena," he groaned. Her body stretched to adjust to him, and he paused, letting her grow accustomed to it before he moved again.

He brushed her hair back from her face, his heart aching at the sight of her passion-darkened eyes gazing back at him. Because for the first time in his life, he felt whole. Complete. Like a piece of himself that he hadn't even known was missing had locked into place.

And if she left, he would never be whole again.

He leaned down to kiss her and she moved her hips beneath him, showing him with her lips and tongue what she wanted from him. Edward was more than happy to oblige.

He moved slowly, setting a careful rhythm that soon had Selena crying out for more.

His hands gripped her waist, keeping her movements slow and steady until she was half frantic with the need to increase the tempo. But he kept his strokes long and deep, filling her over and over until stiffened beneath him. He captured her lips again, muffling her cry as her orgasm crashed over her. He was two strokes behind her, barely keeping enough wits about him to withdraw from her tight grip before he spilled inside her.

He slumped against her, making sure his arms bore the brunt of his weight while the aftershocks rippled through them. Finally, he rolled to the side, keeping her cradled against him. He pressed a kiss to her temple and then buried his face in her neck, trying to ignore the ache taking up residence in his heart.

He knew she might run again. Might refuse him again. But they had this moment. For now, it was enough. Tomorrow they would talk about more.

CHAPTER FIFTEEN

SELENA BLINKED SLEEPILY at the morning sun streaming through her window. Her body was still pleasantly languid, and a bit sore, from their activities last night—

She froze, hardly daring to breathe.

Last night…

The arm banded about her middle tightened as Edward drew her back against his chest and pressed a kiss to her neck, and her heart leapt.

"Edward?" She twisted in his arms, turning to face him.

He gave her a slow smile that had a tingling heat curling low in her belly. Made all the more potent by the realization that…

"You're alive!" Yes, she realized the absolute absurdity of that statement. But logical or no, there had been a large part of her that had thought history would repeat itself yet again. And the sheer relief that he had not succumbed to the curse…She wrapped her arms around his neck in a near stranglehold, his chuckle muffled against her neck.

He pressed kisses along her shoulder and jawline until she loosened her grip enough for him to pull back and look at her. "I told you," he said, rubbing his nose against hers before pressing a heart-meltingly sweet kiss to her lips. Then he lay back, tucking one arm behind his head while the other kept her close to his side. "You really should listen to me more. I'm always right."

His teasing tone meant to rile her, and if she hadn't been so reassured to find him alive and well beside her, she likely would have taken the bait. But for the moment, her relief outweighed the need to best him at his games. So instead of slapping at his distractingly bare chest, she snuggled against him and kissed it instead. A movement that drew a satisfying hiss from Edward.

"Keep that up, love, and I'll be proving to you yet again just how alive I am this morning."

She smiled against his skin and kissed him again. "I'm surprised it has taken you this long to offer."

Her laugh cut off with a yip as he rolled her beneath him with a heated growl that had her body throbbing with instant need.

She tilted her face up for his kiss, but his lips hovered just above hers, tantalizingly close but just out of reach.

"Edward," she begged, arching against him.

"Marry me," he murmured, brushing his lips across hers.

She froze, and he dragged a hand down her thigh, hiking her leg up over his hip as he settled more firmly against her overheated core.

"I've proven virile enough to survive your curse," he said, his lips pulling into that half smile that drove her so wild. "I can handle anything else that comes our way."

"You can't promise that," she said, though she wasn't sure she believed that anymore. It was hard to think with his body covering hers, his hands sparking sensations that set her body afire, overwhelming every ounce of the caution and levelheadedness she'd been clinging to so fiercely. Though she had precious little of that left when it came to him.

He rocked against her, drawing a moan from her. "Come, Selena love. Let's tempt the Fates together."

There was nothing else she wanted more. And she was so tired of fighting it. Fighting her growing feelings for him. Fighting the draw between them. Perhaps it *would* be different this time. Perhaps this time, she would get to keep him.

Her stomach clenched with trepidation and a fine tremor ran

through her. She would never stop fearing that she'd lose him. But, he had survived so far. He'd avoided the horse and the pond at the park. The statue hadn't crushed him. And last night…last night had been more than she'd ever dreamed. And she'd woken up with him alive and well beside her.

She should probably walk away. Be happy with the moments she'd stolen. But she just couldn't. She didn't want to. She wanted *him*. Desperately.

Enough to do as he asked.

So she closed her eyes, took a deep, tremulous breath, and jumped off the metaphorical cliff. "Yes," she whispered.

Edward stilled above her, pushing up enough he could meet her gaze. "Yes? Truly?"

Her heart thundered, partly in fear, partly in exultation, her pulse racing so fiercely it almost deafened her. Now that the word had escaped her lips, nothing had ever felt so right. Absolutely terrifying. But right. She just couldn't deny him again. Deny herself. So she steeled her spine, shoved her fears into the inner recesses of her mind, and smiled. "Yes."

And was rewarded with a smile from Edward that took her breath away.

"You won't regret it, love. I swear it."

He lowered his head, finally capturing her lips. Selena held on to his words, even knowing he couldn't truly control what fate might have in store for them. But for this one moment, she could pretend. Let her fears go and just revel in being with him. The future would bring what it may. She would deal with it later.

LATER, UNFORTUNATELY, OCCURRED much sooner than she would have wished. She would have liked to have spent the day languishing in bed with her new betrothed. Words that still sent tendrils of dread through her heart, along with an almost giddy excitement.

But Jane's guests had returned to London that morning, Edward with them. And she had needed to return to her room before anyone was the wiser. A task that had proved much easier than the one that now awaited her.

Her parents had unexpectedly arrived.

Due to a stroke of good fortune (in her mother's mind), or yet another manifestation of her curse (in Selena's), her parents had arrived before Selena had departed, stopping to refresh themselves on their journey to London to visit her (surprise!) as Jane had given them an open invitation to do. What "luck" that Selena was still there!

She sighed and took a long sip of tea as her mother chattered on about some soiree or another that they had attended during their recent travels. Not that the tea would help much without a healthy dollop of whiskey. But it would have to do for now. Selena loved her mother dearly, but she did grate upon her nerves somewhat. On occasion. Frequent occasion.

Jane caught Selena's eye over her teacup and raised a brow, her eyes darting between Selena's parents and Selena herself.

Oh. Yes. She did have some news then, didn't she.

Anxiety spiked through Selena hard enough to make her hand tremble, and she set down her cup before the clattering gave her away. Really, it wasn't as if this were the first time this particular topic of conversation had arisen. As it was the sixth, in fact, one would think she'd be quite the expert at it. Then again, this was one instance in which practice did not make perfect. It made…problematic.

Truly, it should have been Edward having this conversation with her parents. And he would, soon. But she could hardly not share the news herself.

"Mother. Father. I am to be married. Again."

She sat and waited in the stunned silence, truly at a loss for how her parents might respond. They generally reacted with joy. Though their optimism had dwindled a bit with each subsequent marriage. As had her own.

Perhaps this wasn't such a good idea after all. She bit her lip, anxiety pulsing through her, fueling her doubts. She had been down this road so many times before. And it had ended the same. Every time.

But Edward was different. Stronger. More alive, vibrant. Determined…. Stubborn.

A small smile played at her lips as thoughts of him invaded her mind.

Surely, he would beat the curse. He'd survived her so far.

"Darling," her mother said with a hesitant smile. "That is wonderful. Isn't it?" she asked, looking to her husband.

Selena's father grunted. "Of course, of course. Hopefully this one lasts longer than the wedding."

Selena's mother covered her mouth with her hand, though she appeared more amused than shocked. Selena could not say the same.

"Father, please," she said, her stomach dropping. She hadn't been in love with any of her husbands, but she had been very fond of them all. Especially Charles. She had tried to follow the fortune teller's advice to trust her instincts. She'd taken a leap of faith with all of them. They had all been good men who had made her laugh. Men whose company she enjoyed, who seemed as though they would be jovial and kind husbands. And she had had very high hopes for their future together. Futures she'd thought would be filled with happiness and laughter. The loss of that, the loss of the men with whom she'd hoped to share her life…it wasn't a subject of merriment.

"Oh, don't trouble yourself, my dear," her father said, reaching over with a vague patting motion that barely skimmed her hand. "Surely you won't lose a fifth one. Sixth? What number are we on now?"

Selena threw a pained look at Jane who immediately snapped her own jaw shut and forced a smile. "Oh, I shouldn't think we have anything to worry with Lord Lockhaven. He's hale and hearty, very robust, and has a good head on his shoulders as well. I shouldn't think any untoward accidents will befall him."

Robust? Selena mouthed silently at her.

Jane just shrugged with a teeth-gritted grin. Their exchange was interrupted by her mother's sudden gasp.

"Did you say Lord Lockhaven?"

Selena pressed her lips together. She'd known that would go a long way to erasing whatever qualms her parents might have about this relationship. Though, they had already seemed thrilled in a bored sort of way about the news.

"Yes, Mother," she answered with a bland smile.

"Lord Edward Brelsford, the Marquess of Lockhaven, son *and heir* of the Duke of Haltham? *That* Lord Lockhaven?"

Selena's brows arched. "Is there another Lord Lockhaven of whom I am unaware?"

Her mother scowled at her and waved a hand in her direction. "Oh, such tone from you! Don't you realize if this marriage lasts—" they both ignored a snort from her father—"you will be the Duchess of Haltham?"

That was technically true, she supposed, though she hadn't really thought much about what her future status as his wife would be. She was far too busy worrying about becoming his widow.

"I suppose so, yes," she finally said.

Her mother clapped her hands together. "This is wonderful news indeed! Now," she leaned forward, all serious business. "We must have the banns read immediately. It wouldn't do to risk any chance of anything—" She glanced at Selena as if just realizing her line of thought might not be the most sensitive. "Well, you know," she half whispered to her daughter.

Selena could do nothing but sigh. "Yes, Mother, I know. But I fail to see any reason to rush things. I'm sure all will be well. After all, as Jane said, Edward is quite healthy—"

"Hmm, so was Mr. MacLaren, as far as we knew. And yet, his heart was weaker than anyone knew. Ill fortune and accidents happen." She frowned again, a line furrowing deep in her forehead as the accidents that befell her other husbands obviously ran through her mind. "In fact, we must take care that the ceremony and wedding breakfast are held in safe locations. No standing bodies of water. Perhaps we should water down the wine, just to be safe. Though not so much it is noticeable, of course, that would never do. And all horses and carriages will be kept well away. Guests can walk. Indeed, perhaps it is better if we leave the proceedings as a small family affair. Yes, I think that is best."

She stood and headed toward the door, muttering tasks to accomplish under her breath as she went.

"The banns must be read in multiple parishes, unfortunately, which might delay things slightly. Perhaps not. Surely Lord Lockhaven would be willing to obtain a special license?"

"Mother," Selena said, stopping her just before she exited the room. "We do not need a special license. I have lived in the same parish as Edward long enough that banns should only need to be read there."

Her mother frowned. "Have you? It is so hard to keep up sometimes."

Selena ignored that comment. If ever there was an embodiment of *out of sight, out of mind*, it would be her mother.

"Besides which," she continued, "well, Edward and I haven't discussed yet *when* the wedding should take place…"

They had only agreed just that morning that it *would* take place, after all.

"Well, perhaps an ordinary license then," her mother suggested. "That would at least allow us to dispense with the banns altogether."

Selena frowned again. "Why would we need to do that?"

Her mother huffed as if Selena were being purposely obtuse. "It just seems prudent to avoid the opportunity for anyone to state an objection."

Just when she thought her mother couldn't surprise her anymore, she'd pop up with another astonishing comment that would leave Selena blinking in shock. "But Mother—"

"Though we'll still need to place an announcement in the papers, of course. There's hardly any point in marrying if it isn't in the papers. And to such a prestigious groom." Her mother's eyes turned a bit glassy as she focused on her inner lists again, and she turned to wander out, her mind on the wedding, the bride forgotten. "National and international papers, of course. Hopefully no one who was present at the others will see…We'll need a new dress, the other is growing quite threadbare, and surely, it's bad luck to…"

Her mother's voice trailed off as she disappeared down the hall, and Selena turned to her father, though she already knew it was hopeless. Her mother had been like this with all her weddings. A more formidable general had never been seen when there were nuptials to organize. But this one was her last chance to marry her daughter off, and she knew it. And with a groom of such stature? She wouldn't squander such a miracle. Selena doubted her mother would rest until she and Edward were before a clergyman plighting their troths.

Her father stood and came toward her with a knowing smile. "She'll wear herself out eventually," he assured her. Then he gave her cheek an unexpectedly sweet pat on the cheek. "Don't worry yourself, poppet. I'm sure this one will work out."

Selena forced a smile until he was out of the room, and then let her shoulders slump.

Jane was right there to wrap an arm around her waist with a reassuring squeeze. "They mean well."

A laugh bubbled out of her before she could stop it. "I think that might make it worse."

"They *are* happy for you," Jane assured her.

"I know. Though, I do wish they could be happy for the future without bringing up the past. It feels like courting bad luck."

"Ah now, none of that," Jane said with another squeeze. "Your luck has changed, surely."

Selena smiled though her stomach dipped with another wave of foreboding. If it was one thing she had learned about life, there was no surety about anything. Nevertheless…

One could but hope.

CHAPTER SIXTEEN

EDWARD'S PARENTS SAT blinking at him. Rather like large, startled owls. His brothers, Hugo and Arthur, were equally surprised but seemed a great deal more celebratory.

"Excellent news yet again, brother," Hugo said, jumping up to clap him on the shoulder. "I assume your lady has accepted this time. Unless you have found someone else. Either way, couldn't have happened to a better man. I wish much happiness for you and the lucky lady."

"You haven't even met her yet," Edward said, slightly taken aback at his brother's sheer enthusiasm.

Hugo shrugged. "Doesn't matter. Whoever she is has accepted your proposal, thereby making me the happiest man in England."

Edward's brow furrowed, his confusion growing by the second. "Making *you* the happiest?"

"Absolutely." Hugo stretched and rolled his shoulders, before planting his hands on his hips and sucking in a deep breath. He let it out with a satisfied sigh. "I must say, it feels amazing to have the weight of the family's legacy off our shoulders, doesn't it, Arthur?"

Ah. *There* it was.

"Oh, indeed." Arthur flashed a brilliant grin at him. "We were growing quite worried it would fall to us to continue the family line and whatnot. You have our heartiest congratulations."

"And gratitude," Hugo added with a smug grin that had Edward narrowing his eyes. If they had still been in their teen years, he would have wiped those smiles from his brothers' faces. In fact, he still might.

Hugo and Arthur were nothing if not resourceful when it came to saving their own skin, and were already heading for the door, calling more congratulations over their shoulders as they went. Edward shook his head and turned back to his stunned parents.

His father cleared his throat. "Is it too much to hope that you've chosen another woman than the one to whom you proposed previously?"

The first thread of nervousness wound its way through Edward. He had no doubt that Selena was the woman for him. Well, no overwhelming doubts. Surely it was normal to have *some* doubts. It was a very large step in a man's life after all. And there were questions he still had no answers to. Yet, he couldn't imagine anything that would make a difference in how he felt about her.

"Edward?" his mother prompted, making him realize how long he'd been lost in his own spinning thoughts.

He straightened his shoulders. "Yes, it is Mrs. Selena MacLaren."

For the second time that morning, Edward was treated to the sight of his parents staring at him with wide-eyed astonishment.

She finally blinked. "Oh Edward. You didn't."

"Mother, we have had this conversation."

"Yes, we did, but you apparently didn't listen. The fact that there are rumors at all is a problem, Edward, whether you wish to acknowledge it or not. Your future wife must be above reproach, a woman of comportment, intelligence, good moral character, and the finest pedigree."

"For heaven's sake, Mother, she's a woman, not a horse."

"For all intents and purposes, my dear son, the requirements are not so different. Speaking of which, while she is certainly beautiful enough, elegant, I suppose, and of good comportment and disposition as far as I've seen, I am still concerned about her age. She is rather older than I had envisioned for you."

Edward gaped at her. "You speak of her as if she were a silver-haired crone."

"Oof," his mother scoffed, waving him off. "I am doing no such thing. But you cannot deny she is far closer to a matron of thirty than a girl of twenty."

"And I am thirty as well, which happily makes us of an age."

"All well and good," his mother retorted. "However, it does makes birthing an heir that much more difficult. And gives you far less time to have several."

"We aren't even married yet," Edward said, his head spinning.

"A good thing too!" His mother rounded on him. "If you were, you'd likely already be dead."

He didn't bother choking back his groan. "Mother—"

She held up a hand to stop his protest. "There is little reason to continue an argument in which neither of us will yield."

"I agree."

"I realize you wish to marry this woman—"

"I *will* marry her."

"I am not completely objecting. Frankly, I'm afraid if we don't permit this, you'll never propose again. It's nothing short of a miracle you've done it once. Or twice, I suppose."

He opened his mouth to fire back a marginally disrespectful retort, but his mother, knowing him as she did, pressed on before he had a chance. "*However*, I thought we had agreed you would wait until my investigator returned with his report."

"I agreed to no such thing. I simply agreed not to object to you sending out an investigator. Which you would have done in any case making my objection pointless."

"It is foolhardy in the extreme to marry a woman about whom you know nothing," his mother said.

His father nodded. "Listen to your mother, son. She's always had a good head on her shoulders."

Edward took a deep breath. Losing his temper wouldn't help convince them that he had made a rational choice. To be honest, he wasn't all that certain he *had* made a rational choice. Only that he'd made the only choice he could. Losing her was not an option. Even if it was the safer path.

"What exactly are you proposing, Mother? That I rescind my offer?"

"Of course not. Not just yet, in any case."

He glared at her, and she waved him off again. "Oh, contain yourself. If all is well and she is who she says she is, then your father and I shall offer no more objections to this union."

Edward glanced at his father, somewhat surprised he had let his mother take the lead in this conversation. Then again, when it came to his offspring, the duke did prefer to let his duchess handle matters. The only reason he was likely still in the room was because this particular matter was so sensitive and had such far-reaching repercussions.

"She *is* who she says she is. She is not a murderess, simply a woman with the great misfortune to have lost more than one husband. And I have no intention of allowing her to lose another one. I will not waiver. I will be calling upon the lady and her family on the morrow to ask their permission for her hand."

"Edward, I really think it would be best to wait until—"

"No, Mother. You won't find anything." He hoped. "And I wouldn't care if you did." He was pleased to find he actually meant that. Mostly. It wouldn't change how he felt about her, of that he was certain. There was no eradicating this woman from his heart even if she were to rip it from his chest. In fact…

"If you will excuse me, I believe I shall call upon the Haddons and ask to speak to Sir Rawley. Today."

His mother opened her mouth, likely to object or urge caution or patience. But he had none left and no desire to hear more from either of them.

"If something of, shall we say, an unsavory nature were to be discovered," his father said, "and your engagement is already public knowledge, what little reputation Mrs. MacLaren has left will be destroyed. I will not allow a son of mine to marry a criminal."

"Father, if your investigation discovers my betrothed is, in fact, a murderess, we will both have far larger problems on our hands. As for her reputation, I'm fairly certain a broken engagement will come second to murder in the justifications for its demise. But as I said, you won't find anything. So do what you must. As will I."

He gave them a sharp nod of his head and, though his father continued to glower, he thankfully said nothing as Edward made his escape.

He didn't allow himself to think as he climbed into his carriage and sent it post haste to the Haddons' London home. Before his parents' fears had time to take root.

He had enough of his own.

CHAPTER SEVENTEEN

SELENA JUMPED WHEN the door to the library burst open and Jane bustled in.

"Lord Lockhaven is here," she said.

Selena dropped the book she was holding and lurched from her chair. "He what? Why?"

"I am not sure. The footman said that he asked for your father, who was already in the salon, so he led him there and they are now in there together, discussing...something."

"Asking for my hand?" Selena asked, nearly breathless at the speed with which everything was happening.

Jane shrugged but smiled excitedly. "What else could it be?"

What else indeed. Selena had known, of course, that Edward would need to seek her father's permission at some point. Although, as a widow several times over, that mightn't have been strictly necessary. Though of course her father would appreciate it and oh sweet heaven her mind was rambling, and her heart was pounding and—This felt *real* all of the sudden. Real. And unstoppable. How could a person be so happy and so terrified all at once? Though most brides were probably more concerned with the ceremony going off without a hitch, not the groom surviving through it.

"I should be in there," she said, flying for the door, Jane right on her heels.

She did not wait at the salon door to be announced or invited, but burst in, ignoring her mother's startled gasp as she marched straight to where her father and Edward sat in plush chairs across from each other. They rose with smiles, her father's magnanimous and indulgent, as befitted a man who just made a match for his daughter with a future duke. And Edward's? Full of mischief, and with a determination in his eyes she had grown all too familiar with.

"My lord. To what do we owe the pleasure?" she asked, though she was well aware of the answer.

"Oh, my dear, Lord Lockhaven has been so lovely," her mother interjected. "He naturally asked your father for his permission to wed you—which was happily given, of course—"

No surprise there.

"But he also agreed to get a license—just a common license, my dear, as we discussed—so that you can wed immediately without waiting for the banns. Isn't that wonderful? We'll still have the wedding in a chapel, of course. Perhaps St. George's. A bit expected, I suppose, but then it is popular for a reason, and—"

"Mother, I—"

"Do you object to St. George's, my dear?"

Selena glanced over at Edward. He was still speaking quietly with her father, his hands clasped behind his back as he leaned toward the older man. But his gaze met hers and held, sending her heart racing.

"Well, no," she managed to say, "not particularly. It's only that I thought we had agreed a license wouldn't be necessary. Waiting for the banns—"

"We *had* discussed it, however," her mother said, taking her hand in her excitement. Edward smiled and turned back to her father. "It seems your intended is as eager for this marriage as we. He broached no objection when the question was raised. In fact, we've decided upon a date—the twenty-fourth of this month!"

Selena's stomach dropped to her toes, and she raised startled eyes to Edward again. He couldn't hear what they had said, but he raised a brow at her likely alarmed expression and hastened to her side, despite her father being in mid-sentence.

"What is it?" he asked, his brow furrowed.

"The twenty-fourth?"

The concern cleared from his face, and he beamed at her. "Yes."

She raised her own brows. "That is in eight days."

"Yes, isn't that wonderful?" her mother said with a delighted clap of her hands.

Selena struggled to find the right words that would express her concern without sounding as if she didn't want to marry at all. Though she still wasn't entirely sure she did. "Yes, but isn't that a bit…hasty?"

"Oh," her mother said with a dismissive wave. "Perhaps. I prefer to view it as romantic. When two young people are in love and wishing to wed, why wait? Life can be so unpredictable, after all."

A faint blush stained her cheeks as Selena gaped at her. Her mother genteelly cleared her throat. "Rawley, why don't we give the happy couple a few moments?"

"Oh, well, yes, I suppose a few moments wouldn't hurt, now that everything is all official," her father said gruffly.

Selena blinked in surprise. But then, she was hardly the typical virginal bride with a pristine reputation to protect. And with the wedding apparently only a week away, there was little chance of what reputation she had being ruined whilst standing in her own salon. She looked at Edward only to find him staring at her. His eyes never wavered as her parents left, the intensity in his gaze burning away every other thought in her head except the overwhelming desire to be in his arms again.

They were already moving before the door had fully closed behind her parents. His hands came up to cup her face as their lips met, and she could do naught but hold tight to him and give in to the need surging through her.

There was so much they needed to discuss, so much to say,

so much to tell him. Things had already progressed far too much without him knowing everything about her. Her past. Her curse. But there never seemed to be time, or privacy, to get it all out. The few private moments they'd stolen together tended to be spent doing everything but talking.

Though she could spend an eternity never talking if it meant his lips never stopped moving over hers, his arms crushing her to his chest as if he couldn't get her close enough. When he kissed her like this, she was consumed by him. Utterly. Happily. Every touch laid claim to her so thoroughly she didn't know where she ended, and he began. She could get lost in him.

But she mustn't. They must speak. Now, before it was too late.

"Edward." She pulled back enough to gasp out his name. "Are you sure?"

He chuckled and kissed her again. "Have I not proven so?"

She ducked her head, unable to hold back her smile. "Yes, but so soon? I hadn't expected…"

"Yes. I admit I had assumed our engagement would last a little longer than a week. But I have no objection." He took her hand and led her to a sofa, drawing her down beside him. "It appeases your parents. And if we have made up our minds, there is no real reason to delay."

"I suppose," she said, though her lips had gone suddenly numb. Because, obviously unbeknownst to Edward, there were many reasons to delay. Rushing made it feel as if her parents were trying to get the deed done before Edward changed his mind. Or was dead and therefore unable to follow through. Which…was exactly what they were doing. The fact that Edward did not mind worked in their favor, but it didn't sit well with her. "It is only there are things we still must discuss."

"Yes," he said, clearing his throat. "I confess, there was more than one reason for my unannounced arrival today."

Selena had been referring to everything she needed to tell him about her past, her other husbands. But it looked as though he had secrets of his own to reveal. The thought both brought a sense of relief and trepidation. What could be so terrible that it made a man like Edward squirm?

He steeled his shoulders. "I must tell you that my parents have hired an investigator."

Selena's mouth dropped open. Of all the things he might have said that one hadn't even occurred to her. Though perhaps it should have, all things considered.

"To inquire about me?" she asked.

"Unfortunately, and against my objections, yes."

She sucked in a sharp breath and sat back. While she might not be completely surprised at this turn of events, that didn't mean it didn't sting. The horror of the prospect clawed at her and sent her pulse racing.

Though she had no one to blame but herself. She should have told Edward everything before they had spent the night together. Then this whole situation could have been avoided. And she had intended to. But… The man was just so damn distracting!

"I know it must be a shock, and an unwelcome one at that," he said with a grimace. "If it comforts you any, it isn't a statement on how they feel about you. Not truly. On the contrary, they find you beautiful, elegant, and 'of good comportment and disposition' as I believe my mother put it." He smiled reassuringly. "They likely would have had any woman I wished to marry investigated, under similar circumstances."

Her eyes narrowed. The insult of it all rankled, no matter how understandable their actions. Because while Edward had a right to know some things about her past, his parents were reacting to the rumors that had followed her since she arrived. Rumors that were not only patently untrue but so absurd as to be unbelievable. A widow many times over she may be, but she was not a murderess.

That Edward might ever think so hurt. Greatly. That his parents seemed to be trying to use those rumors to justify denying permission for their marriage added an edge of anger to that hurt. Even more so because if word of this investigation spread, it would only lend credibility to the rumors and make her situation even more unbearable.

How dare they?

Yes, she should have shared a few details with him before they had gotten to this point. She could take responsibility for that. But she still couldn't help a retort.

"I very much doubt they would have taken these steps with anyone else. Formal investigation is hardly a normal precursor to Society marriages. So, to what circumstances are you referring?"

He had the grace to look embarrassed, at least. "It is only that you are not well known in our circles. You have only recently arrived. Your parents, from the little I know, are from Wales. Your father, Sir Rawley, is a baronet and somewhat of an amateur anthropologist who enjoys traveling in search of interesting artifacts for his rather impressive collection. Your mother, Lady Griffiths, is from a good family of minor nobility who mostly kept to their country estates and away from court. And you most recently hail from Scotland where you were married to a Mr. Charles MacLaren. A man with whom few were acquainted. His sister's championship of you has bought you a great deal of good will—"

She raised a brow at that. It was true they weren't throwing rotten fruit at her face when she appeared at society functions, but that is a far cry from actually being accepted.

"Aside from knowing you were married at least once more before that, that is all that I know about you. Which is a great deal more than anyone else knows."

Selena plucked at a nonexistent thread on her dress, her anger fading under the weight of her guilt. "Yes. Well. I prefer to keep private details about my life *private*."

Though she knew that to him at least she owed some explanations. But the thought of being investigated…

"I know," he said, taking her hands, "and if it were just me, I'd say to hell with the rest of the world and let you keep your secrets."

Selena blinked, shocked at his words. "Edward—"

"They do not matter to me. Truly," he said, giving her hands a squeeze. "Well, I admit I am curious," he said with a mischievous grin. "And were I in a different position, I could be patient and trust that if there were anything important I needed to know, you would tell me. Perhaps my family would trust that as well. However, I am my father's heir. My wife will be the next Duchess of Haltham. And with all the rumors—I do not believe a word of them," he hurried to assure her. "But my family wish to be certain."

Her stomach dropped, roiling against the truth spilling from his lips. His family didn't trust her. And she couldn't even blame them. She was a stranger with nothing but salacious rumors to her name. Truthfully, she was a bit surprised it had taken them this long to start investigating her. Unfortunately, she had no doubt they would not like what they found.

"Edward," she said, swallowing past the ache of emotion in her throat. "Perhaps we were too hasty, too foolish to think—"

"No," he said, reaching up to cup her cheek. "*That* I will not accept."

He pressed another kiss to her lips, her heart fracturing a bit more with every lingering brush of his mouth.

"No, wait. I cannot think when you touch me so. There are things I must tell you, that I have been trying to tell you. Things I would rather you hear from me," she insisted, standing up to put some distance between them.

"You can tell me anything, dearest," he said, though his eyes remained troubled, as though he feared what she might reveal.

As well he should.

"I told you that I have been widowed before. That Charles was not the first husband I lost."

His brow furrowed. "Yes. But that does not mean it will happen again. I know you fear that—"

"No, it's not that," she said, needing to get this out before she lost her courage. "Well, not only that. I do fear for you, but I also fear what you might think when you know the full truth."

He stood and wrapped his hands gently around her upper arms. "You needn't fear, love. I swear to you, nothing you can tell me will change anything between us."

She shook her head. "Do not make promises you mightn't keep," she murmured.

"I will stand by your side. Always. Nothing you can tell me will change that," he insisted again.

There was never going to be a better time for this.

"You know about Charles, and how he died after…well, after our wedding night. Or…during, rather," she closed her eyes, her lips pinching together for a moment.

"Yes, love," Edward said with a gentle smile. "And I think I have proven I am more than capable of performing that particular task unscathed. Though I would be happy to prove so again." His husky voice sent a delightful shiver up her spine, and she pressed her palms to his chest, melting into him when he drew her closer.

"Edward," she said faintly, dragging in a tremulous breath when he bent to trail his lips up the column of her neck.

"Wait," she said, pushing away just enough to break his kiss, though she stayed within the circle of his arms. "I must tell you the rest."

"My apologies, love. I seem to have a distinct lack of control when it comes to you."

She gave him a faint smile as it was an affliction she shared. But she must finish.

"Before Charles, I wed a man named Marius Albescu, in Bucharest. My father wanted to bring my mother there to partake in the healing baths and brought me with them."

Edward frowned a little but didn't seem overly upset. Yet.

"Our courtship was brief," she continued. "He was a composer. His music was so beautiful. I think perhaps it was that with which I fell in love."

"It was his song you played at the soiree?" Edward asked.

"Yes, it was."

His eyes widened slightly with appreciation. "Then he was indeed a talented composer."

Selena could do naught but nod. "We hadn't known each other long when we wed. A few weeks only. But...I was infatuated. He was so charming and talented. And about to depart on a tour of the courts of Europe."

"Ah. You wished to go with him."

She nodded again. "My parents had no objection, and so we were wed within the week."

Edward made a noncommittal rumbling noise, though his brow remained furrowed.

She let out a delicate snort. "I'm sure I can guess what you are thinking. I admit the circumstances, at least those surrounding the planning and execution of our wedding, are rather similar to my wedding to Marius."

Edward gave her arms a gentle squeeze, but he didn't respond to that. "What happened to Marius?" he asked instead.

Selena frowned, both at his question and at the answer she must give. "He died on our wedding night. They all did."

CHAPTER EIGHTEEN

EDWARD FROWNED. "WHAT—"

They both jumped when the door opened and Selena's mother bustled in, Mrs. Haddon right on her heels looking very apologetic.

"All right you two," Lady Griffiths said. "There will be plenty of time to hide away together once you are wed. For now, we have so much to do!"

The rest of the afternoon was a whirlwind of planning, paperwork, and preparations that had his head spinning. Lady Griffiths was more organized than a general with his troops. Edward had no trouble believing that the woman had hosted a wedding or two—or possibly three?—in the past.

What had Selena been about to tell him when they were interrupted? They hadn't had another opportunity to be alone since those brief moments when she had finally begun to open up. And while he was glad she had told him about Mr. Albescu, he could have sworn she was preparing to tell him about yet another husband. Had she truly buried three husbands already?

The thought gave him pause. He didn't like that it did, but…there you have it. He couldn't very well stop his thoughts from running off any more than he could stop Lady Griffiths from finally shooing him away so they could head to the modiste's for an emergency trousseau. His objections that all Selena's needs would be met—and could be dealt with after the wedding—fell on deaf ears.

He had not seen hide nor hair of his betrothed since. He had spent the last several days preparing for their impending nuptials himself, so he did not think she was avoiding him. But now that he had a common license in hand and all necessary paperwork had been drawn up and signed to his solicitor's satisfaction, his part was done. All that was left to do was to show up at the chapel at the appointed time and day. Which left far too many hours of the day to brood.

"You're getting broody," Anthony said.

Damn the man for always knowing exactly what Edward was thinking.

Edward squinted at him accusingly before downing what was left in his glass and pouring what was left in the bottle of brandy they had requested be left at their table into their glasses.

Their favorite club was usually bustling at this time in the evening, but the crowd was thankfully sparce tonight. Edward didn't think he could handle any more scrutiny than he was already receiving from his best friend.

"I am not broody," he grumbled into his glass.

"Yes, you are. That is your broody face. It usually prefaces you doing something unbelievably ill-advised. Like riding through Kensington Park without a stitch on—"

"It was the middle of the night. No one saw me. And I was hardly more than a boy."

"You were nearly twenty!"

"As I said." Edward took another drink.

"Very well. How about trying to steal the queen's zebra?"

Edward shrugged. "He looked lonely."

"And stealing that painting from the museum?"

"I didn't technically steal that. It belongs to my family. I just…took it back."

"Without permission or anyone's knowledge," Anthony pointed out.

"I put it back. Must you always spoil things?"

That damned eyebrow quirked up again. "That seems a question better asked of you, my lord."

"Oh?" Edward asked, cocking his own brow. Two could play at that game.

"Hmm. You are rather an expert when it comes to spoiling things. At least when speaking of sabotaging another potential match."

Edward scowled at him and took another welcome gulp of brandy, savoring the smooth warmth as it slid down his throat.

Anthony leaned over the table, letting his glass dangle from the rest of his fingers as he pointed to Edward. "Only this time it would be so much worse because you have already proposed to the poor woman. It may not have been announced, and there will be no banns thanks to the license that was apparently necessary, but the contracts are signed and both families are agreed. You're stuck this time, mate. There is no sabotaging this one."

"I am not stuck. Not," he hurried to add at Anthony's raised brows, "that I have any intention of sabotaging anything."

Anthony slowly nodded. "But…"

Edward's scowl deepened. Then he let out a sharp breath. "Very well, if you must know, yes, I am having a few second thoughts. Not enough to call off the engagement. I would never do that to her," he said, sitting back in his chair while he frowned down at the glass in his hand.

"But…" Anthony prompted again.

He really was quite the nuisance this evening.

"She finally divulged a small bit about her past. A very small bit."

Anthony's eyebrow quirked up again. "And it was enough to put that look on your face?"

Edward didn't answer for a moment but sat rubbing a finger along the rim of his glass while his mind whirled. Anthony, for once, waited patiently. Finally, Edward could stand the silence no longer.

"I have long since been informed that she had been widowed more than once. And it did not give me much pause. These things happen, and she can hardly bear the blame for it."

"Well, she could," Anthony said with a teasing smile. "She certainly wouldn't be the first woman to hasten a man to his grave. That *is* the rumor making the rounds, is it not?"

"Yes," Edward grumbled.

Anthony's eyes widened and he set down his glass. "Are you giving credence to those rumors now?"

Edward did not answer immediately, and Anthony pursed his lips. "I am torn. On the one hand, I would be a poor friend, indeed, if I were not at least somewhat concerned that you are betrothed to a woman who may or may not have a few homicidal proclivities. On the other hand, rumors aside, she seems a perfectly lovely woman who is not only willing to tolerate your presence but actually seems to enjoy your company. A rare find, to be sure. And you seem poised to sabotage yourself yet again."

Edward opened his mouth to speak but Anthony cut him off before he could. "Do not point to all the other women who have thrown themselves at you over the years because we both know they were throwing themselves at your title and bank account. Not *you*."

Well, *that* was painfully true. Edward knocked back the last bit of brandy in his glass.

"*This* woman actually seems to care for you," Anthony said, the amount of confusion in his voice more than a little insulting. "As a man in your station, surely even you are aware that finding a woman who cares more for you than what the match can bring her is a rarity. As your friend, I could want nothing more for you. Providing, of course, she is not actually a murderess making you here next target."

"Of course," Edward said, rolling his eyes.

"And here you sit, ready to throw it all away over a rumor."

"I am not throwing anything away. I have told you, I care deeply for Selena. I would never do something so callous."

"I'm not judging," Anthony said. "Quite the opposite. If I were in your position, I would have run long ago. But then I do tend to put too much stock into the latest gossip. However, you are not me. So then why are you sitting here with your brow furrowed drowning your angst in a bottle of brandy?"

Edward snorted. "Perhaps I am contemplating my fate should the rumors prove to be true."

Anthony shook his head with an indulgent smile. "I suppose I should be grateful she does not have a cat or doesn't seem overly fond of the color orange, or you would have disappeared from her sight long ago."

That put the scowl back on Edward's face and made Anthony chuckle in earnest.

"Come now, what has transpired since I last saw you to put you in such a mood?"

Edward tilted his glass against the table, watching the way the candlelight caught the last few drops of amber liquid inside. "We spoke this afternoon. She has been trying to tell me something important for weeks now. And it seems the rumors are at least partially true."

Anthony's eyes widened again. "Not the murdering bit—"

"No." Edward snorted faintly again. "At least…I hope not." He shook his head. "No, she admitted Mr. MacLaren was not her first husband. And that her previous husband, a Mr. Marius Albescu, also left her a widow." He looked up and held Anthony's gaze. "On their wedding night."

His friend sat back with a sharp exultation of air. "Well. I must admit, two husbands dead on their weddings nights is a pretty strong coincidence."

"Yes," Edward said. "As was the speed with which she wed them. Though, I might even be able to overlook all that. After all, assuming she was not the one hastening their ends, she could hardly be faulted for what occurred. In fact, she should be pitied."

"But?"

Anthony always knew when there was a but.

"But…I am fairly certain she was about to tell me there had been yet another husband."

For once, Anthony sat in stunned silence. Though unfortunately, not for long.

"Are you certain? A third dead husband?"

"No," Edward said, scrubbing his hand over his face. "Perhaps? I am not certain. She started to say something that she was obviously reluctant to share. But I did get that distinct impression. It could have been something else. Or perhaps she had been married a third time, but it had been annulled or…" He threw up his hands. "I do not know. That is the problem."

"Would it make a difference if that *had* been what she was about to say?"

Edward sighed again. "I do not know. That is the problem," he said again.

Anthony blew out a breath. "Is she to be pitied? Or is she to be feared?"

"At the risk of repeating myself for a third time," Edward said with a wry smile.

Anthony chuckled. "You do not know, that is the problem."

"Yes." Edward slumped down in the chair far enough that he could lay his head against the back and stare up at the ornate ceiling. He had been so happy only a few hours earlier. And now…

"Edward."

He moved his head so he could look at Anthony, though he didn't lift his head.

"The wedding is tomorrow."

He moved his head back. "I know."

"If you were to call it off now…"

Edward sighed and sat up, his hand gripping around the glass so tightly he was surprised it didn't break. "I know."

He couldn't do that to her. The gossip mill was already churning about her, it was true. But if he were to abandon her days before their wedding, her reputation would never recover.

"If *she* were to call it off…" Anthony started.

"No, Goodwin. I cannot spend weeks trying to convince her to marry me only to insist she cry off days before. And I do not wish to."

"If your life is in danger…"

"My life is not in danger."

"Are you certain?" Anthony insisted. "Isn't it better to err on the side of caution? People would talk, yes. But it would be assumed the fault lay with you, not with her. A small but important distinction."

Edward scrubbed his hands over his face. "I love her, Anthony. That is all I know."

Anthony smiled. "And that is all that matters then, is it not? However, perhaps it would be wise to speak with the lady again. Orchestrate an opportunity if you must. But sit down and speak with her. At length. Until you have both said all that is needed to say."

Edward nodded his head slowly. He needed to find out what she had been about to say. And he needed to figure out if it mattered.

That he harbored even a shred of doubt that these rumors might be true made his stomach feel as though it were filled with lead. If they were, if her husbands had met their end at her hands? He sighed. The more rational part of him knew that the fact he was even thinking about such a thing meant he thought there could be truth to the rumors. And what did that say about him, or her, that something so dire was beginning to seem more possible by the day?

But a large part of him, the biggest part, did not care. Wanted to wed her and let her do her worst. He wanted to be her husband. Whether that lasted fifty years or fifty seconds. If he found death in her arms…well. At least he would die a happy man. There were a good number of worse ways to die.

He stood with a frustrated growl.

"Enough of this. I will find out what is going on one way or the other."

Anthony grabbed his arm before he could march for the exit. "Where do you go?"

Edward glanced out the window at the darkened streets. Night had fallen while he'd been wallowing in his drink.

"I am going to speak to my lady and discover once and for all the truth."

He retrieved his hat, gloves, and coat and pulled them on before stepping out into the street, Anthony right on his heels.

"And if the rumors are true?"

Edward glanced at him over his shoulder. "Then I guess we shall find out who I love more. Her, or myself."

Though he was fairly sure he already knew the answer to that question.

CHAPTER NINETEEN

SELENA SAT UP, her ears straining to catch the sound that had woken her. Well, disturbed her. Sleep had been evasive the last few days. Her mother had kept her so busy running about town preparing for the wedding that by all rights, Selena should be dropping into bed every evening and drifting off into an instant, dreamless sleep.

That was far from the case, however. Rather, most nights she spent tossing and turning, her mind churning with a bombardment of thoughts that would not stop long enough to let her rest. And when she did sleep, her dreams were filled with Edward. It didn't seem to matter whether the dream was horrible or wonderful (or very, *very* wonderful). She had no peace either way. If she could just speak with him. Alone. Clear her conscience. Ensure he was entering into this marriage with full knowledge of all the sordid details of her past, the danger he might be putting himself into, the men she'd married before him… Perhaps then her mind could rest.

She had little hope of it helping her body though. No amount of sleep would cure her restlessness. Only Edward could do that. Surely there would come a day when she stopped craving his touch. But it likely wouldn't be any time soon.

Truly, it was becoming increasingly embarrassing. Just the other day, they had been sitting in church. He had only spoken a quick hello to her before the service, so he had certainly not said or done anything aside from breathing to inspire the deluge of sinful thoughts that plagued her throughout the sermon. There he was, singing hymns and clasping his hands in prayer. And all she could think of was the wonderfully wicked things he had done to her with those lips and hands. For the rest of the sermon, every time the vicar or congregation said Hallelujah, she thought about how many times she had shouted God's name under Edward's ministrations.

She was going to hell for sure. But sweet heaven, it was worth it.

At least…she hoped so.

They had spoken for a few minutes after the service, but then they had each been whisked away by their families. She must find a way to have more than three minutes alone with him before the wedding.

There it was again!

A sort of muffled…well, if she didn't know any better, she would think someone was outside her window cursing. But that was impossible. Her window was far too high from the ground. Though, there was a balcony. And multiple trees. And a vine-clogged lattice. Now that she thought on it, a more inviting window had never been created. And, as scatterbrained as she had been, she couldn't recall if she had latched the window.

Selena had just swung her legs out of bed to investigate when her balcony doors blew open…and Edward stumbled in still cursing under his breath while he brushed stray twigs and dirt from his shirt and breeches.

"Edward?" she exclaimed, taking a few steps toward him.

His eyes shot to hers, halting her in her tracks. And then they widened and took her in with a gaze that grew more heated with every inch he spied.

Her hand fluttered to her chest in a futile attempt to cover herself. She had been sleeping—trying to sleep—in nothing but a thin chemise. Which obviously left very little to Edward's imagination. Her robe lay across a chair near the fireplace, too far away to help her now.

Not that she would have put it on anyway. Not with the way his eyes devoured her.

"I can't believe you are here," she said. "I was just thinking of you."

"Were you?" His gravelly voice sent a delicious shiver up her spine, his gaze sharpening at the fine tremor that ran through her.

"Yes. We have hardly seen or spoken to each other since we became engaged."

"Well, it *has* only been a week," he said, his lips pulling into a half grin that had her heart pounding.

"Yes," she said with a shaky laugh.

"Have you missed me, Selena?" he asked, his eyes raking over her again.

"Yes." The word was barely more than a whisper, but he heard it.

That crooked smile turned decidedly more heated. "I've missed you," he said, walking toward her as if he thought she might spook, like a skittish horse. But the closer he prowled, the more rooted to her spot she became.

"You did?" She paused, trying desperately to regain some composure. Impossible to do with Edward stalking toward her like she was his prey.

His very willing prey.

She tried again. "I am glad you have come. We must speak."

"Yes," he said, stopping before her, so closely she could feel the heat radiating from him. So close their breath mingled when she raised her head.

Selena sucked in a lungful of air, trying desperately to control the fire raging through her. Her hardened nipples brushed against his chest with her inhalation and her breath strangled in her throat. His hands came up to grip her biceps, and she trembled in his grasp.

There was no stopping this. And if she was honest with herself, she had no desire to stop it. All her desire was for him. *Now*.

"Later." She grabbed his lapels and hauled him against her, raising on her toes so her lips could claim his.

They crashed together, and he wrapped his arms about her, lifting her against him as he carried her back to the bed.

He lowered them both to the soft mattress, his lips devouring hers as they tangled themselves together.

She couldn't think when he kissed her so. Couldn't do anything except cling to him for dear life. Her body cried out for him. As did her heart. She would never get enough of him. If they lived for a dozen lifetimes…

"No wait," she said, pulling her lips from his with a gasp. She couldn't let this happen again. Not yet. Not until they had spoken. Not until he knew everything. "Wait, please. We must speak."

He chuckled and rested his forehead against hers as they both tried to catch their breath.

"What is it, love?" he asked.

"My apologies," she murmured, untangling her legs from his, if only to keep herself from ignoring her own words and immediately resuming their activities. "I hadn't meant for—"

"Don't you dare apologize," he said with a laugh. "I promise you, there is no need."

"Is this why you came?" she asked, looking up at him.

"No. Well," he said with another wry grin, his fingers drawing soft patterns along her shoulder. "It wasn't my first intention. Though I confess, the moment I came through that window and saw you standing there, so beautiful it took my breath away, my intentions took a decided turn. But no. I came so that we could finally have a private moment to speak. We've barely seen each other since our betrothal. And as you've said, there are things to say."

"Yes." She took a deep breath and sat up, willing the nerves in her gut to settle. Moving to the edge of the bed to get some distance from him did not help much. He moved so that he could lean back against the headboard, letting one arm dangle from his propped up knee. Which somehow made him look even more irresistible.

She briefly closed her eyes against the sight in a futile effort to keep her desire in check. It did not help. Later. She could give in later. If there was a later once he'd heard what she had to say.

No matter what though, even if he hated her for it, she couldn't regret the time they'd had together.

Just speak, she chastised herself.

"I am sorry that I reacted so poorly to your news of the investigation."

He was already shaking his head. "Again. No apologies are necessary. Anyone would have felt the same. In fact, your reaction was a fair sight better than most would have been, I dare say."

"Be that as it may, your family has a right to want the truth. Their suspicions are not entirely wrong."

That put a frown on Edward's face. One that sent her stomach reeling.

"You'll have to speak more plainly." he said. "I do not want to misunderstand you. Are you saying…?"

"The worst of the rumors are not true," she hurried to assure him. "I am not a murderess." She gave the word the disdain it deserved.

"Of course not," Edward exclaimed. The fierceness of his immediate defense soothed her soul. Though she did not entirely deserve it.

"But there is a reason why I vowed to never marry again. I am cursed, Edward. No—" She held up a hand to keep him from speaking when he looked like he was about to defend her yet again. Or refute her.

Her words came faster, more clipped, as she rushed to get them out before her nerves failed her. "Please let me speak before you question further. I cannot carry this burden any longer."

"Very well," he said. "I shall endeavor to hold my tongue."

He gave her that half grin that she so loved, surely in an effort to put her more at ease.

Noble of him but, she feared, futile.

"The worst of the rumors may not be true. But there is *some* truth in what has been said."

"What?" he asked, stunned.

"I *have* buried more than one husband."

The relief on his face twisted the knife in her heart. "Oh. Yes, of course. Mr. MacLaren. And you told me of Mr. Albescu."

He said the name slowly, obviously noticing the dread she had hoped to keep from her face.

"Are there…more?"

She could almost see his body tensing as if he were waiting for a blow.

So she did not make him wait for its delivery. "Yes, I told you about Charles. And Marius. But there was also Francesco," she said, her voice cracking. "And Louis."

Edward sat, his eyes widening more and more with each name. "Four?" he asked faintly.

She let out a sobbing sigh and threw her hands in the air, moving from the bed to pace the floor in her agitation. "Yes four. And would have been five if Otto hadn't run off and abandoned me."

"You mean all four are…deceased?" Edward's eyebrows flew up. "Wait, there was a fifth—"

But now that Selena had released all the secrets she'd kept pent up for all these months, she couldn't staunch the flow.

"Yes. All of them. Do you understand now? Why I say I am cursed? Their deaths were too strange to be anything else. I know of no woman who has buried so many husbands. Men, certainly. It may not be common, but it is certainly far from strange for a man to lose so many wives. But, do you know of any other women as unlucky as I?"

"Well…no," he said, obviously reluctant to confirm her argument. "But I hardly think that means you are cursed, love.

Unlucky, perhaps. I will give you that."

He could hardly do otherwise, but that was beside the point.

"But well, these things do happen," he added.

She snorted, not caring how unladylike the sound. "Do they? So many? All happening to one woman? Or…well, of course nothing happened to me except for the loss of them…" Her voice cracked again.

Edward leaned forward, his concern clearly etched on his face. "I maintain, while tragic, these things do happen. Sickness spreads. Accidents befall even the most careful of men. If any of them were of a certain age—"

She shook her head. "Young and healthy all. Do you understand now?" She dropped back to the bed, her face in her hands.

"Not quite," he admitted, not surprisingly. "How *did* they die?"

He asked as if he were afraid of the answer. And so he should be. Though not perhaps for the reason he thought.

She let out a long breath and told him everything. "Louis Dampierre was my first husband. We meet at a ball in Paris. My father always took my mother and me on his travels. Well, not always. But often. Unconventional perhaps, but he loved us and wanted us by his side. Or perhaps he just did not trust my mother on her own," she added, nervous laughter erupting at her own jest. Her parents loved each other dearly, but her mother did love to shop and had a tendency to do so prolifically when her father wasn't around to rein in her more expensive excursions.

"We married six weeks later in a beautiful church in the French countryside. But when we left the church, a flock of geese who had been startled by the raucous laughter of Louis's uncle flew across our path. Poor Louis got caught up in the flock as they tried to flee and stumbled into the path of a carriage whose horses had been likewise startled."

She closed her eyes. Poor, sweet, gentle Louis. He would have been mortified at such a ridiculous death. Yet, she pressed on. If she stopped now, she'd never get it all out.

"I met Francesco in Venice."

Edward held up a hand. "My apologies, but would this be Francesco Fiorentino? The Francesco Fiorentino from the painting at the museum?"

Her eyes narrowed. "The one you tried to touch?"

He scoffed with an impatient wave. "Not the point."

"It should b—Never mind. Yes. That Francesco." She sighed, her mind refocusing on her dearly departeds before she lost her nerve again. "His paintings were so lovely. Breathtaking. From the first moment I saw them, I was captivated. First by his work. Then by him. He was such a dreamer. So sweet, exuberant, romantic. Too romantic perhaps. Too exuberant, certainly. After our wedding breakfast, we traveled to his lodgings by gondola. He stood up to sing to me as we went along.

"But he did have a tendency toward the theatric. Especially when singing. He gesticulated just a bit too wildly during a particularly poignant part of the aria and…well, the reigning theory is that a particularly tenacious pigeon thought Francesco was offering food in his upraised hands and it grew impatient waiting for its treat. Whatever the cause, it flew at him, and he lost his balance."

"He drowned?"

Selena shook her head. "He gulped too much water and whether it was from the cold or something in the water, he caught a fever and was dead by nightfall."

Edward's eyes widened, and Selena didn't need to ask why. She knew exactly how preposterous everything sounded. Their deaths were perhaps even more tragic for the sheer ridiculousness of them. If it weren't for those damned geese…and pigeons…and just-deep-enough, possibly poisonous water. And Marius's love of a good sparring match.

She took a deep breath and plowed on. "Then Marius. Poor, dear Marius. We were in Bucharest while my father met with a few of his contacts. There was a concert at the palace. Marius was the court composer. He played the most beautiful music. So beautiful I think I was half in love before the night had ended."

"Another whirlwind romance," Edward said. Not unkindly. But perhaps with a slightly wary tone that resettled her dread about her like an old, familiar friend she could never escape. After all, their own romance was less than two months old. And they were to be wed in the morning. If he would still have her, that was.

But how else could she respond but to say, "Yes." She pursed her lips briefly, willing herself to go on. "We were married just a few weeks later. After what happened with my first two marriages, I would have wished to wait. But my father was scheduled to return to court shortly afterward. We could not wait if we were to wed before my parents left.

"Our wedding celebration lasted the entire day and well into the evening. There was so much music, and laughter. And wine. Marius imbibed perhaps a little too much. He was so full of life. At odds, it sometimes seems now, with his seriousness when it came to his music. Perhaps he saved all his solemnity for his music and saved none for the rest of his life."

She smiled a bit wistfully, lost in her memories.

"What happened?" Edward asked quietly.

She pursed her lips again. This one she really did not want to share. Finally, she let out an exasperated breath. There was nothing she could do to change the situation now. She might as well tell him all of it.

"As I said, he'd had quite a bit to drink, as had his friends. So when one of them placed a wager that Marius could not beat a horse in a wrestling match…"

"Oh bollocks. He didn't."

She blinked at his curse. But really, at this point, she was rather more surprised he wasn't filling the rafters with his curses.

"He tried," she answered. "The horse won." She let out another long sigh. "The poor creature had so many limbs flailing about it was a wonder he only stuck Marius the once. But that was all it took."

"Indeed." He shook his head, utterly bemused. "Your husbands did seem to have an unfortunate time with horses."

"And birds," she said, crinkling her forehead.

"And birds," Edward said, his lips pulling ever-so-slightly into a faint smile.

"Edward," she said, not bothering to keep her voice down. "It is not funny."

"No, of course not. My apologies if I seemed to be amused. But you must admit—"

"Yes, I know how it all sounds. I would probably laugh as well if it were not my life we were discussing."

"I am sorry, Lena, truly."

His use of her nickname made her pause. He had never used it before. And the sound of it on his lips sent her heart racing.

"I promise you, I am not making light of your troubles. However," he said, making her eyes narrow. "I still maintain that *you*, perhaps, are making too much of them."

"Too much?" She stood again, the nervous energy coursing through her too much to keep bottled up. "My mother had to take me to the Highlands of Scotland to escape the rumors that were spreading all over the Continent about me. And instead of learning my lesson, I went and found yet another husband who again didn't survive a marriage to me."

Edward's mouth opened and closed a few times as he apparently struggled to find a retort to that.

"Did his death involve birds or horses?" he finally asked.

"Edward!"

"I'm sorry," he said with a laugh. "I know this is no laughing matter—"

"Your current behavior to the contrary," she said, crossing her arms. Though…she wasn't deaf or blind. She knew exactly how ridiculous this whole situation was. Or seemed from the outside in any case.

"My deepest apologies. Truly. It is only that Mr. MacLaren obviously died of very natural causes…" His gaze flashed to her. "Am I correct?"

"Yes. The physician who examined him said that he must have had a weak heart that had never made itself known until…"

Her cheeks flushed hotly as the doctor's exact words echoed in her head. If she had remembered them earlier, or been a little less distracted with what she had been saying and who she had been saying it to…

"Until?" he prompted.

She groaned under her breath. "Until he…overexerted himself," she muttered.

Edward's gaze intensified, knowing immediately to what she referred. Having so recently engaged in a little overexertion with her himself.

"Well then," he finally said, though his voice had grown decidedly more gruff. "There you have it. An unfortunate, but unquestionably natural death."

"Edward, there is nothing natural about a woman losing a fourth husband in as many years."

He frowned. "Perhaps. But—"

"No buts, Edward. I am cursed. Do you see now why I refused you. Why agreeing to your mad proposal has put you in danger?"

He stood, blocking her way to stop her pacing, and took her hands. "No, love, because despite all you have told me, I still do not believe in curses."

"How can you not? After all the accidents that have happened when you are near me?"

He frowned. "Such as?"

She gaped at him. "The carriage that almost ran you over in the park. The fountain. The horse that kicked you in the skull." Her eyes narrowed. "Perhaps he kicked you too hard if you cannot remember such a recent injury."

"Selena," he said, pulling her into his arms again. "Those are silly little accidents that could happen to anyone."

"Very similar silly little accidents killed three of my husbands."

"Coincidence," he insisted.

"*Fate.* A curse. My curse."

"Then one that has been broken. I am still standing here."

"For now," she said, cupping his face in her hand. "But we aren't wed yet."

"So this particular curse requires a clergyman's blessing to trigger it?" he asked with an amused smirk.

"Oh," she growled, shaking him off. "You aren't taking this seriously."

"Of course not!" He chuckled, then tried to control himself, rubbing a finger across his lips in a futile attempt to erase his smile. He cleared his throat. "You've had a spot of bad luck, I'll give you that. But—"

"A spot of bad luck?" she nearly shouted. "With four dead husbands and a fiancé who abandoned me the day of our wedding which I could not even blame him for becau—" She hiccupped and slapped a hand over her mouth. Whether she had breathed in too much air while trying to talk or hadn't breathed enough, the rather embarrassing squeak was enough to make her pause.

"What? Who was the fifth?" Edward asked, his brow creased. "Where? When?"

Selena covered her face with her hands and spoke through them, not caring if the sound was muffled.

"In Geneva. My father took me there after Charles died to rest and restore my health. I needed someplace tranquil, he said, after all that had happened. But again. I met a man, handsome enough, and kind enough. A bit boring perhaps, but who seemed strong and capable and frankly, was one who, while I found him agreeable enough, I did not love. I thought perhaps that would make the difference. Or at least wouldn't hurt so badly if I lost him as well, God forgive me. My poor parents had married me off four times and were still stuck with their daughter. And I could not bear losing someone else I cared for.

"He needed my money. I needed to remove myself from the

marriage mart, and despite all I had been through, a convent held little appeal. I wanted to be married. Have a family of my own. Children. Security. So I agreed. I had hoped that our arrangement was more of a business transaction than a love match would save him. But the day before the wedding, he came to me and said he couldn't go through with it because h—"

"Oh good heavens!" Jane exclaimed from the doorway, making Selena jump with a startled yelp while Edward yanked her behind him, ready to defend her from the invader.

He relaxed slightly when he saw Jane.

"What are you doing in here?" Jane hissed to him. "It is bad luck for the groom to see the bride before the wedding!"

Selena covered her mouth with her hand to keep in her groan. The last thing she needed was more bad luck at one of her weddings.

Edward seemed to know exactly what she was thinking because he was already shaking his head, his eyes boring into hers. "I don't believe in bad luck."

"Well you should have a healthy respect for irate fathers," Jane snapped. "It's one thing for a discreet liaison when there is no one about…perhaps…but shouting at each other loud enough to wake the dead the night before your wedding when the bride's own parents are in the house is sheer folly. Shoo!"

She marched toward Edward, waving her hands at him and herding him toward the window like she was ushering a rodent from the pantry.

"Wait," he said, tripping over his feet as he tried to keep from being pushed out the window without physically moving Jane aside. "We must finish discussing—"

"You can finish tomorrow," Jane said. "After you are safely wed. You have your whole lives to discuss whatever you wish. Now out the way I assume you came in!" she said, all but shoving him onto the balcony.

"But, what did Otto know that made hi—"

Edward's words were cut off when Jane closed the balcony

doors in his face.

"What were the two of you thinking?" she said, rounding on Selena and shaking her head like Selena was a mere maid caught flirting with the stable lad.

"I had to tell him everything before the wedding, Jane. It felt too much like I was keeping secrets from him otherwise."

A muffled thump and curse sounded from outside the window and both women turned. Jane opened the window and glanced out, then closed it again with a roll of her eyes. "He's fine."

Selena frowned slightly, and Jane crossed her arms. "So, did your clandestine meeting help? Hmm?"

Selena sank onto the edge of the bed. "I…am not sure."

Jane just cocked a brow, waiting for Selena to elaborate. Except, she wasn't sure she could.

"I told him everything. About all of them. How we met. How they…died."

Jane sat beside her. "You cannot continue to let a few bad experiences rule your life."

Selena pursed her lips. "They are a little more than mere bad experiences."

"Yes," Jane said, patting her hand. "But my reasoning stands. What happened is your past. He," she jerked her thumb at the window, "is your future."

Selena let out a sigh that felt as though it were being dragged from the depths of her soul. "I hope. You chased him away before I could discover if his feelings for me had changed," she said with a wry smile. "Perhaps he hates me now. Or at the very least would prefer not to marry a woman who has been widowed so frequently. He did seem wary, at the very least. And very concerned over Otto." Her brow creased in a frown. "What if he does follows Otto's lead? What if he does not come tomorrow?"

"Oh, dearest." Jane pulled her into a hug. "He will be there."

"But how can you be sure? I certainly divulged enough to shake even the strongest constitution. And even if he does come…what if what I told him has changed his feelings for me. Being the sixth man in a woman's life could prove daunting to any man. He may be too honorable to refuse me, but it will make for a cold and lonely marriage if he marries me out of obligation alone."

"That will not happen," Jane said firmly. "That man just climbed through a window for you in the middle of the night. Most men, once the deal is sealed, cease applying any effort into their relationships at all. Your marquess is a rare one. And he loves you. Even a fool could see that. He will be there."

Selena nodded and laid her head on her friend's shoulder.

He will be there, she repeated to herself.

Perhaps if she repeated it often enough, she would believe it.

CHAPTER TWENTY

ANTHONY'S RAISED BROWS when Edward stumbled into his study told him all he needed to know about his appearance. He plucked another twig from his hair with a grimace.

"Did she throw you out the window?" Anthony asked, watching with amusement as Edward dropped into the seat opposite him.

"Not Selena. Mrs. Haddon. And very nearly, yes."

Anthony's brows rose even higher if that were possible. "You were discovered by Mrs. Haddon?"

Edward leaned forward and took the glass Anthony had set down, downing the liquid in one gulp. "Yes." The word was more a sound as he grunted at the burn of the liquor than an actual word, but Anthony understood well enough.

"Well. I assume she did not raise the alarm since you are here and not marching toward a duel with Sir Rawley. Though, I suppose as the wedding *is* in the morning, so even if there were…complications from your pre-wedding visit, the timing would not raise any ques—"

"We did naught but talk," Edward said with a scowl.

Anthony's lips pulled into a grin. "Hmm. Looks like it went well."

"It…" Edward sighed and ran a hand through his hair, grimacing when his fingers snagged on more shrubbery. "In truth, I do not know how it went."

"Oh?"

Edward slumped back against his seat, his mind churning over everything Selena had just told him. Some of it he knew, of course. And some he had suspected. That there might be more than two husbands, for one. Four, he had not guessed at. Three, he thought possible, though even that number had seemed too large. But four…no. And a possible fifth?

He gave Anthony a quick rundown of what he had learned, watching with some gratification as Anthony's expression changed from interest to shock to wariness.

"Four dead husbands?" he finally asked.

Edward nodded and poured himself another glass of bourbon.

"And she did not mention any inquires or suspicions?"

"No. That does not mean they did not exist. I do not know. There were witnesses to the events, after all. At least according to Selena. Whose testimony, albeit is biased."

"True. I suppose it is possible she poisoned their drink to make them act out of character or lose control of their faculties to make such accidents more likely."

Edward frowned. "I cannot see my lady doing such a thing."

"Nor can I. But it is a possibility nevertheless."

That it might be, but it wasn't one that Edward would lend any credence to. Though that did not mean that other people would follow suit.

"Regardless, it seems Sir Rawley and Lady Griffiths always removed their daughter rather quickly after these tragedies befell," he continued.

"To other countries?"

"Yes."

"Where the same thing happened again?"

Edward's frown deepened. "Yes."

"And her intended fifth bridegroom disappeared the night before the wedding?"

Edward gulped down his second glass. "Yes."

"That is…interesting." Anthony's own brow was furrowed, and he wouldn't quite meet Edward's gaze.

Edward let out a long sigh. "Yes."

Anthony toyed with his glass for a few moments, though Edward could see the questions stewing in his mind. "And her explanation is…"

"That she is cursed," Edward reluctantly answered.

Anthony stared at him a moment, long enough Edward had to repress the urge to squirm.

"Speak your mind, man," Edward finally said, unnerved at Anthony's uncharacteristic quietness.

"My apologies, Lockhaven. I suppose I am just surprised that you are still sitting here."

Edward scowled. "And where else should I be?"

Anthony shrugged. "When you caught Viscount Mulford's daughter trying to slip a love potion into your ratafia at the Haliford's ball two seasons ago you disappeared to Mallorca for a fortnight. This is a good sight more severe. I would have thought it warranted a trip to Greece, at the very least."

"Are you saying you think I should be on my way to Mallorca?"

"No," Anthony said slowly. "Only that it is odd you do not seem more concerned that the rumors about her seem to be proving true."

"They are hardly proving true. Only that she has been widowed more than once—"

"Four times," Anthony cut in.

Edward ignored him. "But she did not murder them."

"As far as you know. As I said, she could have added something to their food or drink to addle their brains. Or at the very least cause them some discomfort. Enough that they were not as aware of their surroundings as they should have been. She could have chased the first one in front of the carriage herself. Pushed the second into the water. Encouraged the third into overindulging. Even without a potion. And the fourth…"

Anthony's lips twitched, and Edward shot him a warning glance. "Be careful, Goodwin."

"I was merely going to suggest that he could have been urged into likewise… *overindulging*," he said despite Edward's glare.

"I very much doubt he did anything of the sort. She did *not* murder them," Edward insisted again, though it sounded defensive even to his own ears.

"You are satisfied with her explanations then?"

Edward exhaled heavily again. He wanted to say *yes* with an urgency that bordered on desperation. And yet…he could not. "I do not know. I believe that what she told me was the truth. Or at least that she believes it is the truth. But I also think there could be information she is withholding. And I understand why she hasn't been more forthcoming to this point. Frankly, I likely would have behaved the same if our situations were reversed.

"Yet I cannot help but be hurt that she kept so much from me for so long. That she let things between us go as far as they have before revealing her secrets. She may have told me everything there is to tell, but…can I truly trust that now that she has revealed her willingness to keep things from me? Though, I suppose she didn't have much of a chance to tell me earlier. And, in all fairness, can she ever trust me to always stand by her when I seem to be faltering already? It is our first test, and I am failing miserably."

"Well, in fairness to *you*, my friend, this is quite the test. Most men are faced with a petulant bride or meddling mothers-in-law. Few must worry over whether they will be killed on their wedding night."

Edward snorted, slightly mollified. "I can't deny I desperately wish to know what happened with her last fiancé. Why did the man leave? Had he found something of a nefarious nature? Or was he just a scoundrel? Perhaps it should not matter. But I cannot keep from wondering what would cause a man to take such a drastic action."

Anthony raised a brow at that, and Edward huffed. "I'll admit in the past I have been…shall we say reluctant to fall prey to the confines of marriage."

"Reluctant?" Anthony repeated with a growing smile.

"Disinclined."

"Disinclined?" His smile grew larger.

Sometimes he enjoyed having a friend who knew him so well. Now was not one of those times. "Oh, very well, I was unwilling. Loath."

Anthony chuckled. "Petrified, some might say."

"That is taking it a step too far." Not really, but Edward didn't feel the need to admit that. "Nevertheless, even I would hesitate to abandon a woman at the altar. And would never do so without just and dire cause."

"Hmm." Anthony's gaze burned into him. "And what about the night before?"

"I should like to think I am a better man than that," Edward said, his brow furrowing. "Under normal circumstances, at least," he added with a mutter.

"Is your resolve faltering then?" Anthony asked.

Edward scrubbed a hand over his face again. "No." He paused with a frown and then shook his head. "No," he repeated more firmly. Then he glanced at his friend. "Do I seem to be?"

Anthony shrugged. "Your words are perhaps a bit ambiguous," he said with a smile. "But I'd say the fact that you are still here proves otherwise."

He let out another long sigh. "I hope that is the case. And I hope Selena will continue to trust me." He shook his head. "I fear I haven't given her much reason to put her faith in me."

Anthony gave him a supportive smile. "You are too hard on yourself, my friend."

"Am I?" He shook his head again. "I do not think so. I have proclaimed my love, but not my support. And I have done neither publicly. I have not addressed the rumors that have only intensified over recent weeks, especially with the news of our hasty marriage."

"That was insisted upon by her parents," Anthony reminded him.

"Yes, and I had agreed thinking it would help matters. But I fear it has only made everything worse. I confess, I thought perhaps hastening the wedding would remove the temptation for us both to change our minds. As we both seem wont to do," he added wryly.

Anthony chuckled. "Well, I cannot refute that."

Edward ignored him. "However, perhaps a lengthy engagement would have been better. Given me time to show Society that I am her champion. That I do not believe the rumors about her."

"Or perhaps you simply do not care if they are true," Anthony said.

Edward froze for a second. Was that the truth? Did it truly matter to him?

He thought back over every moment he'd spent with her. Thought of that first moment when he'd walked in the ballroom and their gazes had met. The instant feeling of *home* that had permeated his being the first moment he'd heard her voice. The happiness that enveloped him in her presence. The utter bliss of being in her arms. He was more himself with her than he had ever been on his own.

Did it truly matter to him what had occurred in her past?

His breath left him in a rush.

No. No it did not.

The firmness of that realization did not waiver, even as he sat with it for a moment. Examined it. Poked at it. There was truly no scenario he could fathom where he would willingly give her up.

He laughed, the shadowed weight that had been hanging over him finally lifting. "I believe you are correct. I do not care. Let her be a murderess."

Anthony's eyes widened though he smiled a bit bemusedly. Still, he raised his glass. "To your murderess."

Edward grinned again, raised his own glass, and drained it.

To his Selena. Murderess or no, as long as she remained *his*.

God help him, he was fairly certain he would not only stand by her side were it ever necessary to defend her even against the Crown itself if her rumored crimes proved true but would even help her escape whatever consequences came her way. Might even willingly lay down his own life if she asked it. Let her have it. As long as he spent his last moments with her.

He could but hope that she put her faith in him long enough to make it to the church. If she did not come, he would understand. That she had been able to put her fears aside long enough to even accept his proposal was nothing short of a miracle. He could only pray she met him at the church.

Even if he knew that they might both fare better if she did not.

CHAPTER TWENTY-ONE

THE MORNING OF their wedding dawned long before Selena was ready. She had not slept a wink after Edward disappeared out her window. And judging from the strange quiet that permeated the house (aside from an occasional crash, raised voice, or muffled curse that echoed through the halls), she was not the only one whose nerves were on edge this morning. In fact, it seemed as though everyone, from Jane to her parents to the servants, were poised as though they would be plunged from a cliff at any moment.

"I'm so sorry, ma'am," Morris, Jane's abigail, said for the third time after snagging an errant curl in the brush.

Selena forced a smile and tried to keep still as the maid continued to style her hair. It was hardly the poor woman's fault that everyone was so tense. Selena took a deep breath and let it out slowly, making a visible effort to relax. Worrying herself sick would not help anyone.

"It is all right, Morris. My hair does tend to tangle."

The maid gave her a grateful smile and finished sweeping Selena's hair into an elegant, braided bun, leaving soft ringlets around her face. Then she placed tiny sprays of flowers and small pearl pins throughout her hair, the white blossoms and gems nestled like delicate stars in a midnight sky.

When she had finished, Selena stood and looked herself over.

She didn't know how the modiste had accomplished it, but she had somehow fashioned a beautiful ivory gown embellished with embroidered rosettes and a fine lace overlay in mere days. Whatever her mother had paid for the gown, the woman deserved twice the amount. It was truly the most beautiful wedding gown Selena had ever worn. And she was certainly the expert on the matter.

A nervous laugh escaped her lips and Selena clapped them shut, hoping no one else had heard the sound.

If they had, they ignored it. Everyone seemed to be doing their best to ignore the fact that the bride looked as though she was ready to bolt at the slightest provocation. Her nerves were strung so tightly they could be plucked like a harp. It wasn't as though she weren't happy about her upcoming nuptials. If she let herself imagine life as Edward's wife, she became near giddy in her happiness. Distressingly so.

Because she just couldn't make herself believe that they would actually happen. Even if Edward were actually in that chapel waiting for her (and she had very serious doubts he would be) she just couldn't let herself hope that their story would end happily. The pain if he were not there would be unbearable. Yet the pain if he were and something were to happen to him—as all her experience promised it would—was frankly unimaginable. Unsurvivable.

She wanted so much to believe everything would be well. He would be there, waiting for her with a smile upon his face. They would wed. And neither horse nor bird nor ill-advised drunken altercations would separate them.

Their wedding night was a separate matter entirely. Though at least with that, he had proven he had the constitution to survive her affections. Of course, they had not been wed at the time so if the curse was matrimony specific, he could still be in danger.

"You are thinking so hard your brow will be permanently creased," Jane said softly, her smile so full of sympathy Selena nearly sobbed.

She looked around, noticing for the first time that she and Jane were alone.

"I sent everyone to the carriages. We have a few moments to ourselves. I thought you could use a brief respite."

Selena squeezed Jane's hand. "I do not deserve such a dear friend."

Jane pulled her into a rib-cracking hug. "Yes, you do. You deserve so much more. And that man you are marrying had better realize it."

Selena laughed, though there was little mirth in the sound. "If he is wise, he will have immediately quit town after you so unceremoniously tossed him from my window last night."

Jane laughed heartily. "He was perfectly fine. Agile as a cat, that one."

Selena couldn't help but smile at that.

"You fear needlessly," Jane said. "He will be there, waiting for you."

Selena took a slow deep breath. "I hope you are right. While I think my heart would shatter completely if he were to abandon me, I really wouldn't blame him. In fact, I would commend him for being intelligent enough to save his own skin."

"Oh." Jane waved that away. "You worry for naught. This time is different. *He* is different. I can feel it."

"I hope so," she said again. "But if he does change his mind, as much as it will destroy me, it is a much better option than him dying."

Which would surely happen if they actually went through with the marriage.

Jane gave her a stern look. "No one will be dying today. Or tomorrow," she added with a guilty afterthought. "However, you will never know for sure if you will be standing in that church alone if you never arrive. I fear we have used up our reprieve and must now make haste if we are to arrive in time ourselves."

Selena let out a sharp laugh. "You are right. Very well," she said with a sigh. "Let us depart."

"Before we go—" Jane turned to the maid who had just entered carrying a beautiful bouquet of flowers. She took them with a grateful smile and turned back to Selena.

"I know it isn't strictly necessary to carry flowers, but I thought it couldn't hurt."

Selena took the bouquet, blinking back the tears that rose to cloud her vision.

"Lavender, peonies…" She sucked in a tremulous breath. "Daffodils." She looked at her friend with emotion clogging her throat. "All flowers that denote luck." Especially the daffodils, a particular sign of good fortune and hope in Wales. Fortuitous indeed that Jane had found any this late in the season. Selena was happy to have a bit of her homeland represented.

Jane nodded, her own eyes suspiciously misty. "Also rosemary for loyalty, basil for lasting love, sage for long life." Jane reached out to adjust the embroidered capped sleeve of Selena's gown, before stepping back to look at Selena with so much love and pride that Selena nearly sobbed.

"I am certain Fate is smiling down on you and your groom today," Jane said. "But I thought a little extra help wouldn't come amiss."

Selena raised a brow at the other herbs in the bouquet. "Dill and mint?"

Both herbs that symbolized sensuality, even lust, as well as protection. Jane laughed and shrugged with one shoulder. "Just a bit of fun. And it needed more greenery."

Selena laughed and held the bouquet tight to her bosom. "Thank you," she said, her throat tight again. "They are beautiful."

"Not nearly as beautiful as the bride," Jane said, taking her hand with a quick squeeze. "Now. Let's get you to the church."

Selena took a deep breath and nodded. They hurried down the stairs and bustled into the carriage where her parents waited impatiently. Her mother looked her over with an approving and proud smile. Then her forehead creased slightly.

"I do wish you hadn't felt the need to tell him *everything*," her mother finally mumbled.

She had let her parents know about their conversation. Though she had kept the details of when and where it had occurred to herself. They had a right to know that yet another marriage attempt might prove futile. If she knew her father, he was already planning their next trip abroad. Just in case.

"I know, Mother. But he had a right to know. I could not have wed him without telling him everything. If he is not there…" She shrugged and tried to pretend her heart wasn't rending in two. "If our positions were reversed, I likely wouldn't be."

"I don't believe that for a second," Jane whispered to her.

Her mother grunted. "Neither do I." She sighed and settled back against the cushions. "Well, no matter the outcome of this morning, we will be by your side," she said, giving Selena a reassuring smile before turning her gaze out the window and muttering, "Out of sheer morbid curiosity if nothing else."

Selena laughed her first genuine laugh of the morning, and the mirthful moment lasted right up until the others hurried inside, and she was left standing outside the church door with her father.

"Are you ready?" he asked, giving her hand a squeeze where it lay against his arm.

Was she ready to find out if her future waited for her behind that door, or yet another humiliating, soul-shredding reiteration of her past? No. She wasn't. Not even a little.

But it was too late to turn back now.

"STOP FIDGETING," ANTHONY commanded, swatting at Edward's hands where he had been tugging at his cravat.

Edward scowled but made a concerted effort to drop his hands and keep them away from his neck. He was not normally so restless. Then again, he was not normally on the precipice of a monumental, life-changing decision either. That the decision was not entirely in his hands certainly did nothing to soothe his nerves.

"Look again," he ordered, jerking his head toward the door that closed the clergyman's office off from the rest of the sanctuary. He wished he had obtained a special license instead of merely the common license so that they could have married in his parlor instead of their parish church of St. George's. Fashionable though it may be, it was far too large and too public for the disaster that could be awaiting him.

"Calm yourself," Anthony chastised again before poking his head out the door. "There. You see. Her mother and Mr. and Mrs. Haddon are seating themselves now."

Edward raised an eyebrow. "But you do not see the lady herself?"

"No, but—"

Edward threw his hands up and paced away only to turn back at Anthony's groan.

"What?"

Anthony just shook his head with a chuckle. "I thought the bride was supposed to be the one worrying a path into the floor, not the groom."

"Humpf," Edward grumbled. "I would worry a good sight less if I knew there *was* a bride."

"Her family is here, all but her father, which only serves to prove further that she is here as he will be waiting with her to walk her down the aisle."

Edward frowned, but he couldn't find any fault in his friend's logic. "I somehow still do not feel better. Even if she is there, that does not mean she wishes to be. Perhaps her parents forced her. Or she does not wish to be ruined or fuel the gossip mill more than she already does."

"She has never seemed to care about the gossips before, I doubt she does now. If she were to cry off, it would likely have more to do with her guilt than anything."

"Her guilt? Over what?" Edward frowned and then rolled his eyes with a frustrated breath. "Bloody hell, Anthony, you don't still believe she murdered her husbands, do you?"

Anthony shrugged, his hands upraised. "I cannot say if she did or not. I *will* say, having gotten to know the lady, that if she did hasten their ends, they likely deserved it. However, she could, and should, in my opinion as your oldest friend, feel some bit of guilt over not divulging all her secrets *prior* to mere hours before your nuptials."

Edward snorted. "If you are expecting any woman, especially your future wife, to divulge all her secrets you are going to die a very disappointed man."

Anthony wasn't wed yet. But he would be some day. It would be wise to manage his expectations now. "A woman is entitled to her secrets, Goodwin. Pity the man who tries to pry them out."

Anthony scowled. "Yes, well, be that as it may, there are some secrets that should be shared."

"Agreed," Edward nodded.

"She should have told you sooner."

Edward shrugged at that. "Perhaps."

"I am only looking out for you, my friend. Playing the role of *advocatus diaboli*, if you will. What does it say for the type of relationship you have if she could not bring herself to do so?"

"Likely nothing aside from being a woman who has been judged too harshly by too many for far too long." Edward planted his hands on his hips. "I have been over this a thousand times since last night."

"Yes. I know. As I have been with you through every moment. If you are still this troubled, perhaps it *would* be best to call off the wedding. I have never seen you in such a state. This surely cannot be healthy. And if the bride already has a habit of burying her grooms, at least one that we know of from a failed heart, the last thing you should be doing is helping the curse along."

That stopped Edward in his tracks. "I have no intention of crying off, despite what my current demeanor might insinuate. I am a man of honor. I would never ruin what little reputation Selena has left by leaving her at the altar."

Not to mention how much *he* would be hurt by such an action. He had fought too hard to win her. He would not give her up now. For any reason. If he lost her…he would never recover.

"Then what is all this?" Anthony said, nodding his head at Edward's obviously agitated state.

He let out a long sigh. "I suppose I worry if she will have me at all. While it wasn't entirely my fault that I was not given time to react to her news before being chased from the house, Selena still has no assurances from me. No declarations. The last she saw of me, I was still too much in shock. And by the time I had recovered enough to give her the response she likely hoped for and deserved, I was clinging to the trellis outside her window for my dear life."

Anthony chuckled and then held up a placating hand at Edward's glare.

"My apologies, my friend. I know this is not a matter for amusement, but I simply cannot get the image of you clutching at the wall like an insect in the dead of night from my mind."

Edward pursed his lips and narrowed his eyes at his friend, though frankly had their positions been reversed he would have been howling with laughter. "I'm sure it is very amusing."

"It is," Anthony said, wiping the mirth from his eyes. "Truly."

"Glad to be of service," Edward said wryly.

"Oh, be at ease." Anthony clapped a hand on his shoulder. "I am certain your lady awaits her moment right outside that door."

Edward nodded though he still felt far from confident. Selena had been very upset, rightly so. And after such a revelation—one which she had only withheld because of her fears that he would reject her—to have him not immediately reassure her of his love and commitment might have devastated her. Disappointed her, certainly. And possibly been enough to discourage her from meeting him in front of that clergyman today.

Yes, her family sat opposite his in the pews waiting for the ceremony to start. But that didn't mean she hadn't taken the opportunity to run once they were out of sight. She had certainly run from him before.

"It is time," Anthony said, holding open the door into the main sanctuary.

He took a deep breath and shook his arms out, then straightened his jacket and cravat and followed his friend to his place in front of the vicar. Anthony nodded at him once more and left him to take his seat.

His mother gave him a surprisingly gracious smile, considering her initial objections to this union. His father checked his pocket watch. His brothers smiled at him like buffoons. And his sisters, busily fanning themselves and nudging their husbands now and then, smiled at him, smugly delighted he would be joining the ranks of the happily wed momentarily.

At least he hoped he so.

"Are we ready?" Mr. Burgess, the vicar, asked.

Edward gave him a sharp nod and turned to face the aisle though custom typically indicated one should face forward awaiting one's bride. He wanted to see Selena for himself the moment she walked through that door. If she walked through it.

And if she did, he would marry her just as fast as he possibly could. Yes, they still had a few issues to work out. And they would do so. But first, he would make her his.

The vicar nodded and two attendants opened the outer doors, letting in the sunlight.

CHAPTER TWENTY-TWO

S ELENA'S HEART POUNDED so furiously in her chest she could scarce hear anything else. The second the doors opened, her eyes searched for him. Momentarily blinded by the sun streaming through the stained glass windows, her panic nearly took her over, clawing at her throat and stealing her breath until her father squeezed her hand.

"Your betrothed awaits, my dear. Shall we go meet him?"

Selena jerked her head to look at her father and then turned back to the church interior. Searching until she found what she was looking for. *Him.* Edward. Standing at the front of the aisle, waiting for her. Just as he'd promised.

Her breath left her in a rush, and she started down the aisle, nearly dragging her father with her. Her gaze met Edward's, and the smile he aimed at her stole her breath and stopped her in her tracks. Edward didn't hesitate. He stepped down and rushed toward her, not slowing until he was right before her, his hands cupping her face, his lips upon hers.

Pandemonium broke out around them, and she didn't care. She dropped her flowers and clung to her love, kissing him as though he were the very air she needed to breathe.

They broke apart just long enough to smile at each other. "You came," she said, her smile so wide it made her cheeks ache.

He kissed her again, and she reached up to grasp his hands in her own. He brought them to his lips, kissed each one, and then held their clasped hands against his chest.

"I will always come for you," he said, kissing her again so sweetly she nearly sobbed.

"In truth, I was not certain *you* would come," he confessed.

"I?" she asked, eyes widening. "Why would you doubt me?"

"After the way I left last night…"

"Well, Jane aided in that a bit."

He chuckled. "True. But after everything you told me, I should have said something. Should have stopped Mrs. Haddon from expelling me. Not until I told you that I loved you. That nothing you had told me had changed that. That if anything, it only made me love you more. And that I couldn't wait to marry you."

She dropped her head to his chest with a happy sob, laughing when he lifted her face back to look at him, brushing his thumb across her cheeks.

"It is I who should apologize," she said. "For waiting so long to tell you. For doubting you, even for a moment. I love you, too. And I have never been so happy in my life to see someone standing inside a church."

He laughed again but she sobered slightly. "I do still fear for you though, Edward. Perhaps even more so. What if—"

"I promise you, I shall avoid all birds, horses, and bodies of water until at least a fortnight after we have signed that register. I will drink nothing but water so that my wits will not become addled. And I will eat healthily, sleep regularly, and rest as often as needed after we—"

A clearing throat snapped them out of the little world they had carved for themselves, and Selena glanced about with growing embarrassment to realize that not only did her father still stand mere feet away (and therefore had likely heard a fair bit of what they had just said, if not everything), but that the vicar had also followed Edward down the aisle and was standing purple faced and stuttering behind him. Her mother, Lord Goodwin,

Jane and Mr. Haddon, and Edward's entire family seemed to be greatly amused by it all, at least.

"While I am glad to see you have decided not to abandon my daughter after all," her father said, "however, perhaps we should continue with the ceremony before Mr. Burgess has an apoplexy." He nodded at the vicar who truly looked as though he might suffer from the vapors at any moment.

"Yes, please," Mr. Burgess said, gesturing them toward the front. "It is customary to save such…activities for *after* the ceremony. When in *private* and *not* in the church," he hissed, though more out of embarrassment than anger it seemed. In fact, once they had gotten themselves situated before him and he'd taken a deep breath, he looked quite amused.

"I suppose I do not need to ask if you are giving yourselves freely," he said with a little chuckle. "Now then, let us begin. Dearly beloved—"

"Wait!" someone shouted as the door crashed open, sending an echo through the church. "I object to this union!"

Mr. Burgess threw his hands up. "I haven't gotten to that part yet. We've barely begun."

"Well…" The man, who looked disturbingly familiar, frowned, a great deal of his bluster deflating with the lackluster response to his interruption. "I object all the same. This union cannot be allowed."

"And why is that?" Edward said, his face darkening with anger. He stepped off the dais, and the gentleman audibly gulped and took a step back.

Selena gasped, suddenly realizing why the man looked so familiar. "Herr von Richter?" she asked.

"Are you acquainted with this man?" Edward asked, turning to her with a confused frown.

"Not personally but…I believe he is Otto's brother."

"Otto?" His eyes widened again. "Number five?"

"Yes," she said faintly.

She had never met the man, Johann, but he and Otto had a

similar look about them. This man had darker hair, was a bit shorter, stouter. But the eyes were the same. The cut of his jaw. The angle of his nose. She could definitely see her last betrothed in the man before her.

He glanced at her with a slight sneer but gave her a sharp nod.

"What is your business here? What possible objection could you have to our union? Especially after the foul treatment of my betrothed at your brother's hands."

"My *brother's* hands?" he said. "It is *her* hands that have blood on them, my lord."

Selena and the other women—and Mr. Haddon—gasped at the accusation. Edward's brothers just watched as if they couldn't decide if they should be entertained or ready to defend her honor. Which she found quite sweet, all things considered.

Edward stepped in front of Selena, shielding her from the man before them. "Careful," he said, his voice a growl of warning.

"That is quite a serious accusation," Lord Goodwin added, placing a restraining hand on Edward's shoulder. "One for which I doubt you have evidence."

Selena's spirits were buoyed somewhat by their defense of her, and she straightened her spine. "I have no blood on my hands, Herr von Richter. I do not know what happened to your brother, but my conscience is clear."

"There. You have your answer," Edward said.

"No. She lies."

Edward took a step forward with a growl, but Anthony held him back.

"You have thirty seconds to explain yourself before I let him go," Lord Goodwin said.

Johann watched Edward uneasily, which at least showed he had a healthy appreciation for just how tenuous his current predicament was.

"If she had nothing to do with his disappearance," he said,

"then why has no one has seen nor heard from him since the day he was set to marry that woman." He jabbed his finger at Selena and for a moment, she thought Edward might just reach out and break it off.

She stepped around Edward, despite his grunt of protest. No matter how angry or confused Johann was, she knew she had nothing to hide. And she was well enough protected by not only Edward, but her father who had come to stand beside him. And Lord Goodwin who flanked his other side. And Edward's brothers and father who hadn't yet moved closer but who stood near their seats, watching and waiting. Even Mr. Burgess had moved closer. Though she wasn't sure how much protection the man could offer. He looked as though a strong wind might blow him right off his feet. But she appreciated the support all the same.

Besides, Johann didn't look murderously angry. More confused and frustrated. And that was one thing she could understand.

"Herr von Richter," she said, "what do you mean no one has seen or heard from your brother? I assumed he had been home this past year."

He shook his head in sharp, jerky movements. "No. According to the servants, he left the morning of your wedding, and he never returned. I have searched for him for months and haven't found a trace."

"What?" she said faintly. She let out her breath in a rush and dropped onto the nearest pew. "Forgive me, but I cannot make any sense of that."

"Sense of what?" Johann said, following her, though a slight movement from Edward stopped him from coming too close. "It is obvious what happened. You married him and disposed of him, as you do of all your husbands. And then you came here to find your next victim. You should thank me for saving your life," he said, glancing at Edward who was staring at him with a dangerous fire in his eyes.

Lord Goodwin's grip on Edward's shoulder tightened visibly. "You should thank me for saving yours," he muttered, though Selena wasn't sure if anyone heard him but her…and Edward, whose stance relaxed slightly as he snorted.

She turned her attention back to the problem at hand. "I have no victims, Herr von Richter, past or future." Then she frowned. "How did you find me? I left no word to where I'd be traveling."

Johann's eyes narrowed. "This!"

He pulled a piece of paper from his pocket and unfolded it. Selena leaned closer to see the wedding announcement her mother had placed in the paper.

"I knew your father's name and thought to appeal to—"

Selena could do naught but laugh. Out loud. And once she started, she couldn't stop. Nothing about this situation was funny in the least, but at the same time it was so ridiculous she could scarce believe it was happening. Of all the catalysts to this monstrosity of a situation, that her wedding announcement was what could possibly ruin everything was one insanity too far.

Johann seemed dumbfounded for a moment but then pointed at her, his anger flaring again. "You see? The evil woman laughs at her misdeeds. She should be arrested and—"

Her father's outraged grunt was matched by Edward's. She bit her lip to keep her laughter from turning hysterical.

"I will not warn you again," Edward said, stepping in front of her once more. "While I understand your concern for you brother, I will not tolerate you threatening or insulting my wife."

"Not wife quite yet," Mr. Burgess leaned in to quickly point out.

"Close enough," Edward growled, making Mr. Burgess scurry back a few paces. Edward turned his attention back to Johann. "Do not do it again."

Johann swallowed hard. "I deserve answers," he insisted. "I was willing to let things lie, despite my questions, when I thought she truly grieved him as a proper widow should. Assuming he is dead as she has told everyone."

"I have said nothing of the sort to anyone," Selena insisted. "The last I saw him, he was alive and well. I was humiliated when he abandoned me the day of our wedding. The last thing I wanted to do was bandy about that sordid tale. And my laughter just now was not due to my amusement. Far from it. This is all just so ridic—"

"I will not stand for her becoming a marchioness," Johann interrupted, "a future duchess, conniving such an exalted future for herself whilst my brother likely lies rotting in some roadside grave!"

Mr. Burgess stepped forward once again, and Edward flashed him a warning look, moving closer to block Selena from anyone who might try to get too close. Her heart swelled at his protectiveness, but she hardly thought she was in danger from the vicar.

She reached out to take Edward's hand in her own. He gave it a gentle squeeze and did not let go. But he didn't look at her either, his entire focus on the man he considered a threat.

"Edward," she said, tugging his hand until he dropped his gaze to her. "I believe Mr. Burgess has a suggestion?" She glanced at the vicar, hoping she was right.

He nodded and gestured to the pews as if he were trying to gather everyone together without actually touching anyone.

"There is obviously a discussion to be had. Perhaps you would like to use the table in the office?" He gestured toward the back.

Edward's eye narrowed, but Mr. Burgess glanced at the sun coming through the windows. "It is only, there are several other weddings scheduled for this morning and the next one is due to begin shortly. I am assuming you'd prefer to keep this all priv—"

He cut off his words at another glare from Edward. "Right. Just so. Well then, I will again offer the use of the back room to get this all sorted out."

"But what about *our* ceremony," her mother broke in.

Mr. Burgess shook his head. "I'm afraid I cannot proceed once an objection has been lodged. Unless the objection is retracted?"

he added, glancing hopefully at Johann.

Who simply jutted his chin into the air and crossed his arms. "Not unless my questions are answered to my satisfaction."

"You cannot do this!" Despair flooded through Selena. It was her curse. It had to be. Edward may not be dying—yet—but fate had once again intervened to take him from her. "Herr von Richter, if I had the answers you seek, I would tell you. I swear it on my soul. But I do not know what happened to your brother."

"That is not good enough for me," Johann said. "And if you will not confess, then I will have no choice but to take it up with the magistrate."

⤖⤕

"OH, NO YOU will not," Edward said, squeezing Selena's hand again. "I warned you not to threaten my wife again."

"You should be grateful I came, or you would have been her next victim," von Richter insisted again.

Edward dropped Selena's hand, his own hands clenching into fists. Every word, every threat, from von Richter's mouth had Edward seeing red. The thought of any harm coming to Selena, in any form, had a rage so furious burning through him it nearly made his head spin. That the rage was laced with fear only served to heighten the emotion, and his blood pounded through him, urging him to do something.

He would never allow any harm to come to the woman he loved.

"I do not know your brother or what kind of man he is," he said, his words vehement with every ounce of love and faith he had in Selena. "But I do know my wife." He glared at Mr. Burgess, daring him to contradict the moniker again. "She is no murderess." His voice broke no argument.

Von Richter let out a derisive snort. "If even half the rumors about her are true, then she could be nothing but."

"Well," Anthony said, drawing out the word, "she's had a spot of bad luck, surely. But she's no murderess. Cursed, perhaps. But not a criminal."

Edward glowered at him. "Stop helping."

Anthony held up his hands with a slight grin and backed away a few steps. "Apologies. Simply trying to lighten the mood."

"*My* sincerest apologies," Mr. Burgess broke in, "but I'm afraid I really must insist—"

"I am not going anywhere until I get some answers!"

"If you levy one more accusation at my daughter I—"

Everyone started shouting at once. Everyone but Selena, who sat staring in stunned silence at the pandemonium breaking out around her. Selena, breathtakingly beautiful in her wedding down, her midnight hair swept up from her elegant column of a neck, pearls and diamonds dripping from her ears and throat, glitteringly beautiful and somehow still paling in comparison to the sheer beauty of *her*. His sweet love. Who looked up at him, her sapphire eyes filling with tears.

And that was suddenly all he saw.

He reached out, his thumb caressing her cheek. And then looked around at the arguing people around him.

"Enough!" His voice thundered from the rafters, stunning everyone into silence.

"Excuse me," a hesitant voice called, drawing everyone's attention to a slight man with ginger hair and an armful of papers in the back of the room.

"Who the bloody hell are you?" Edward snapped.

"Edward," his mother gasped.

"Apologies," he muttered to her, though he was anything but sorry. This lot was going to drive him mad.

"I am Mr. Travers," the man said.

"I'm afraid that doesn't help—"

"He's the investigator, dear," his mother said, leaning in to speak quietly.

He turned incredulous eyes to her. "You invited him to my

wedding?"

"Well, no. Not exactly. But he arrived this morning and rather than have him wait, I thought…if there was a lull…"

Edward's jaw dropped, and for the first time in his life he was struck well and truly speechless.

"You'll be pleased to know he found no impediment to your wedding," she said, offering that morsel up like a peace offering.

He just blinked at her, unable to find a response that would be both appropriately damning and still respectful to the woman who gave him life. Saying nothing at all seemed the wisest course of action. But he couldn't just leave the man standing there, milling about. And if he did have information that could help sort this mess…

"Investigator?" Herr von Richter asked, his surprise turning triumphant. "You see! You suspect her too! Someone must fetch the constable—"

"No one is fetching anyone!" Edward shouting, then looked around absolutely nonplused. This lot would be the death of him. "We will get to the bottom of this. Right now!"

Selena stood and he took her hand. "You and you," he said, jerking his head at Herr von Richter and the investigator, Mr. Travers. "The rest of you stay."

There was another rash of voices of protesting voices until Edward held up his hand to silence them. Anthony leaned in. "Perhaps I should accompany you. Just in case."

Whether he meant to offer his services in helping to quell Herr von Richter or to keep Edward from doing so, Edward was not sure. Either way, his presence was likely a good thing. Edward nodded. "Very well."

"Wait a moment," Lady Griffiths said. "My daughter should hardly be ensconced with three men, alone—"

"I will go with her," Mrs. Haddon said, glancing at Edward. He nodded, though he had a feeling she had been informing him, not asking his permission.

"Well, if they are going, I should go," his mother insisted.

"After all, he is *my* investigator and—"

"Later," his father said, giving his mother a stern glance. "They don't need our presence mudding the waters just to ease your curiosity."

She looked as though she would argue but finally sat down with a huff.

"Any more objections?" Edward asked, glancing at everyone with a look that dared them to speak. He nodded sharply. "Very well, then. You lot, with me," he gestured to the relevant people. "The rest of you, enjoy the next wedding."

"But—" Mr. Burgess started to object, but Edward thoroughly ignored him, instead marching for the back room with Selena at his side, his best friend at his back, and the rest bringing up the rear.

They were going to get this mess cleared up so he could marry the woman he loved or by God he would make every last one of them disappear and whisk her away to Gretna Green.

CHAPTER TWENTY-THREE

THERE WAS INDEED a good-sized table in the back, but only Selena and Jane pulled out chairs. The men were too wound up to do ought but stand around the table glaring at each other.

Finally, Selena slumped into a seat. If she was going to try to do the impossible, she may as well be comfortable.

"Herr von Richter," she said, trying not to flinch when he turned to her. "I do not know how I can convince you that I had nothing to do with your brother's disappearance," she said. "I have no proof I am innocent. However," she said, when Johann looked as though had just won the argument, "I am certain *you* have no proof that I am guilty. There could be no such evidence as I am not."

"My brother did not simply vanish into thin air, Mrs...MacLaren, is it now?" he said with a slight sneer.

"Very soon to be Lady Lockhaven, so mind your tone," Edward reminded him with that growl in his voice that sent delightful shivers up her spine.

Johann's lips pinched together but did not argue back.

"If I may?" Mr. Travers said, raising a finger.

He waited for Edward to nod before he took a seat. The rest of the men likewise sat, though they did so more warily, watching each other like they expected someone to attack the moment their backsides hit the seat.

"Lord Lockhaven, as you know, your mother hired me to look into…" He paused, glancing nervously at Selena.

She sighed. "I am aware of your instructions, Mr. Travers. Please do not hesitate to be candid on my account."

He nodded with evident relief. "First, I had to discover if there actually *had* been multiple marriages. Which is not so daunting a task as it might seem. Servants know far more than most people realize. A few well-placed coins and I had most of the information I sought."

Selena blinked in surprise. Who would have betrayed her? Though, while she knew all the staff at her parents' home, she wasn't well acquainted with them all. There did tend to be the regular bit of turnover amongst the lower staff, but anyone who had been with her family for a few years would know everything that had transpired. And it wasn't as if they had been keeping the information secret, so betrayal was likely too strong a word.

That lessened the sting a bit. But not entirely.

Mr. Travers, however, had noticed her surprised start and nodded sagely. "Oh yes. It always surprises me how little attention people pay to those who serve them," he mused. "Such a wealth of information, just ripe for the plucking. Do you know," he asked, leaning an elbow on the table with a conspiratorial smile, "I once discovered that a certain duke's mistress had had a secret child with His Grace's brother simply by bribing the man's valet?" He chuckled. "Truly, you would be astounded at—"

"That is all rather fascinating," Edward said tightly, "but perhaps we could return to the matter at hand."

"Oh, yes, of course. My apologies. Now, I thought I would need to travel to the home countries of all these men to interview their families. Which would have presented quite a bit of trouble considering the distances involved. Though I can still do so if I'm given more time. And funds, of course."

"Of course," Edward said, his voice implying the eye roll he somehow managed to keep contained.

"However, as luck would have it, I needed only travel to the home of the first. Umm, a Mister…" He began shuffling through his papers, and Selena let out a sigh through her nose.

"Monsieur Louis Dampierre," she said.

"Yes," Mr. Travers said with a grin. "Very good. Thank you. Monsieur Dampierre. In Paris. He perished in a terrible carriage accident. Caused quite a stir at the time. Stumbled into the path of the carriage because of…" He squinted down at the paper. "A flock of geese?" He shrugged. "In any case, it was reported on in all the papers and gossip columns for quite some time. And even the subject of a few cartoons I was able to find. Mostly due to the sudden disappearance of his newly wedded wife."

Selena's cheeks grew hot. His news was both unexpected and decidedly unwelcome. She had assumed there might be some tattle about Louis's death in the gossip columns, but it had never occurred to her until that moment that her disappearance afterward might have caused comment. Though…now it seemed a foolish thing *not* to realize.

Louis had been popular at the French court. The younger brother of a minor noble, so no one of importance politically, perhaps. But a jolly fellow who was well liked and well connected. However, when his family voiced no objection to her leaving, she had thought nothing of it and accompanied her father to Italy where he planned to peruse some newly discovered ruins hoping for a few bits of crockery for his collection. That her departure added to the rumors over Louis's death, over all her husbands' deaths, made the entire affair even more soul-wearyingly dreadful.

Edward again took her hand, bringing it to his lips. His gaze held hers as he pressed a kiss to her skin and remained on hers as he lowered her hand. One brow quirked up slightly, as if he were asking if she were all right. The tension that had taken up residence in her shoulders eased, and she gave him a grateful smile. She could do this. He was by her side.

She turned back to Mr. Travers, who had continued prattling on about the fascinating tidbits one could pick up in a gossip column, completely oblivious to Edward and Selena's little interlude, or the rest of their audience's growing agitation.

Edward cleared his throat. "Yes, yes, Mr. Travers. That is all well and good. You have told us what you discovered about Monsieur Dampierre. Do you have anything else to report?"

"Oh yes! As I was saying, there is a wealth of information in the gossip columns. One in particular, as it mentioned interesting stories not only from Paris, but a few from other locales as well. As I did have an idea of timelines, it then just became a matter of finding columns, cartoons, and newspaper articles from the correct dates. As luck would have it, some enterprising soul had heard rumors from multiple courts and wrote a column about Lady Death—"

"Lady what?" Selena exclaimed, sitting bolt upright in her seat.

"Lady… Death," Travers repeated. "I had thought it rather clever, but yes, I can see where that might be, well, where you might find that…" He cleared his throat, growing more nervous and fidgety by the second the longer Selena stared at him in dumbstruck horror.

"There," Johann said, jabbing a hand toward Mr. Travers. "Just as I said."

"A few gossip rags are hardly grounds for condemnation," Edward said.

"Lady Death," Johann snorted. "Putting on airs even as a murderess."

"She will be a duchess someday so wouldn't Duchess of Death be more apt?" Anthony suggested.

"Oh, now that does have a nice alliterative ring to it," Travers said.

Edward glowered at them both, and Anthony held his hands up and apologized with a chuckle. He sobered when he caught Selena's narrowed gaze and cleared his throat.

"And were you able to find information on all of Mrs. MacLaren's husbands?" Anthony asked, getting back to the task at hand.

"Yes." Mr. Travers gave them all another delighted grin. The man was positively glowing with pride in his work. Which was, in all fairness, rather impressive.

"And?" Johann prompted impatiently.

"Oh, yes, well…" He shuffled more papers.

"How does it say these men died?" Johann insisted.

Mr. Travers gulped and glanced at Selena, clearly not wanting to answer. "Poison."

"Oh, this is ridiculous." Selena sat back, crossing her arms with a grumble.

Jane patted her arm and shot a glare at Mr. Travers for good measure. God bless the woman.

"It is only, the deaths are so strange, so naturally people are prone to provide an explanation for how such things could occur." Mr. Travers said, looking at his papers again. "Well, not so strange perhaps in occurrence—accidents do happen, after all. But in sheer quantity, certainly. People assume so many accidents befalling the husbands of one woman, surely she must be facilitating such mishaps in some way. Poison is always a popular theory."

"Surely," Selena echoed, not bothering to hide how insulting-ly preposterous she found that argument.

Mr. Travers glanced at her two or three times but wisely chose not to respond. Instead, he continued on with his story.

"Your second husband, madam, Francesco Fiorentino, died from a fever after a falling in the canal. There was quite a bit about him, as he was a very popular painter. As well as about Marius Albescu, a composer who died after an unfortunate incident involving a horse. And Mr. MacLaren I have not yet looked into, having assumed, as his sister is an obvious champion of Mrs. MacLaren, that his death, at least, was not under consideration."

"Correct," Jane stated firmly.

"So, while they did all die," Lord Goodwin said, "all the deaths were legitimate—if unusual—deaths. No murder. Pure bad luck."

"Bad luck?" Jane scoffed.

"Yes. Tragically extreme bad luck, but still, bad luck all the same. Not malicious murder."

"Is he always this helpful?" Selena muttered to Edward.

"You grow accustomed to it," he murmured back.

"Unfortunately, Mrs. MacLaren," Mr. Travers said, "while I do understand why you may have wanted to hide away after everything that occurred, it was your disappearance after each death that caused the most stir."

She let out a sigh, having suspected as much. Yet, at the time, she couldn't bear to do anything else.

"But," Travers continued, "I did speak to the physician who examined Monsieur Dampierre. He confirmed that the death was accidental. No signs of poison or anything other than the injuries sustained in the accident. I must assume the other deaths were similarly ruled accidental, though I would need more time to prove so conclusively."

Selena nodded with a grateful smile. At least now she had proof for anyone who wanted it that she wasn't what the rumors claimed.

She turned to Edward with a smile, and he lifted her hand to his lips once again.

"That is all very fascinating," Johann said with a scowl, "but you have told me nothing of my brother. Nothing that would cause me to withdraw my objection. She may not have killed these other men," he said, waving his hand toward Mr. Travers's stack of papers, "but that does not mean she did not harm my brother. Or perhaps they did, indeed marry, and then she left him. Which would render her equally ineligible to marry again."

"Ah, yes." Mr. Travers thumbed through a few more pages. "I confess, this one was a bit more difficult. I feared I would not find the information in time, however…"

He pulled a letter from his stack of papers with a flourish.

"What is that?" Johann leaned forward, squinting at it.

"It is a letter for you, from your brother."

"What?" Johann shouted and jumped up, startling Selena enough that she jumped as well. As did everyone else at the table.

"Where did you get that?" Johann leaned over and snatched it from Mr. Travers, who seemed confused as to why there was such commotion all of the sudden.

"I called at your residence yesterday evening—"

"I was not at home," Johann grumbled, dropping into his seat so he could read the letter.

"Yes, as I discovered. However, your footman did offer to let me wait a bit if I wished and placed me in the salon. I confess after a time I did grow quite bored and, well, I may have engaged in a small bit of snooping. Hazard of the trade, I'm afraid. There is quite a lot of mail on the desk in your study that has yet to be opened along with a rather urgent piece from your solicitor—"

"You stole this letter *from my desk*," Johann thundered, causing Mr. Travers to yip in fright and duck behind Lord Goodwin who gallantly stood to defend the man.

"I borrowed it!" he said, peeking out from around Goodwin's broad shoulders. "It was vitally pertinent to my investigation. I would have brought it back this evening. And now I don't have to. Isn't that fortunate?"

Johann growled and made to reach for the man again, but Edward held up a placating hand.

"What's done is done, and I'm sure Mr. Travers is very sorry for his transgression." He glanced at Travers who appeared to be not only thinking about the truthfulness of that statement but seemed ready to deny it. Until he caught Edward's look and nodded with the enthusiasm of a man trying to save his skin.

Johann grumbled but seemed, for the moment, more intent on reading his letter than murdering Mr. Travers.

Edward rubbed at one temple with a finger and nodded at the investigator. "The damage is done, Travers. At least share with us what you found."

"Oh, yes. Well, it seems that Herr von Richter—err, Herr

Otto von Richter, that is—left the evening before his nuptials to Mrs. MacLaren due to…well, to put it kindly, a lack of desire to engage in any marital responsibility and a healthy fear of falling afoul of Mrs. MacLaren's curse."

"That's kindly?" Jane muttered, making Selena snort softly. She'd heard worse, certainly. But if that was Travers's idea of kind, she didn't want to hear him be cruel.

The investigator continued, oblivious to their commentary. "Apparently, while in the tavern not long before the wedding, someone shared with him the rumors regarding Lady Dea—err, Mrs. MacLaren's past marriages, and rather than risk his life for a life of responsibility he did not want, he decided to go on an extended holiday."

Selena listened to this all with growing agitation. The nerve of that man, leaving her as he did without any regard to her feelings or reputation, over a few tawdry rumors. Of all the… She blew out a sharp breath and narrowed her eyes at Mr. Travers.

"And where has my erstwhile fiancé been all this time?"

CHAPTER TWENTY-FOUR

EDWARD COULDN'T STOP his frown at the reminder that Otto had been betrothed to his soon-to-be wife. But he had to admit to a morbid curiosity about what happened to the man. He raised a brow, waiting for the skittish investigator to regale them with the tale.

"Oh…well, I'm afraid…" Travers stuttered.

His obvious reluctance to avoid sharing the information only served to convince Edward Selena might not wish to hear the answer as much as she thought. But he doubted he could persuade her. In her place, he would want to know.

"In Greece," von Richter said, tossing the letter to the table with a disgusted huff.

Travers deflated a bit at someone stealing his biggest reveal. But when one dawdled, one dealt with the consequences.

"Greece?" Selena repeated, sounding thoroughly astonished.

The sigh that dredged from the depths of von Richter's soul was one with which Edward, with two younger brothers of his own, was intimately familiar.

"With an opera singer named Maria with whom he is apparently completely infatuated."

Selena flinched, a movement so slight Edward doubted anyone but he noticed. He took her hand again, cradling it in his own, and she gave him a grateful smile.

"He asks my pardon for his prolonged absence and requests that I give his love to our mother." Von Richter snorted and pushed his chair away from the table. "He can do so himself. I do not wish to be within a day's ride of our mother when she discovers where he's been."

He began striding for the door without another word. But they still had one rather important matter of business to discuss.

"I take it this means you withdraw your objection to our marriage?" Edward asked.

"Do what you must," he said, not pausing until he reached the door. "I still say there is something dangerous about that woman," he added, glancing over his shoulder at her.

"You have no idea," Edward said, giving her a heated look that he knew didn't come close to conveying the fire that burned in him for her. She sucked in a trembling breath that had him aching to toss her over his shoulder, marriage certificate or no.

Herr von Richter snorted. "If you insist upon taking your life into your hands by marrying her, then by all means do so. I have a brother to fetch."

"Wonderful," Edward said, grabbing Selena's hand and pulling her with him. "Tell the vicar on the way out, would you?"

Von Richter marched out the door, Edward and Selena not far behind him, and Anthony, Mrs. Haddon, and Mr. Travers on their heels if his hearing did not deceive him.

They all barreled out of the back room, only to stumble to a halt when they reentered the main sanctuary to find the vicar in mid-marriage ceremony, staring at them with wide, shocked eyes while the bride and groom looked on with growing horror.

Johann, however, continued his march to the main doors.

"I withdraw my objection, vicar," he shouted over his shoulder, with an apathetic wave. "Marry whomever you please."

"Lovely," Mr. Burgess said. "Would you mind if I finished this ceremony first."

"My apologies everyone," Edward said with a wave. "Please carry on. You three, have a seat," he said to the others. "You…"

He grinned at Selena. "Come with me."

He grasped her hand again and towed her back into the back room. She, thankfully, did not protest but followed him with a delighted smile.

The second the door shut behind them, he pushed her up against it and captured her mouth with his, groaning as her lips opened for him and welcomed him inside.

He plundered her mouth for a blissful few seconds until she squirmed against him. Which only made him groan louder.

"Edward," she said, briefly breaking from his lips to speak.

"Hmm?" He didn't bother to lift his lips from hers.

"The handle," she murmured, before going right back to kissing him.

"Hmm?" He stopped and glanced behind her. "Oh." He chuckled and spun her a few feet away, then pressed her back against the wall.

"They'll hear us," she said with a gasp as he moved to her neck.

"I don't care." He nipped at her collarbone, and she shoved her fingers into his hair, holding him in place.

"Glad to hear it." She tugged on his hair, dragging his face back to hers so she could crush her lips to his once more.

His hand trailed up her side to her silk-and-lace-covered bosom, squeezing at the bounty he found here until she arched against him with a moan.

He heard the click of the latch just in time to unhand her breast before the door swung open.

"My lord!" Mr. Burgess said, properly scandalized at the scene he'd walked in upon. He would have needed a doctor if he had walked in a few seconds earlier. "This is a house of worship! You must desist at once!"

"Then marry us with haste, Mr. Burgess, because I cannot guarantee my good behavior for much longer."

"What? Here? Now? We can go out into the—"

"I will not move another step until this woman is my wife."

He leaned down to press another kiss to Selena's radiantly smiling mouth, ignoring the sputtering of the vicar.

Selena could do naught but laugh as Edward stayed right where he was, arms around her, while the vicar stammered with indignation.

"My lord, I must insist…" Mr. Burgess said trying in vain to get them to move toward the door.

Frankly, even if Edward wanted to, he could not move, or it would become even more evident to all what had been going on behind that closed door. "We will stay right here until—"

"What is happening?" her mother's voice carried in from the doorway. "Edward, don't you dare get married until you come out from that room."

Never mind. That handled matters quite satisfactorily. Selena, by this point, was clutching her stomach from laughing so hard, though she was somehow managing to do so without making a sound other than a faint wheezing. Fascinating, though he much preferred the actual sound of her laughter. He couldn't wait to get her alone and find out what other sounds he could tease out of her.

"Very well," he said, "let us remove ourselves to the chapel proper. Post haste!" he said, pushing his way through the small crowd of their family and friends who had gathered at the door.

He and Selena took up their positions while their guests scrambled back to their seats, and a remarkably flustered vicar fumbled to liberate his hands from his voluminous robe and open his prayer book.

He finally got himself situated and glanced around to ensure everyone was in place.

Edward waved his hand at Mr. Burgess to begin.

"Dearly beloved…"

"I'm sure we can skip through a fair bit of this, vicar. We all know why we are gathered here today."

"Oh, well, yes, I suppose…let's see…First, it was ordained—"

Edward waved his hand like he was rolling a ball of yarn.

"Yes, yes. Ordained for children, against sin, mutual society, et cetera, et cetera. We've all heard the ceremony and understand all the important bits. Yes?" he asked Selena, the only person whose opinion mattered to him in this moment.

"Yes," she said, smiling up at him with those shining sapphire eyes.

"Well, this *is* unusual," Mr. Burgess muttered. "Very well, therefore, if any many can show any just cause—"

"We already did that bit. I am certain there is no one else here who plans to object," he said firmly, not bothering to turn his warning gaze on everyone. No one would dare.

"Oh, good Heavens, very well, let's see…I require and charge you both—"

"Mr. Burgess," Selena said, making Edward glance down at her with delighted surprise. "We both swear to you on our souls that we know of no impediment, as we have already stated."

"Very well," he grumbled, his finger skimming along the lines of the ceremony. "Oh, now I *must* insist upon this part," he said, looking at them with surprising sternness. "You must recite your vows."

"Gladly," Edward said, smiling down at his bride.

"Happily," Selena agreed, smiling back at him.

"Oh. Truly? I expected a bit of an argument there," Mr. Burgess said. He shored up his shoulders, obviously pleased to be able to perform his duties at last.

"But, just the vows and the ring. Let's just skip through all the prayers and psalms shall we? I swear upon my eternal soul we shall offer up enough prayers and psalms at a later time."

"This is most unusual—"

Edward cocked an eyebrow, and the poor vicar sighed. "But very well."

Edward would have to remember to donate a goodly sum to the parish to make amends for haranguing the man. But later. For now, he just wanted this ceremony legal and binding so he could start his life with his wife at his side.

"Edward Colwyn Laurence Brelsford, wilt thou have this woman to they wedded wife…"

Edward beamed down at his love, letting each charge of the vow settle into his soul. And when the vicar asked, 'so long as ye both shall live?', Edward did not hesitate to state, "I will," with every ounce of his being.

The vicar pulled out a small slip of paper upon which had been written Selena's full name.

"Selena Dampierre Fiorentino Albescu MacLaren nee Griffiths—good heavens, that is quite the name isn't it," the vicar said with a little chuckle. "Shortly to add one more for hopefully the last time!" He grinned at them but choked it back when he saw their mirrored expressions of surprise. Though Edward was quite sure he heard Anthony's quiet chuckle from the pews. He would glare at him later. At the moment, he was too busy gazing at his breathtaking wife.

"Yes, my apologies, where were we? Oh yes. Selena Dampierre Fiorentino Albescu MacLaren nee Griffiths, wilt thou have this man to thy wedded husband…"

She turned her lovely, joy-filled eyes back to him and proclaimed, "I will," with a smile that made his heart skip a beat.

Sir Rawley waved the vicar on when asked who gave this woman away. He had already played that part several times over.

Then finally, Edward turned to Selena, took her hands in his, and they plighted their troths. He took the ring the vicar blessed, that Anthony, bless him, had kept hold of during all the commotion. And when he slipped it on Selena's finger, it felt like he was locking in the last puzzle piece that had been missing his whole life. He lifted her hand to his lips and kissed where the ring lay against her skin, ignoring the surprised breath the vicar sucked in. At this point, Edward had no doubt the man would be neck deep in a bottle of wine before they were fully out the door.

"Now, let us…no, you wished to skip this part…and the psalms, no song I suppose, then this, then…ah yes. Amen. Forasmuch as Edward Colwyn Laurence Brelsford and Selena…MacLaren have consented—"

Selena made a strange squeaking noise and Edward looked down to find her biting her lip in a vain attempt to keep from an all-out smile. Though her shoulders were shaking with laughter. He was finding it quite hard to contain his merriment himself. Of all the things he insisted the vicar skip over, he was tempted to make the man repeat her full set of names. Before he could say anything, the vicar proclaimed—with more relieved gusto than he likely did at most weddings—"I pronounce that they be Man and Wife together. In the name—"

"Excellent!" Edward said, gripping Selena's hand as they hurried together toward the back room where the register had been laid out.

The vicar was attempting to stumble through the rest of the prayers and psalms at a truly remarkable speed, but Edward wanted only to sign the register and take his wife home. They had fought too hard to get to this moment. He did not want to wait any longer.

"Witnesses!" he called over his shoulder, laughing when Mrs. Haddon and Anthony jumped from their seats, beating out any number of others who could have served just as well.

The vicar wisely wrapped up the rest of the ceremony and hurried after them, sputtering about the sin of impatience and likely a few other choice utterances as well.

Edward, Selena happily smiling at his side, waited only long enough for their witnesses and the vicar to get through the door before signing his name with a flourish in the register. Selena took the quill from him and did the same. And then laid it down, glancing at him, her brows raised in question.

He looked to the vicar. "Is the ceremony complete and binding now?"

Mr. Burgess glanced at the register—unnecessarily in Edward's opinion, seeing as how the man had just watched them sign—and nodded. "Congratulations."

Edward beamed. And then he turned to Selena, wrapped one

arm about her waist, and hauled her to him for a resounding kiss.

"Lord Lockhaven!" Mr. Burgess exclaimed again. "I really must protest this behavior. You are in a church, my lord, not a tavern!"

Selena broke away from him with a laugh. "Our apologies, Mr. Burgess. But this is the first moment in my life where I have truly understood the twenty-third psalm. My cup truly runneth over. It is difficult to contain such happiness."

"Oh, well, yes, of course," he said with a slight blush to his cheeks.

Selena could charm the devil himself when she smiled as she was smiling now. That he had even a little to do with such an exquisite expression gave Edward a greater sense of pride than anything else in his life so far. He would do a great deal, commit any number of sins, to keep such a smile on her lips.

Mrs. Haddon handed Selena her bouquet of flowers and gave him a smiling nod.

"Shall we?" he said, holding out his elbow for his wife to take.

She did so with a smile, though there was still worry shadowing her eyes.

He tucked a finger under her chin and lifted her face until she met his gaze. "Do not worry so, love. I have taken all the precautions I can to ensure we end this curse of yours."

She blinked at him, eyes wide. "You have?"

"Oh yes." He wrapped her hand through the crook of his arm and escorted back down the aisle toward the door.

"My stable hands were instructed to choose the most docile horses to pull our carriage this morning—and I will stay well away from them aside from riding in the carriage. My cook will serve only lemonade, cider, tea and coffee, and water at our wedding breakfast. Not a drop of anything more spirited. Avoiding bodies of water should be easy enough, but I have had the servants erect a temporary barrier around the fountain in the garden at Brelsford House just in case. And the doctor has been placed on call and will be passing the night at Lord Goodwin's residence, which is just a few doors down from ours. Just in case he should be needed."

They'd reached the doors to the chapel and stepped out into the sun.

"You truly did all that, just to allay my silly fears?" she asked, her eyes shining up at him with so much love his heart ached.

"Your fears are never silly to me, my love. I will always battle them with you."

"Let us go home then, husband."

He beamed at her and led her through the columns to the steps of St. George's. Startling a group of wood pigeons that had been loitering about the columns. Two flew directly at him and his foot missed the first step. He had a split second where he realized he was going to topple down, and he immediately loosed his grip on Selena so he wouldn't bring her down with him.

Or he tried.

Instead, she grabbed his arm and yanked hard enough his shoulder popped as if he were cracking his knuckles, then turned with a banshee yell to chase down the birds, swatting at them with her bouquet until every last one had flown off.

He hurried toward where she stood, chest heaving, bouquet upraised like a conquering knight with his sword. She heard his step and rounded on him, dropping her arm once she saw it was he.

"I think you got them, love," he said, unable to keep his grin hidden.

"I thought you...you started to...the birds..." Her words tripped over themselves, stumbling from her lips in a jumble of concern and righteous fury.

He just nodded and pulled her into his arms. "Yes, the birds nearly made me fall. But you saved me." He pressed a kiss to her lips. Then another one, and another, until the tension that fear had put into her body changed to a different kind of tension. One that was sweeter. Hotter. And infinitely more delightful.

"My lord," Mr. Burgess said. "I feel I should remind you, you are still on the steps of the church. Perhaps—"

"Oh, give them a minute, vicar," Anthony said, laughing. "They just broke a curse, after all."

CHAPTER TWENTY-FIVE

SELENA GLANCED BACK, belatedly realizing they had an audience. And finding she didn't care overly much. Once again, she had nearly lost her newly wedded husband. But…Lord Goodwin's words echoed in her mind. Had the curse been broken?

Edward laughed while Mr. Burgess sputtered in confusion. "We shall defile your church no longer, Mr. Burgess, I assure you." He held his elbow out to Selena again. "Shall we attempt this again?"

She raised a brow but allowed him to carefully lead her down the stairs and into the carriage. Though she kept a careful eye on the horses the entire time. She wasn't taking any more chances.

The moment she climbed into the carriage and the door shut behind them, Edward hauled her into his lap. "I will make no such promises about defiling our carriage, however."

"Edward," she laughed, holding onto him to keep from falling when the carriage took off with a lurch.

He dipped his head to give her a searing kiss that had her arching back against him.

"My love," she said again, trying to get the question out while she still had the ability to speak. Because if his hands kept wandering the path they were currently taking, she would be incoherent with need very shortly.

"Do you believe we have broken the curse?" she gasped out when his hand delved into the neckline of her dress.

"If there was ever a curse to break, then yes, we must have. You saved me." He kissed her again, even more thoroughly. "We are married, the birds did their worst, and I am still here."

"Yes," she gasped again. "But, what about our wedding night?"

He frowned down at her. "I thought we had allayed your fears about that," he said. "We have already challenged that one." His heated lips trailed down her neck again while his fingers worked their magic inside her gown. "I survived."

"But. Oh!" She pushed back against him, trying to get as close as she could to give as much access as she could. "But we were not married yet."

His hand froze, and she whimpered in protest.

"Hmm. You are right." He pressed his lips to her ear. "But we are married now. Let's find out who is stronger, shall we? Me or this curse."

He sucked her earlobe into his mouth and gently bit the soft flesh. She gasped and arched into his fingers when he freed a breast from her stays, bringing one arm up to wrap around his neck to draw his head down to hers.

"Should we be doing this here, my lord?" she asked, crushing her lips to his in a searing kiss. His answer was moot already. They were both too far gone to stop now.

His fingers found her nipple and a moan escaped her, his mouth capturing the sound.

"No time like the present," he managed to say, trailing his lips down her neck.

She sucked in a breath, tilting her head to give him better access. "Agreed."

Her words cut off on a choked breath when the arm banded about her waist tightened, bringing her backside up against his deliciously hard shaft.

"I think the carriage is slowing," she murmured, wriggling

against him, trying desperately to find the friction she needed.

"Keep driving," he called out.

She giggled. "Don't you think it will be a bit obvious what we are doing if our guests see our carriage driving in circles."

"Hmm, I do not care," he growled in her ear before nipping gently at her earlobe. She shuddered against him, pressing her hips back in an effort to feel him better through their layers of clothes.

He seemed to have the same idea as he grasped her skirts and started raking them up, his hand dragging along her skin as it was exposed.

"I very nearly dragged you into the vicar's office the second the ceremony was over," he said.

She laughed, the sound low and throaty. She opened her mouth to speak again but instead cried out as his fingers found her aching core.

Edward chuckled, his other hand leaving her breast to cover her mouth while he pushed a finger inside her.

"You will give us away, wife. My sweet…" he pushed a second finger inside and she dropped her head back onto his shoulder, bucking against his hand to bring his fingers even deeper, "…beautiful, wife."

She tried to keep quiet, turning her face into his neck as she rode his hand, every stroke bringing her closer and closer to that crest. She rucked up the rest of her skirts and reached behind her to fumble with his fastenings.

"Edward," she nearly whimpered, "I need you. Please."

He growled, her plea snapping his control. He reached between them to unfasten his breeches, freeing himself from the confines. She looked over her shoulder, trying to see. Wanting to touch him. But perched upon his lap as she was with the carriage bumping along the uneven road made it difficult to do much more than feel his hard length slipping between her folds.

And he was done waiting. He gripped her hips and pulled her down, sheathing himself with one thrust. She moaned. The feel of him stretching her inner walls never ceased to draw her wonder and awe. It was though if he had been made to fit her perfectly. Fill her to the brink. Every inch of him caressing every inch of her. She never wanted the feeling to end.

Yes, perhaps they were playing a dangerous game right now. She had saved him from the birds. The stairs. Hopefully the horses. But there was still the wedding night to come.

Unless now, this moment, broke the curse for good. Curse or no, it didn't matter. She wanted this moment. Needed it. The more he touched her, the more she craved him. It had been bad enough when she'd wanted him from afar. When she had only the fantasies in her mind to dream about.

But then he'd touched her, kissed her, made love to her. And now, she wanted him with an intensity that frightened her. She would never be whole again without him. And it had been far too long since that first moment between them. She couldn't wait any longer.

His thrusts quickened, his rhythm thrown off now and again from the carriage movements which jostled them about. Every bump and hole hidden in the road had Selena clutching at his thighs and writhing on him, chasing that high that kept building and building. When his hand reached around and found that sweet bundle of nerves at the apex of her thighs, she ground herself back against him as he thrust up and she went careening over the edge, clenching around him as she orgasmed.

His hand wrapped around her throat, and he pulled her back against him so his mouth could capture her cries. His mouth ravished hers as he thrust into her again, and again, before finally reaching his own release. He held her close, his lips and tongue still plundering hers while he held onto her, riding the combined waves of their climaxes.

Her head dropped back against his shoulder as they panted, both trying to drag in a breath through tortured lungs.

"Can we ask the driver to take another turn around the block?" Selena asked with a shaky voice.

Edward laughed, and the movement made them both gasp as he was still nestled inside her.

"Our guests will already be waiting. I'm afraid we must go inside."

She let out a long sigh. "Very well."

He chuckled. "Is that a bad thing?"

"I don't know. I've grown quite fond of this carriage in the last few minutes."

Edward barked out a laugh and pressed a kiss to the long column of her neck.

"Come," he said, pulling his handkerchief out of his pocket. "We must be quick."

He did his best to clean them both while she hastily righted her skirts and patted her hair back in the place. They gave each other a quick look over to ensure everything was in place and as it should be, and she slid back onto the seat opposite him just as the carriage pulled to a stop in front of the house.

He opened the door and stepped down first, holding out his hand to help her down. "Well?" he asked, glancing at her with his eyebrows raised. "We have broken the curse have we not?"

She pursed her lips, tilting her head as she regarded him. "Have we?"

"Do you not believe so? After all, we just—"

"Edward," she hissed, hushing him as they stepped into the hall of Brelsford House. "Someone will hear."

"Let them," he said, pulling her into his arms again. "I've found I quite enjoy being the scandal of the town."

She laughed and wrapped her arms about him. "Well, I confess it will be a relief not to be alone in their scrutiny any longer."

He cupped her face and pressed a heartachingly sweet kiss to her lips. "You will never be alone again, my love. I will always be by your side."

She raised on her toes to deepen the kiss, her heart so full she had to choke back tears.

"And as for the curse?" he asked again.

"I confess, I am not certain," she said hesitantly.

"But how is that possible?" Edward asked, eyes wide. "After all, we just—"

"Edward!" she chastised again, lightly slapping his chest.

He laughed and caught her hand, bringing it to his lips. "We just took a wonderful carriage ride," he said, with a heated half grin that had her quivering with need again. "And here I stand, hale and hearty."

"Hmm, yes," she said, leaning back to look him over. "I suppose that could mean the curse is, indeed, broken. Then again…"

"Yes?" he asked, his eyes alight with interest.

"It is only that the last time the curse struck, it was the morning after the wedding. Not the morning of."

"Ah. Yes. Well then, I suppose there is only one thing to do."

"Wha—" Her words cut off with a surprised squeal as Edward picked her up and tossed her over his shoulder.

"My lord, what are you doing? Our guests!"

"Our guests can wait," he said, hurrying up the steps toward his chambers. "We have a curse to break."

EPILOGUE

The next morning

EDWARD LAY PROPPED on his elbow, watching his wife as she slept. Despite the worries she still expressed, something seemed to have eased in her. The circles were gone from beneath her eyes. The tension she always seemed to carry with her was gone. And a small smile graced her lips, even in her sleep.

He didn't wish to wake her, but he couldn't help reaching out to touch her. He lightly trailed a finger across the delicate skin of her cheek, then dragged his thumb gently across her bottom lip.

The rhythm of her breathing changed. She didn't open her eyes, but she smiled beneath his fingers touch.

"I take it you are sufficiently rested, my lord?" she asked, her voice slightly raspy from sleep.

"Hmm. Even if I were, how can I sleep when there is such a tempting beauty in my bed?"

"Perhaps because you spent the entirety of the night, trying to break a curse that—" Her eyes flew open. "Edward!"

"Yes, my love?" he asked, kissing her neck.

"It is morning."

He glanced at the sun streaming through the window. "So it is. I suppose that means we have finally vanquished your curse."

Her smile grew mischievous. "Hmm, perhaps."

"Perhaps?" He frowned, genuinely confused now. "It is the morning after our wedding. And I am still here. Alive. After a

230

very vigorous wedding night, if I do say so myself."

Her low chuckle had him pulling her even closer against him, until the sound cut off in a ragged gasp.

"Yes," she said, the breathless word sounding more like a moan. "However, I have suddenly realized that the last time the curse struck was on a Thursday. And it is only Wednesday today. Therefore, I do not think we can truly consider the curse broken until at least Friday."

He rolled her beneath him, grinning when she wrapped her legs around him. Little minx. Luckily, he was very willing to play this game. "Two whole days. Well, if that is what we need to do to ensure the curse is truly broken…"

He slid inside her, gritting his teeth at the exquisite grip of her body around his.

"I am happy to oblige," he managed to say.

Friday

SELENA WATCHED EDWARD over the top of the book that she had not been reading for the better part of an hour while he sat at his desk, not going through the paperwork scattered around him. She had woken the morning after their wedding with a sense of peace that she had not felt in many years. As if a weight had finally been lifted. And the feeling had persisted every morning since.

Perhaps it had been silly to believe so whole-heartedly in a curse. But, as strange as it seemed, a part of her needed to believe in that curse. To believe that there was a reason for the tragedies that had repeatedly fallen. That it wasn't just random. That there was something she could do to prevent such things from happening again.

And then she'd met Edward. He had broken past all her defenses. And kept doing so. She would always mourn her other husbands. Mourn the possibilities their relationships had offered.

Mourn the kind, talented men who had met such pointlessly tragic ends.

But even with them, Selena had never dreamed such happiness was possible. She had hoped for companionship. Contentment. But she had never dreamed such a depth of love was possible. She loved Edward with an intensity that frightened her even as she rejoiced in it. And a large part of her was still afraid to believe it would continue. Believed that something would happen to take it all away.

And…it could. Accidents happened. People got sick. They grew old. Someday, she *would* lose him.

But not today. Today, he was hers. And she was going to continue to make the most of their time together for as long as she could.

He finally laughed and put down his quill.

"You haven't turned a page in almost a quarter of an hour," he said.

She gave him an impish smile. "I am a slow reader."

His lips spread in an answering grin. "Your book is upside down."

"Is it?" She glanced down. "Hmm. So it is."

He leaned forward, resting his crossed arms on his desk. "Is there something on your mind?"

"I believe it is Friday, my lord."

"Hmm. So it is." He leaned back and spread his arms wide. "And the curse has yet to strike."

"So it seems." Her smile grew wider.

"You *still* don't believe the curse is broken?" he asked, his gaze growing heated.

"I wish we could be sure. It is only that I just realized that three of my four marriages were in June, and one in July. It is still June now. So how can we be sure the curse is truly broken until August?"

Edward rubbed a finger over his chin, as if he were truly contemplating what she said.

"You may have a valid argument there." He crooked his finger at her. "Come here, wife."

August

"It is August, love," Edward said, running his hand over the tiny bump of Selena's belly as she lay her head on his lap under the large tree in the back garden. They had finally allowed the fountain to flow again, and though the water attracted birds, Selena did not seem to mind anymore. Though he still took care not to go too near it, just in case.

He would never get over the miracle of having her in his life. Especially now that she was gifting him with a miracle of their own. He would go to his grave thanking his lucky stars for bringing this woman into his life. Whether his life ended the next day, the next year, or fifty years from now. He would cherish every moment.

"Hmm yes," she said. "But I have been thinking…"

"Oh?" He grinned as she smiled at him and threaded her fingers through his.

"You see, every other time the curse has struck, it has been summer, and we are in summer still. So perhaps, just to be completely sure, we should wait until autumn."

"Hmm, that does seem prudent. Perhaps after a summer of flouting the curse, the Duchess of Death will no longer be a threat, and her curse will finally be broken?"

She narrowed her eyes at him. "Not amusing."

He chuckled. "It's a little amusing."

"Besides, it was Lady Death."

"Hmm." He pulled her into his lap until she straddled him. "But you shall be a duchess, my lady. The cartoonists have increased your rank."

"Have they really?" She pursed her lips in surprise. "I should think they'd have grown bored of the story by now."

"Truly?" He gripped her hips and dragged her against him until she threw her head back with a gasp. "I believe the tale of Lady Death marrying the Marquess of Lockhaven will be a story for the ages."

Her deep, throaty laughter had him burying his face in her neck with a groan.

"We can but hope," she said, draping her arms around his neck as he pulled her close. "Now, don't we have a curse to break?"

His hand slipped up her skirts. "As always, I am happy to oblige, my love."

His heart soared as their lips met.

Autumn

"I HAVE BEEN thinking," Selena whispered, leaning against Edward as they sat in the chapel watching Anthony say his vows to a lovely woman he definitely hadn't seen coming.

"Oh?" He placed his hand over where hers pressed against another little kick pummeling her belly.

"It is the end of autumn, and the curse has yet to strike."

His brows raised. "Ah. Has it finally broken then?"

"One can only hope. It is hard to say for certain, though. A good friend of mine had been wed just before the curse struck for the first time. And a good friend of yours has just been wed."

"Hmm. Again, a valid point, my love. Perhaps we should redouble our efforts in breaking the curse. Just to be certain."

"I would not be adverse to that, my lord. In fact, we might want to spend a few more months redoubling. Just to be safe."

Mr. Burgess finished his prayer with a loud "Amen," glaring at Edward as he did so. Which had Selena slapping her hand over her mouth to keep in her laughter.

The wedding concluded, the vicar turned to lead the couple into the back to sign the register.

"I'll fetch the carriage," Edward said with a wicked grin that had Selena laughing even harder.

Edward slipped out of their pew and began hurrying toward the doors.

"Lord Lockhaven," Mr. Burgess chastised. "You are a witness."

Edward cursed under his breath and hurried back up the aisle to stand witness for his friend, while Selena clutched her belly, her eyes watering with laughing tears.

A few months later

EDWARD TOUCHED THE tiny head in his wife's arms with awe. The love he felt for the precious being Selena had brought into the world was unmatched. How could anyone love anything so much? He looked at his wife, his heart near bursting with pride and love and happiness. He thought the same thing every time he looked at her. Never had a man been as lucky as he.

"Edward," she said quietly, gazing up at him with so much love in her eyes he ached with it.

"Yes, my love?" He sat beside her on the bed, wrapping one arm around her back and the other around her arms so they could cradle their son together.

"I believe the curse has finally been broken."

He pressed a reverent kiss to her lips and gazed down at his family.

"Yes. I believe it has."

About the Author

USA Today bestselling author Michelle McLean is a jeans and t-shirt kind of girl who is addicted to chocolate and Goldfish crackers and spent most of her formative years with her nose in a book. She has degrees in history and English and is thrilled that she sort of gets to use them.

Her love of historical romance began in the pages of a Victoria Holt novel. A love that is entirely to blame for both her degrees and her current career. Her days are spent working in her local high school library and writing…or avoiding deadlines by fixating on a variety of hobbies or, if really desperate, cleaning something.

She currently resides in PA with her husband and two kids, the world's most spoiled dog, and a cat who absolutely rules the house. She also writes contemporary romance as Kira Archer. Her novel Truly, Madly, Sweetly, written as Kira Archer, was adapted as a Hallmark Original movie in 2018.

Social Media Links:
Newsletter: landing.mailerlite.com/webforms/landing/b6c0h6
Website: michellemcleanbooks.com
Instagram: michellemcleanbooks
Facebook: michelle.m.mclean
Tiktok: @authormichellemclean
Pinterest: michellemcleanbooks
Amazon: amazon.com/stores/Michelle-
McLean/author/B0041OFZSS
Bookbub: bookbub.com/authors/michelle-mclean

www.ingramcontent.com/pod-product-compliance
Lightning Source LLC
Chambersburg PA
CBHW072115300726
48975CB00003B/816